MOVING
TARGET

Books by Lynette Eason

WOMEN OF JUSTICE

Too Close to Home

Don't Look Back

A Killer Among Us

DEADLY REUNIONS

When the Smoke Clears

When a Heart Stops

When a Secret Kills

HIDDEN IDENTITY

No One to Trust

Nowhere to Turn

Nothing to Lose

ELITE GUARDIANS

Always Watching

Without Warning

Moving Target

ELITE GUARDIANS [3]

MOVING TARGET

LYNETTE EASON

a division of Baker Publishing Group
Grand Rapids, Michigan

© 2017 by Lynette Eason

Published by Revell
a division of Baker Publishing Group
P.O. Box 6287, Grand Rapids, MI 49516-6287
www.revellbooks.com

Printed in the United States of America

Library of Congress Cataloging-in-Publication Data is on file at the Library of Congress, Washington, DC.

ISBN 978-0-8007-2324-8 (pbk.)
ISBN 978-0-8007-2854-0 (print on demand)

Scripture used in this book, whether quoted or paraphrased by the characters, is taken from the Holy Bible, New International Version®. NIV®. Copyright © 1973, 1978, 1984, 2011 by Biblica, Inc.™ Used by permission of Zondervan. All rights reserved worldwide. www.zondervan.com

This book is a work of fiction. Names, characters, places, and incidents are the product of the author's imagination or are used fictitiously. Any resemblance to actual events, locales, or persons, living or dead, is coincidental.

Published in association with Tamela Hancock Murray, The Steve Laube Agency, 5025 N. Central Ave., #635, Phoenix, AZ 85012

17 18 19 20 21 22 23   7 6 5 4 3 2 1

This book is dedicated
to the amazing brains behind it!
Thank you to Colleen Coble, Ronie Kendig,
Carrie Stuart Parks, Robin Miller, and Michelle Lim.
Your input made the story shine!

Special thanks:

To Dru Wells and Wayne Smith
for keeping me on the straight and narrow
when it comes to law enforcement. :)
I appreciate you more than I can say!

To my family.
I love you for letting me write.

PROLOGUE

". . . for it is written: 'It is mine to avenge; I will repay,' says the Lord."

The words grabbed the man by the throat. He pushed the half-eaten plate of spaghetti away and studied the passage again. He had read those words before, but never had he understood them to mean what was so clear to him now.

It had been six years.

Six years and the Lord had not exacted his vengeance. And it suddenly occurred to him why.

He was to be the instrument used to ensure justice. *He* was the one the Lord had chosen and had just now revealed to him how he was to carry out the plans that would set the world right again.

He was the chosen one.

Stunned at the revelation, he set aside the Bible and picked up the other book he'd been studying. Just one book in the hundreds he'd read over the past six years.

"Sweetheart?"

He looked up. "Yes?"

"Could you get me a glass of water, please?"

"Of course."

He stood and walked to the sink to fill the glass. As the water ran from the spigot, he stared at it.

And knew what he had to do.

Because he was the Chosen One.

[1]

Maddy McKay smiled at the man across the table from her. "Congratulations on graduating from physical therapy." Detective Quinn Holcombe wore khaki cargo pants, a long-sleeved black T-shirt that he did *GQ* things to—and a scowl. "Be careful, your face is going to freeze like that."

He lifted a brow. A slight improvement. "That's something you congratulate someone on?"

She sighed. He was always so grumpy. She smiled again. This one forced. "Of course it is. Do you have no social skills whatsoever? You were almost crushed to death. You lived. You finished your physical therapy. I'd say that's cause to celebrate— and something to offer congratulations for." Six months ago, Quinn had been investigating a case and the killer had used a backhoe to flip Quinn's car, trapping him inside and slamming the arm of the machine down on the vehicle. Quinn's broken legs had healed and now he walked with only a slight limp.

11

This morning, they'd run three miles without stopping. "You've come a long way, Quinn."

He grunted. "Maybe so."

She pursed her lips and leaned back, crossing her arms.

His eyes softened. "You're right, I'm sorry."

"For which offense?"

He sighed. "For everything. My lack of social skills for one. My surliness for another. So . . . thank you. I . . . uh . . . couldn't have . . . uh—" he cleared his throat—"gotten through all of this without you. You know that, right?"

The words combined with the flash of vulnerability reminded her of what she saw in the man in spite of his acerbic personality. She gave a short soft laugh. "Of course I know that." She eyed him and wrinkled her nose at him. "Although, with your sunny disposition, I can't imagine why you didn't have people lining up to volunteer to take care of you."

He blinked and shook his head. "There's no one I would have wanted there more than you, Maddy. I know I'm a bear sometimes, but . . . yeah."

"Yeah, you're a bear sometimes." She reached over and squeezed his hand. His willingness to just admit that he'd needed her, *wanted* her to be there, touched her. She'd been so close to smacking him in the head and walking out on their relationship—if one could call it that. Several times.

Now his words gave her hope that one day he'd open up to her. Confide in her. Let her share the pain that never left him.

"I wanted to ask you something," Quinn said.

"Okay. Ask."

"Why do you hang out with me?" he asked softly. "Why did you stay with me in the hospital? Through physical therapy?"

She swallowed. "I . . . uh . . . well, because of your charming personality, of course."

12

He let out a short bark of laughter. "Right. Really. Why?"

"We've been through a lot together."

"Yeah."

"You didn't leave my side last year when that lunatic slit my throat and left me to die."

He looked away. "That was a bad time, Maddy. I really didn't think you were going to make it."

"I know. I didn't think so either."

He caught her gaze. "Is that why you stayed with me? Because you felt obligated?"

"No."

"Then why?"

"Because, Quinn. Just . . . because." She sighed. "I don't know. Maybe obligation was part of it, but . . . not really." Silence descended. She took a sip of her water. "So, how's the puppy doing?"

He shot her a look that said he didn't want to let her off the hook that easily and she tensed. His scowl deepened. "Sherlock is a pain in my neck."

"But you like having him there."

He shrugged and sipped his water.

"Oh just admit it, you do." She and her co-workers Olivia Savage, Katie Matthews, and Haley Callaghan had all gone in together and gotten him the puppy. A black lab with massive amounts of energy. Quinn had a large fenced-in yard, and she knew the two went jogging every morning and evening.

"Maybe." The scowl faded and a small smile played at the corner of his lips.

"Not a resounding yes, but I'll take it." She also knew if he hadn't wanted the dog, he'd have given him back with a simple "Thanks, but no thanks." And he hadn't done that. She cut into her steak and took a bite. The savory piece nearly melted

13

on her tongue. She swallowed. "Have you made any progress on finding the serial killer?"

"No. I mean, I don't even know if there *is* a serial killer."

"But the messages keep coming and the people keep disappearing, right?"

"Yes." He shook his dark head. "So maybe it's just a serial kidnapper? We're missing something. Why can't we find them? Alive? Or even dead?"

"He's got a good hiding place."

"Unfortunately." Quinn's scowl deepened. "It's like they've just fallen off the face of the earth. We're stumped."

"That's the way it always seems to go, doesn't it?"

"Yes. Usually. Until he makes a mistake."

"How many victims now?"

"Eight. That we know of—over a six-month period of time." He ran a hand through his hair. "Or maybe none. I don't know."

She shuddered. "I worked several serial killer cases when I was with the FBI. I don't miss it."

"Well, that's not what I was hoping to hear."

Wary, she eyed him. "What do you mean?"

He reached across the table and took her hand. "I need your help on this case."

She shook her head. "You've turned it over to the FBI. Let them handle it."

"I'm part of the task force and I want to recruit you."

She pulled her hand from his and ignored the flutter in her pulse at his touch. It was her turn to scowl. "I'm a bodyguard now. I quit the FBI for a reason, remember?" She shrugged. "And besides, I'd have to be sworn back in as a special investigator or analyst or something, go through the whole background check thing, et cetera. Is it really worth it?"

"That wouldn't take any time at all. You're just trying to come up with excuses."

She grimaced. "Maybe so."

He leaned back and studied her. She resisted the urge to squirm and took another bite of the steak. While she chewed, her gaze went from person to person in the restaurant. No one alarmed her or caused the hair on the back of her neck to stand on end.

When she realized what she was doing, she let her eyes lock back on to Quinn's. He was simply waiting. She sighed. "Why me?"

"Because you can get in his mind," he murmured. "Just like you did with the Butcher."

The serial killer who'd dismembered his victims and cooked them on the gas grill in his backyard. She still got nauseous thinking about him. "I don't want to be in his head, Quinn. It's too . . . damaging to my own peace of mind. We're not meant to think stuff like that."

"Unfortunately, we have to have people like you to catch people like him. That's why you studied psychology, right?"

"Partly."

He sighed. "He's going to kill again."

"Of course he is. They always do." The steak now sat like lead in her stomach.

"Unless you help me catch him."

She was losing her appetite. "Did you get another note or something?"

"Yes." The notes came to the station with the victims' names and pictures attached—and then the victims disappeared. And no matter how fast the cops moved, the victims were always already gone.

"And what did it say?"

He drew in a deep breath. "'Judgment Day is coming.'"

"And whose name and picture were attached to this one?"

"No one's."

She frowned. "That's odd. Out of eight letters, he's never deviated from his pattern. Are you sure you didn't miss the name and picture?"

"I'm sure."

She rubbed her forehead, the idea of helping grabbed hold. He was right. She was good at her job. Correction. *Had been* good at her job. She'd tell him about her note in a moment. Right now, her thoughts were spinning as to who might be sending the notes. "Could be a copycat," she said. "I know you released information about the notes to warn the public, but there was nothing about the kind of stationery or if it was handwritten or typed and you never revealed that the victims' names were on the notes, right?"

"Exactly. I thought the same thing. A copycat."

"So, it could just be someone getting his kicks by emulating what he learned from watching the news. It wouldn't take much to figure out who the lead detective on the case was and that's why you got the notes."

"Could be." He shook his head. "But this feels weird."

"I'll think about it."

"Thanks, that's all I ask. Now do you mind if we talk about something else?"

"Actually, I was going to tell you—"

"Seriously, no more work stuff tonight, okay?"

She shrugged. She'd tell him about the note tomorrow. "Okay then, I have something I'd like to discuss."

"What?"

"Your birthday party tomorrow. You want to come by and pick me up or you want me to meet you there?"

16

His fork thunked on his plate. She raised a brow and he shook his head. "I don't need a party. Why would anyone want to throw me a party? Do I look like a party person? When have you ever known me to attend a party? I don't party." He picked the fork back up and viciously jabbed his own piece of meat. Then he pointed it at her. "They obviously know nothing about me and are not my friends if they'd do this."

"Right. Because they want to celebrate your birthday with you and went to all the trouble to set this up. I can see how you would come to that conclusion." Maddy could no longer find her smile. Her irritation was easy to locate though. And anger.

"Now wait a min—"

"No, I won't wait. Look, Quinn, apparently they see something in you to care about." She tossed her napkin down. "I'll tell them to cancel it. In fact, why don't I just tell them to cancel their friendship? If you want to be alone the rest of your life, then so be it. Enjoy your dinner. Alone." She stood and gathered her purse.

"Maddy—"

His shocked expression was gratifying, but she'd had enough. More than enough. "I'm getting off the Quinn Holcombe roller coaster. Congratulations. You've managed to push me away. In fact, I think you've managed to shove me straight over the edge of the cliff. Goodbye and have a nice life."

She headed for the door and she felt his eyes on her back. Her heart nearly broke in two, but she was done. She loved him, she freely admitted it, but he was too broken, too damaged to ever fully trust her, and she couldn't live with the stress of loving him anymore. So she'd live with the stress of loving him and losing him.

Because the fact that he let her walk out the door, get into her car, and drive away spoke volumes.

17

The Chosen One stood about ten feet from the house and, aided by the gibbous moon, read the directions he'd printed from the internet one more time. How to disable a home alarm system. He'd done his research. He knew the kind of alarm system she had. It was a good one. A pricey one. And a wireless one. And as he'd found out, all wireless alarm systems rely on radio frequency signals. The signals bounce between the door and window sensors. When the system is breached, the alarm sounds and sends a silent alert to the monitoring company.

But what most people didn't know was that the signals could be jammed using radio noise. Radio noise prevented the signal from getting through the sensors and to the control panel. Easy peasy.

Within seconds, he had the alarm disabled and was through the back door. He smiled. Now that he'd found his calling, everything was falling into place.

From watching the house over the last several days, the Chosen One knew she'd enter through the kitchen. Every time she'd come home, she'd parked in the garage, shutting the door behind her.

Now. He looked around. Where to hide? He would have to act fast. She was very skilled in self-defense. He'd never beat her in a hand-to-hand fight. He hefted the canister in his right hand. She'd be no match for the friend he brought along.

After studying her house plans, he knew she had a small closet off the great room. When she came in through the garage, she would enter the laundry room, pass the small utility room and into the open kitchen and dining area. No place to hide there. Now that he was actually in her house, he could see that the closet was his best option. As long as it wasn't packed to the brim. He walked over and opened the door.

He smiled. Two coats, two filters that probably fit the ceiling vent in her kitchen, two tennis rackets, and a box of children's toys. His smile slipped. She didn't have children, but she catered to the mass of nieces and nephews she had. They would miss her.

For a brief moment remorse flickered. He snuffed it out. He was fulfilling his calling, living out his destiny. Just two more and his work would be done. He could go back to living his quiet, simple life and no one would ever know of his greatness. And that was fine.

Because he would know and the raging need for vengeance would be satisfied. His phone pinged and he glanced at the screen.

What do I do about the pits?

What do you mean?

You wanted changes. Should I have some driftwood or a tree limb lying around for them to use to get over some of the pits safely?

Do that for several pits around the perimeter. But space those out so that they have to find the right ones to cross to live. Camouflage the others. Wrong area = death. Right area = they live.

Good idea. Thanks.

Anytime.

He tucked his cell phone into his coat pocket, then slipped inside the closet to wait for Maddy McKay to arrive home.

[2]

Quinn stared at the napkin Maddy had tossed down only seconds before. He felt the startled gazes of the other diners on him and didn't care. He closed his eyes and blew out a slow sigh. He was an idiot. A complete and total jerk. He admitted it.

Slowly, it dawned on him that he didn't want to push her away like he did everyone else in his life. He wanted to grab her and hold her close, look into her sapphire blue eyes and tell her how much she meant to him. But there were things she didn't know. Things he couldn't share with her. With anyone. Not even his partner, Bree Standish. Things he wouldn't even admit to himself.

Only now he was truly afraid he might have lost Maddy for good.

And that couldn't happen.

He'd lost everything and everyone that had ever mattered to him. What would he do without Maddy? The thought terrified him.

The black hole of his life had widened considerably when the door shut behind her, but he'd been so shocked he hadn't been able to move. What should he do? He absently watched the television attached to the wall above his head. Closed captions played across the bottom of the screen as the announcer spoke. "Three men are still missing from Key West. Gabriel Clemmons, an architect, disappeared approximately nine months ago." Pictures flashed and he noted their faces absently while he tried to decide the best way to proceed. "Two construction workers from Henry and Roach Construction Company still haven't been heard from for the past two months. Lamar Henry and Jason Roach were thought to have met a client for lunch, then disappeared shortly after they left the restaurant. The client they met with has yet to be identified, and authorities have stated foul play is suspected. If anyone has any information, please call the number at the bottom—"

Go after her, you idiot.

Quinn grabbed his phone and car keys from the table, tossed three twenties on the table, and bolted out the door.

After punching in the code for her alarm, Maddy slammed the door that led from the garage into the laundry room. It made her feel only slightly better. How could he? Tears threatened, but she held them back. Crying would only make her stuffy and Quinn wasn't worth crying over anyway. Okay, he was worth it, but she wasn't going to do it.

She exited the laundry room, passed the small utility room, and made a right into her kitchen, where she slipped out of her light jacket and unhooked the shoulder holster. Maddy set it on the counter, her weapon still in the holster, and took a mental inventory. She needed coffee. Or something. She needed to go running or pound on a bag for a while. Instead, she pulled a mug from the rack and popped a K-Cup into the machine. As she waited for the water to heat, she filled the empty hole in her K-Cup tree with a fresh pod, then walked into her bedroom and slipped into her jogging pants and a short-sleeved T-shirt. She pulled a long-sleeved tee over that and grabbed her running shoes.

Maddy sat on the bed and thought about the note she'd received.

"Divine perfection is overrated." The small index card had been on her car windshield when she'd walked out the door to meet Quinn at the restaurant. Now that she knew he'd received one as well, chills shivered up her spine. It could be the same guy, even though there were some subtle differences in the style. Or was it a copycat? The other victims had notes, but the notes had gone straight to the police department, not to the victims themselves.

She needed to send it in and have it analyzed, even though it only faintly resembled the notes of the other victims. She'd planned to mention it to Quinn tonight and hadn't because he said he didn't want to talk about work stuff anymore. She sighed. She'd give it to him tomorrow.

For now, she'd go running.

Thunk.

She straightened from tying her shoes and stilled.

What was that?

Maddy rose from the bed and her hand went to the weapon that wasn't there. She'd left it in the kitchen on the counter. Her pulse rate skyrocketed.

She took several deep breaths. It was probably just the ice maker. It was always loud. Although she had to admit, she didn't remember it sounding quite like that. She peered out of her bedroom door into the great room. It looked like it always did. Calm and peaceful. Maddy crossed the room, looked into the dining room and then the kitchen.

22

Nothing. She grabbed her Glock 21SF from the counter, feeling slightly foolish at the comfort it brought her in her own home. Her empty home. But still . . .

Her phone pinged and she rushed back into her bedroom and grabbed it from where she'd tossed it on the bed.

A text from Quinn. *I'm sorry. Let me make it up to you. I'm coming over.*

She ignored it and slipped the device into the armband she used when she ran. He could come over, but she wouldn't be here.

A floorboard creaked.

Maddy froze. That was *not* the ice maker.

Was someone actually in her house? She gripped the weapon. But how? She had her alarm on. Didn't she? Had she rearmed it when she stomped inside, still fuming about Quinn and his behavior? And her reaction to it?

She couldn't remember.

Maddy moved slowly, gun held in front of her. She stepped to the door of her bedroom and peered around the frame. Seeing nothing, she slipped out of her bedroom, then looked at her front door. It was shut. Her gaze moved to the closet to the left.

It was cracked. She never left her closet doors cracked. She liked them firmly closed. Heart thundering in her chest, but her training overriding her fear, she moved closer.

She reached for the knob.

A spray of liquid caught her in the face.

She gasped and dizziness immediately hit her. The weapon fell from her hand with a thud.

Maddy stumbled to brace herself against the wall, heart racing, fear choking her. She reached for the gun, but weakness invaded her, and she sank toward the floor while flashes of the last time she'd been attacked raced through her mind at warp speed.

She felt the hard floor beneath her knees. The room seemed to tilt, nausea swirled. Maddy tried to stop the darkness, to push it back, even while she knew it was a losing battle. She saw the masked face hovering above her and tried to order her muscles to cooperate, but the face quivered, then faded to black.

Quinn pulled to a stop in front of Maddy's home. He didn't see her car but knew she usually parked in the garage. Darkness was falling quickly. He and Maddy had shared a late dinner—or at least a part of one—and he wasn't ready for the evening to end. At least not the way it had.

He grabbed his Yankees ball cap from the dash and slipped it on his head. He was using it as a figurative barrier he could hide behind should he need it when he ate his plate of crow, and he couldn't bring himself to leave it in the truck. It gave him the nerve he needed to climb out and shut the door. He scanned the area and noticed the gray van two doors down and the green pickup across the street. He took note of the next-door neighbor on her front porch talking on her cell phone. She saw him and went inside.

He glanced at his phone. Still no text from Maddy. He climbed the front porch steps and knocked on the door.

No answer. "Come on, Maddy," he muttered, then raised his voice. "I know you're home. I just want to talk to you."

He knocked again, then rang the bell.

Maddy's home backed up to a small man-made lake. He knew she loved the water and had always dreamed of having a back porch where she could sit and hear the water lapping against the dock. Maybe she was out back.

Quinn walked down the steps of the house and around to the back. The light was on, but she wasn't anywhere to be seen. He took the two steps up to her porch, then rapped his knuckles on the sliding glass door. "Maddy? You here?"

Again, no answer. He dialed her number and paused when he heard the ringing from inside the house. Now he knew she was home. She wouldn't go anywhere without her cell. He knocked again, even as an uneasiness slithered through him. "Maddy? You okay?"

The blinds in front of the glass doors blocked most of his view of the inside, but he found a gap and looked through. Maddy lay on the floor, her hand outstretched, eyes closed. "Maddy!" Quinn grabbed the handle to the door and yanked.

Locked. He fumbled for his phone to dial 911.

A rustling sounded behind him. He spun, caught a glimpse of a figure in dark clothes, then caught a face-full of some liquid spray. He choked and dizziness hit him. He tried to backpedal and weakness flooded him. "What—?"

Darkness that had nothing to do with the time of day closed in on him, and he lost his balance and hit the ground. He rolled and stared up at a shimmering, fading figure.

"The time of judgment has come," it whispered.

Quinn struggled to stay awake, to verbalize a response, but finally had to give in. His last thought was that he'd failed yet another person he cared about.

[3]

Maddy groaned. Her head pounded a painful rhythm and she lifted a hand to her temple as she tried to force her eyes open. At first they didn't want to cooperate, but finally, she got her lids up. Slits, but at least they were moving on demand. What had hit her?

Light filtered through her lashes and she finally took note of her bed. Only it wasn't her bed. It was a hard surface. She moved her fingers. Concrete. The pounding in her skull intensified and she shut her eyes again as she struggled to remember what had happened. Had she fallen and hit her head? Did she have a concussion?

She lay still as the minutes passed. Finally, the painful vibrations receded and she was able to blink her eyes open once again. She slowly eased her way into a sitting position, but the nausea that swept her nearly took her back down.

She focused on the far wall and took several deep breaths, and gradually the feeling passed. She raised her hands to her head and pressed her fingers to her skull, massaging, touching, looking for anything that would indicate she'd been clobbered.

Nothing. She processed that. She had no head wound. Okay, if she hadn't hit her head, why did it hurt so bad? Drugs? The aftereffect. That seemed most likely.

She took note of her surroundings. The wall she'd fixed her gaze on was concrete, like the slab she now sat on.

She let her eyes travel upward. Probably about ten feet tall. Her gaze skimmed the ceiling. It was a blank slate with tiny holes dotting the surface. So where was the light coming from?

Slowly, ever so slowly, she turned her head. Another wall greeted her. A large mural, perhaps five feet by six, covered part of the surface. She stood and walked over to it, touched it. It was a painting of an island, a very skilled, detailed piece of work.

She studied it carefully, even kneeling to get a closer look at the bottom part. But her mind was foggy and she couldn't seem to process the painting. On her knees, she turned ninety degrees to her left and found a third wall that held a toilet, a sink, and what looked like a blank digital clock. And finally, the fourth wall that was exactly the same as the first wall.

Only it had a body on the floor near it. He lay faceup with his eyes closed and his complexion a pale gray.

"Quinn," she whispered. He lay still. Very still. She stood to go to him, only this time the nausea won. She launched herself at the toilet just in time and lost what little she had in her stomach. When she could move again, she rinsed her mouth in the sink, then crawled on all fours and pressed her fingers against Quinn's wrist.

A steady pulse beat and she nearly wept with relief. Again, she scanned the room. Where were they? How had they gotten here? Where was here?

She pushed the ball cap from his head and ran her hands through his hair. Also no injury that she could feel. "Quinn, wake up."

No response. Panic pushed her adrenaline into overdrive. Again, she had to stop and take deep breaths. When she had her pulse somewhat under control, she turned her attention back to Quinn.

Maddy cupped his cheeks, felt the stubble under her palms. "Quinn. Come on, please. I need you to wake up." Her voice cracked on the last word and she realized just how scared she was.

Because it was obvious. They'd been drugged and kidnapped. She didn't even bother feeling for her phone or her gun. Whoever had taken her wouldn't leave those where she could find them.

A groan from Quinn had her squeezing his hands. "Wake up, Quinn."

"No. Go 'way." He didn't open his eyes.

"Quinn Holcombe, we've been kidnapped. If you don't open your eyes right now, I'm going to—to—" What? What would she do? "Cry," she finally whispered.

Another groan slipped from his lips, but at least he cracked an eye. "Maddy?"

"Yes, yes, keep waking up."

"Man. Did I drink too much or what?"

She stifled a sob and pinched the bridge of her nose. "No. You don't drink anymore, remember?"

"Oh. Right. What happened?"

"You don't remember?"

"No. Do you?"

"Not all of it, but I'm getting flashes." She bit her lip and closed her eyes. Quinn sat up, pulled her to him, and wrapped his arms around her. Then immediately shoved her away.

She blinked. "Wha—? Oh."

His green face spoke to her. She helped him to the toilet. Then heard him being sick. Maddy grabbed some toilet paper from the roll and handed it to him. He rinsed his mouth and fell back to the floor.

"So, yeah," she said. "That's a side effect of whatever we got hit with. Give it a minute or two and it'll pass."

He groaned. "What do you mean?"

"I mean, I think we were drugged."

"Drugged?" He scooted to the other wall and leaned against it, his elbows on his knees, head lowered against his right forearm. "Yeah, that feels about right. I'll go with that." She slipped up next to him and he grasped her hand. "Are you okay?" he asked.

"I don't know. I know I'm scared." The admission tasted like dust on her tongue but was true nevertheless.

His eyes bounced from wall to wall just like hers had moments ago. "Okay, I'll admit to being a member of that club as well."

"You? I didn't think anything scared you."

His eyes flashed with a pain she'd never seen before. "A lot of things scare me." His nose twitched. "I smell food."

She grimaced. "That's not what I smell." But then she did and her stomach rumbled. "Where's it coming from?"

"I don't know." He shook his head and pointed. "Are those speakers?"

Maddy looked. In the ceiling corners of the room, there were four little black boxes. "Possibly. Or cameras?"

"Or both."

"But . . . why?"

He shrugged. "So whoever did this can communicate with us, probably." He stroked her hair, his hand gliding down to rest on her shoulder. "How's your head feeling?"

"Better." She liked his touch. Right now, it gave her a security, a sense of gladness that she wasn't alone. Not that she wanted him to be trapped in this nightmare, but if she had to be stuck with someone, she was glad it was with someone who knew how to fight back should it come down to that. And she had a feeling it would. "How's yours?"

"Getting better by the minute. I wonder what he hit us with?"

"I don't know. I don't even care at this point." She touched his cheek, then the bridge of his nose. "You have lines right here. Like you were wearing a mask."

He studied her. "You do too. Light ones, like they've faded. It's probably how he kept us from waking up until he had us where he wanted us."

Scenes flashed in her mind. "He was inside my house," she whispered. "In the coat closet just outside my bedroom. Now I remember. He sprayed something in my face." She frowned. "How did he get you?"

"I came looking for you. He ambushed me at the back of your house." His eyes continued to roam the room. He muttered something and she missed it.

"My memory is like fragments, but it's starting to come back to me," she said. "We were at dinner and we fought."

"Yeah, you left me."

She narrowed her eyes. "You let me leave."

He grunted. "Just for a moment. I told you I came looking for you."

He sounded distracted. "What are you thinking?" she asked.

"The door," he said. "Where is it?"

She sniffed again. "I don't know, but there's ventilation. I still smell the food you were talking about and it's a lot stronger now."

Quinn rose to his feet and walked to the far corner of the room. He placed his hands on the wall and felt every inch of the wall and floor that he could reach, then moved on to the next.

"There are grooves in this wall," he said of the one opposite the painting. "They're faint, but they're there."

"What do you think they're for?"

"Probably to deliver things into the room without fear of being attacked by the occupants."

"Like a prison cell, only without the bars."

"Exactly."

She nodded to the map on the wall. "What do you make of that?"

He blinked and walked over to it. Touched it just the way she had moments before. "It's a painting."

"I figured that part out."

"Of an island."

"Yes, I got that far on my own." He shot her an exasperated look and she shrugged, then hugged herself and clasped her arms. "Sorry, I'm a bit off-balance right now."

"Can't think why," he muttered. He reached out to squeeze her hand, then continued to study the mural. "Tell me your thoughts. What do you think it's for?"

"Could it be a representation of where we are? Like a map?"

"Could be. But why put it on the wall?"

"So we'll see it?"

"You're feeling better, you're getting feisty."

"Greetings, my friends."

Maddy jerked and Quinn's arm came around her shoulder to huddle her next to him. A gravelly voice filled the room, compliments of the speakers. "So glad to see you're awake with only a few nasty side effects from the medication. It wears off pretty fast, though. Have you had ample recovery time?"

Maddy's fear swept back. Along with anger. She refused to be a victim again. "Who are you?" she asked.

"Just someone who's been waiting a long time for this day. I apologize for the lack of privacy, but I haven't kept more than one person at a time in there until now."

"Why are you doing this?" Quinn asked. He returned his gaze to the map.

Maddy did the same, doing her best to memorize it. She didn't know why, but she had a feeling she needed to.

"All in due time, Detective Holcombe. All in due time. But for now, you need to eat."

A space in the wall opposite them opened up. A rectangular area with dimensions that allowed a tray laden with food to slip through. Four chilled water bottles lay on their sides next to the tray.

"What's this for?" Quinn asked, his eyes still on the map.

"Just a little something to make things a bit more even. You have an hour. Be ready."

"Ready for what? Why are you doing this? Who are you?" Maddy demanded.

Silence echoed and for a moment Maddy wondered if he would answer.

"You may call me the Chosen One," he finally said. "I'm doing this because I'm a hunter. I wasn't always one, but then certain things happened in life to show me that this is my calling, my purpose. There are many choices outside of those walls you're trapped within for now. Choices that will determine whether you live or die. Because, you see, I also like games. If you play the game and play it well, you will discover the way off the island. However, should you play poorly, then you will die. And just for the record, no one has managed to beat me at this game."

"Probably because you don't play fair," Maddy said. "Why are you hiding behind those speakers? Get in here and face us."

Silence. Then a chuckle. "Yes, you'd like that, wouldn't you? But you see, I know all about your martial arts skills, so I think

I'll pass." Another pause. "As for not playing fair, that's not completely true, is it? I did give you a good meal to fortify yourself with, didn't I?"

"Why do I need to be fortified?"

"For the games, of course."

"What are the rules?"

"Hmm . . . no one's ever asked that before. I suppose there's really only one rule. If you survive, you win. Now, my dear friends, the clock is ticking. Eat up."

A soft click told her he'd disconnected. Maddy stood still. The feel of Quinn's arm around her shoulders brought comfort. "If he's the hunter, does that mean we're his prey?"

"That kind of sounds like what he was saying, doesn't it?"

"I don't think I like this game very much." She heard the shakiness in her voice and rubbed a hand over her eyes.

Quinn moved away from her and she bit back a protest. He reached out, snagged a water bottle from the tray, and twisted the top off.

She rushed to him and caught his arm. "Don't drink that! Are you crazy?"

Quinn hesitated. "You think he would poison it?"

"Of course I do. Or drug it with something. He seems to be pretty handy that way."

"But why? He told us we have an hour. And to be ready. If he needs us to be ready, he wouldn't do something to make us *not* be ready. Would he?"

"Who knows?" She threw her hands up. Fear had been an ever-present lump in her chest since she'd awakened to find herself trapped in the room. She wanted to sit on the floor and just cry. She wanted to wake up in her bedroom and find this had all just been a bad dream. She wanted her gun. "Maybe it's a trick. Maybe he just wants us to think we need to—"

She stifled a gasp and stared as he took a swig from the bottle. They waited. The minutes ticked by. He shrugged and continued to drink until he'd finished off half the bottle. He handed the rest to her. "Here."

She chugged it, then tossed the bottle to the floor. "There. Happy?"

"Yeah."

"Now what?"

"We eat."

She pressed a hand to her stomach. "I don't think that's a good idea."

He reached for the plastic steak knife and fork, then met her eyes. "Wasn't about to give us weapons, was he?"

He cut into the steak and stabbed it with the plastic fork. He examined the utensils like he'd never seen anything like them before. "They're not bad. Not good enough to defend ourselves with, but good enough to eat the meal."

She put a hand on his. "You're really going to eat it, aren't you?"

He turned serious eyes on her. Glanced at the speaker/camera in the nearest corner. "Yes. I don't know how much time has passed between getting knocked out and waking up in here, but my stomach says it's past time to eat. I think we should."

Her fear multiplied. She pressed a hand to her head. She had to start thinking. She'd been in tense situations before. Life-and-death situations. She could handle this. She took a few more deep breaths. "All right, he said be ready in an hour. That was eighteen minutes ago." She glanced at the clock on the wall as she picked up the second fork. "We have forty-two minutes left."

[4]

Quinn finished the last bite of his steak and glanced at the clock on the wall. Truly, he wasn't quite as confident about the water or the meal as he'd let on to Maddy. But he figured the odds were in his favor. Whoever had gone to all the trouble to knock them out and transport them to this room wasn't going to poison them. No, this guy wanted something.

"There's not a way out of here, is there?" he said.

"Not that I can find. You've gone over every square inch. The whole room is concrete except for the ceiling. I don't know what kind of material that is, but there's no way to balance well enough to try to bust through it with anything." She shrugged. "No going through the ceiling, no going through the floor. We're stuck until he decides to let us out." A muscle jumped in her jaw and he could see her pulse fluttering in her throat.

"I'm supposed to meet my mother for lunch tomorrow," he said. "At least I think it's tomorrow. What's today?"

"Saturday. I think." She blinked. "And that was random."

"Sorry, I was thinking." He looked around. "Like you said, we're kind of stuck. I'd gladly try to bust through the wall, but would rather wait and see if he's serious about letting us out of here."

"I think he is. That's what worries me."

"So let's take our minds off of it. Let's talk."

"Talk? That's a first for you." He scowled and Maddy cleared her throat. "All right. You were thinking about your family."

"Yeah," he said softly.

"You don't ever say much about them."

He pinched the bridge of his nose. Maybe he didn't want to talk after all. "There's a lot of regret there," he finally said. "I don't like to talk about them because then the regrets rise to the surface and—"

"I understand that," she whispered with a glance at the cameras in the corner, then back at him.

He locked eyes with her. "You don't talk about your family much either." He kept his voice low as well.

She pursed her lips and nodded. "Like you, I also have some regrets."

They fell silent. "How long have we known each other?" he finally asked.

"Almost four years maybe? I met you a few months after starting with the bodyguard agency." She paced the room, rubbing her arms and touching the walls as though something might have changed since she'd last examined the area.

"I remember." He studied her face and realized he had regrets about more things than his family. He went to her and placed his hands on her shoulders, turning her to face him. "I remember being blown away by you. You made such an impression on me that I couldn't get you out of my mind."

That caught her attention. "What?"

"Seriously. You were just so professional." He smiled. "You never looked at me as a potential."

"A potential," she said. "A potential . . . what? Boyfriend?"

"Yeah."

She snorted. "That's because I wasn't interested. No offense, but I was going through a hard time and a relationship wasn't even on my radar." She moved from under his hands to the next wall. Tapping, listening.

"I know. That's what caught my attention."

"So you went out of your way to make sure I noticed you?"

He shrugged. "Maybe a little. You just intrigued me. And that fact alone made me want your attention. So I set out to get it."

She huffed a soft laugh that held very little humor. "Do you realize how arrogant that sounds?"

"Yes. I don't mean it to be, it's just you know how a badge attracts some women. When I met you, it seemed like I had been dodging cop chasers left and right." He felt the heat rise in his cheeks but was determined to say what was on his heart. For once. "But you didn't care about the badge. When we talked, I could tell you listened. You weren't humoring me and wondering what your next move should be to get me to ask you out. You just . . . were you. And I was me and . . . it was nice. It made me wonder if you could care about . . . me."

She paused in her restlessness. "I get the badge thing with other women, but surely you've worked with enough female cops over the years that were just like me. A woman who could see beyond that."

He blew out a slow breath and gave a low laugh. "Maybe, but like I said, there wasn't anyone who caught my attention like you did. There's no one like you, Maddy. Trust me on that one." She flushed and he took her hand. "That was a compliment."

"Thanks." Maddy looked at the speakers. "What if he's listening?"

"What if he is? He already knows all about us. I think we've kept our voices low enough that he can't hear what we're saying, but frankly, I don't care what he hears. Mostly because I plan to take him down at some point."

Maddy's eyes hardened. "Yes. Definitely."

Quinn locked eyes with her. "Anyway, we'd just started . . . uh . . . seeing more of each other a year ago when you were attacked and almost died. Then I got hurt and . . . we've spent a lot of time together, working with and helping each other, and yet I'm just beginning to realize that I barely know you."

She gave a slow nod. "It's called dating, Quinn, but I could say the same about you."

"Okay, dating. So why is that? Why do I barely know you?"

She didn't look away from him. "You tell me."

More silence. Then he sighed and looked at one of the speakers. "I'll have to think about that one." He looked around the room. "You think there's more than one person involved in our kidnapping?"

She hesitated, then shrugged. "Going with my first thought, yes, I would think there have to be at least two. You're a big guy, Quinn. Unless he's your size, I don't think he could have carried you out alone. Me? Easy. You? Doubtful."

"Maybe." He pushed that thought away as another intruded. "'Judgment Day is coming,'" he whispered.

She frowned at him. "What?"

He shook his head. Could it be related? "When he sprayed me in the face, he muttered, 'The time of judgment has come.' Or something like that. It's similar to what my note said."

She froze, her eyes widened. "*Your* note? What note?"

He paused. "You remember the note I told you about at dinner?"

"Yes." She crossed her arms. "The one you said had no name on it."

"Well, technically, it didn't. But it was definitely meant for me. When I came out of work a couple of days ago, I found it stuck under my windshield wiper. It said, 'Judgment Day is coming.'"

"So you lied to me."

"Noooo, not really. It didn't have a name on it."

Her jaw tightened. "A little bit of omission is still a lie."

He grimaced. "I didn't mean it to be a lie. I just didn't want you to worry about it." She rolled her eyes. "And truthfully, while it did occur to me that it could be related to the possible serial kidnapper/killer, I didn't think much about it *because* it didn't have my name on it and it was sent to me personally, not through the police department. It wasn't like the other victims' notes." The other notes had been very specific. The kidnapper/killer had put the victim's name in the right-hand corner, then a one-line message in the middle of a four-by-six index card.

"You should have told me about it," she said. "Or someone. Did you tell anyone?"

He opened his mouth to respond, then snapped his lips shut and shrugged.

She sighed. "I got one too."

"What?"

"I got a note too. Same as you. Under my wiper the day before we met for dinner."

"And you didn't say anything?"

She sniffed at his outrage. "I was going to at dinner tonight . . ." She frowned. ". . . Last night?" A sigh. "Whenever. But things went south with us and I forgot."

"So we both got notes."

"Apparently."

He scowled. "Did yours have your name on it?"

"No, it didn't."

"And yet we've both been kidnapped."

"I think that's a given."

He ignored her sarcasm. "You know what this sounds like, right?"

"Yes, of course. It's like your serial killer case and the missing people. The ones who also received notes shortly before their disappearances and the ones you think have been killed by a serial killer."

"Unfortunately."

"But mine was definitely different than the notes the other victims got." She bit her lip. "Someone at the precinct will put two and two together and realize you're missing because you received a note, then disappeared, right?" She snapped her fingers. "Oh wait, you didn't tell anyone about the note."

Once again he ignored the sarcasm. "Bree will turn this country upside down looking for us. They'll figure it out. I hope."

She swallowed. "You can hope, I think I'll pray."

"Good luck with that." He paused. "Actually, when we don't show up for the party, people will start wondering where we are."

"Yes. Either that or they'll just assume you're blowing them off."

Offended, he frowned. "I wouldn't do that."

"Sure you would."

"Would not."

"But then they'll eventually search our houses and they'll find my note on my kitchen counter."

"Let's hope they do that sooner rather than later." He turned his gaze first to the clock, then to the picture on the wall. "Nine minutes."

"I wonder what happens in nine minutes?"

"Guess we're going to find out."

She fell silent, but he noticed she'd finished most of her food. He snagged the bread and stuffed it into one of the pockets of his cargo pants. She got up and walked back over to the painting. Placed a finger on the ocean's edge. "Being out there would be better than being in here, wouldn't it?" she asked.

"I don't know."

"Yeah."

"At least in here, there's a measure of comfort," he said. "And he let me keep my hat." He placed it on his head.

She walked the perimeter of the room, tapping the walls. She stopped at the back wall and tapped again. "I don't know why I keep doing that. It's still concrete. Not like it's going to change," she muttered sarcastically.

He moved and felt the area, and all around it, just as he had before. "We do it because it's *doing*. Anything is better than just sitting. So, this is our new normal," he mused aloud. "A new comfort zone. I'm feeling nervous, a little afraid—and yet nothing bad has happened yet, so I'm slightly comfortable. However, I'm on edge and nervous because I don't know what's to come."

She spun and looked at him, anger blazing in her dark eyes. She flipped his hat off his head and poked a finger in his chest. "You know, I really don't feel like analyzing the psychological aspects of this. I don't want a new comfort zone, I want my old one back. I don't like this and I want out of this room, so quit being all accepting and let's figure a way out of here." She punctuated her ire with her finger in his chest.

Quinn grabbed her hand and she curled it into a fist. He wrapped an arm around her shoulder. "I'm sorry, Maddy. I'm not taking this lightly, I promise. I'm with you."

She let out a shaky sigh and leaned in to him. Minutes passed and he just held her. She finally pulled back. "I know you're with me. You're doing what I need to be doing. Thinking. I'm sorry I blew up."

"You needed to."

"Yeah." She paused. "You were getting into the other victims' heads, weren't you?"

"Yes. If this is where they were kept before . . ."

"Before . . ."

"Before whatever happened outside of the room, then I want to know how they felt, what they experienced."

"I don't think that's going to be an issue, do you? I can tell you in detail what they experienced."

"Yeah."

Together they stood there and watched the clock on the wall count down. "Five seconds," she whispered.

"Four, three, two . . ."

"One."

No sooner had the words slipped out than a rumble started. He wouldn't have thought it possible, but Maddy's shoulders tensed even more under the weight of his arm, and she slipped into a fighter's stance as she faced the rising wall that worked like a simple garage door. Quinn let his arm fall from her and did the same. They stood back-to-back, to face the unknown.

The wall continued to rise and Quinn blinked when the sun hit his eyes.

Maddy's heart trembled like a leaf in the wind. Now that the door was open, she wasn't sure she wanted to leave the perceived safety of the room. She took a step back from the opening. "What if we don't leave?" she said. "He wants to hunt us. What if we don't give him anything to hunt?"

"Then you die anyway," the voice said. "It will make it less interesting, of course, but the end result will be the same." He chuckled and the sound sent chills racing up her spine. "I

LYNETTE EASON

have to say," he said, "I appreciate you making this so much fun. I've never had anyone not bolt out the door the second it opened." Smoke released from the ceiling. From the tiny holes she'd noticed when she first regained consciousness. "So, I'll just say, you have less than a minute before the room fills up with poisonous gas and the door shuts. Fifty-nine, fifty-eight . . ."

Maddy glanced at Quinn. The gas continued to fill the area. The door began its descent. Quinn leaned down, snagged his hat, then grabbed her hand, and together they raced from the building.

Within seconds, the door shut behind them.

Maddy grasped Quinn's hand in a death grip. "What now?" She looked around, liking that her back was to the building. Not liking the open jungle in front of them.

Something whooshed by her cheek and she heard a thud behind her. She spun, pulling her hand from Quinn's and ducking at the same time. A crossbow bolt protruded from the door they'd just exited.

Quinn reached for her again. "Let's go."

Maddy wrapped her hand around the bolt and pulled. She wasn't strong enough. "Get the bolt, Quinn."

"He's going to kill us while we stand here."

"Not if you hurry up. Get the bolt."

Within half a second, he had the bolt in his hand. She took off for the cover of the trees and heard his footfalls right behind her. Another bolt thudded into the trunk of a tree as she passed it. She veered right and tried to picture the map of the island in her head. The problem was, she wasn't sure where the building they'd been trapped in was located on the island. So even with the map in her head, she didn't know which way to go.

Except away from the crossbow and the deadly bolts.

Quinn stayed right with her. After several minutes of running, she stopped and slipped behind a large tree trunk. Quinn pulled up beside her, panting. "What are you doing?"

She tried to slow her breathing and her heart rate. "Listening. We can't keep running. We have to come up with a plan and outsmart him."

He fell silent. Maddy closed her eyes and tuned her ears to the sounds around her. Birds singing, insects clicking.

Dogs barking.

Dogs?

"He's set dogs on us," she whispered. "They're coming this way."

"Well, like you said, he doesn't play fair."

"Then we won't either."

"What do you have in mind?"

She looked up, then around until she found what she was looking for. "There."

"What are you doing?"

"I'm going to climb that tree. When the dogs focus on me, you get the handler. Use that bolt and drive it straight into his evil heart."

"That's not going to work," he said.

"You have a better idea?"

"Yeah. If we can't outrun them, we're going to have to outfight them. Grab a weapon."

She pursed her lips. The barking dogs drew closer. "What weapon?" She looked around. "The little stick or the tiny one?" She heard the hysteria in her voice and didn't care. She was scared. Terrified. And figured that was all right as long as she didn't allow it to cloud her thinking.

He moved deeper into the thick area, scoured the ground until he found what he was looking for. She watched him break a large piece of tree branch in half and at an angle. "Use the pointed end."

"I hate to hurt the dogs. They're just doing what they've been trained to do."

"I know, but if it comes down to us or them, it's got to be them."

"I know."

She raised the stick in the direction the dogs were coming from and slipped into a fighter's stance again. From the corner of her eye, she saw Quinn do the same.

Then the dogs burst through the trees. One large pit bull and a golden retriever. "Stay!" The word burst from her lips. "Sit!"

The golden skidded to a stop and dropped to his haunches, tongue lolling sideways. The pit bull launched himself at Quinn.

"No!" Maddy cried.

Quinn lifted the bolt and caught the dog mid-flight. The two went down in a tangle of flailing limbs. Maddy hurtled toward the animal and slammed her stick across his head. He howled and spun to face her. And that's when she saw the bolt sticking from his side. He whimpered and went to the ground. Quinn rose to his feet panting, blood streaming from his forearm.

"He got you."

"Yeah, but I'm more concerned about where his owner is."

A rustle in the bushes alerted them. The golden retriever rose to his feet and bolted into the bushes. Quinn gave her a shove. "Go."

She didn't hesitate. They wove their way through the trees, Quinn cradling his bloody arm, following a rough path up a rugged hill. Up, up, and then up some more. She caught his uninjured arm. "There."

"A cave." He hesitated. Looked behind them and then nodded. "All right."

They made their way to the dark opening and slipped inside.

The interior was in stark contrast to the exterior. "It's about ten degrees cooler in here," she whispered and wiped the sweat from her face. Her hair hung in her eyes and she shoved it back. She'd lost her hair tie. "Stay close to the entrance and let me see your arm."

"It's all right."

"Let me see."

He held it out while he kept watch. He had on the same long-sleeved black T-shirt that he'd worn at dinner the night before. "I don't think I can push the sleeve up without hurting you."

He glanced at her. Then reached up and, in one swift movement, ripped the sleeve off at the shoulder. He gave a low hiss when the cloth pulled at his wound, but other than that, he showed no sign that he was in pain. He started to toss it, but she grabbed it from him. "I'll use it as a bandage."

"Yeah. Good idea."

She bent over and once again her hair fell over her eyes. Once again she pushed it back. She shot a quick look at him and saw his jaw tighten. Pain or something else? "You okay?"

"Yeah."

She wrapped the piece of fabric around his forearm and pulled it tight. When she tied it off, it dawned on her what had him seething—besides the obvious. "You didn't have a choice," she said softly. "You said if it came down to the dogs or us, it had to be us. It's not your fault."

"I know."

Yes, he knew, but she could see that the knowledge didn't really make a difference to him. He was still furious. Angry that someone would use an animal like that. Her heart twisted. He was a good man, he just needed . . . something. Someone to understand him. Someone he trusted.

She rested her hand on his arm. "Quinn . . ."

He reached up and pulled his cap off. "Here." He dropped it on her head. "Use it to hold your hair back."

She didn't argue, she simply pulled her dark hair into a ponytail and shoved it through the hole in the back. "Thanks, now will you listen to—" A rustle reached her ears.

She snapped her lips shut at the same moment he placed a finger on her lips. She moved closer to the entrance and could almost feel the air vibrating. He was out there. Waiting. Watching. Ready to pounce. To kill.

She turned her ear toward the opening and closed her eyes. Her heart hummed in her chest, but she could hear over it. It was silent now, but she knew the man waited.

Quinn's body practically vibrated under her hand.

Uneasiness slithered through her. They couldn't stay here. No doubt their attacker knew about the cave, and it would probably be one of the first places he looked for them. She motioned for him to follow her.

He frowned. She insisted. Maddy moved to the edge of the entrance, keeping her back against the rock wall. Quinn stayed with her. She let her eyes scan the area.

She saw nothing.

Heard nothing.

But that didn't mean he wasn't out there. With certainty, she knew he was just waiting for one of them to exit. Then he would pick them off with either his crossbow or a rifle.

"We need a plan," he said. His low voice rumbled in her ear, his breath brushing across her cheek. "We're sitting ducks."

"He won't expect us to run," she said.

"He wants us to think we're safe and that we've gotten away from him," he murmured.

"So what do we do?"

"Run fast."

[5]

"Where are they?" Katie Matthews asked with another glance at her watch.

Olivia Savage shrugged and sipped her punch. "Maddy said she'd have him here at six."

"Well it's six thirty and neither one of them are here and neither are answering their texts."

Katie frowned. "That's kind of odd. Worrisome odd."

"No kidding."

Olivia looked around Katie's home. Her friend and co-worker had finally put the finishing touches on it two months ago. It was a beautiful place, but comfortable and relaxing. Olivia had already spoken to Wade, her husband of one month, about having Katie work her magic on their home.

After one look at Katie's handiwork, he'd readily agreed.

Olivia looked at the clock. 6:35. She hated to admit it, but she was a bit concerned herself. She pulled her phone from her purse and dialed Maddy's number. Straight to voice mail.

She hung up and tried Quinn. Same thing.

That low curling in the pit of her stomach started. The feeling she got when something was wrong. Not just wrong, but *very* wrong. She slipped across the den and into the kitchen, where she found Wade talking to Daniel Matthews, Katie's husband, and two detectives from the police department. Friends of Quinn's who'd, when invited to the birthday party, stated they wouldn't miss it for the world.

She shook her head. She wasn't completely sure what Maddy saw in Quinn, but Olivia trusted Maddy's judgment and knew her friend wouldn't invest so much of her time in someone who didn't deserve it. So that made Quinn Olivia's friend too. Whether he liked it or not.

Wade slipped an arm around her and drew her close. She grabbed his hand and tugged on it. He excused himself and followed her into an unoccupied corner of the dining room. "What is it?"

"I'm not sure. I think something's going on with Maddy and Quinn."

"Where are they?"

"That's the problem, we don't know and they're not answering their phones."

"You want me to ride over to his house and see if they're there? She was picking him up, right?"

"Supposed to."

"When was the last time you talked to her?"

She bit her lip as she thought. "Yesterday. She and Quinn were going to have dinner."

"But nothing today? You didn't confirm that she was picking Quinn up?"

Olivia shook her head. She'd been so busy helping Katie get her house ready she hadn't bothered to check on Maddy. If Maddy said she would do something, she would. She looked at the time again. Only now they were running close to forty-five minutes late. "Something is wrong, Wade. This isn't like Maddy. Or Quinn."

"He didn't really want the party, though, did he?"

Olivia grimaced. "No, not really, but Maddy wasn't giving him a choice."

"Maybe he decided to skip out and she's chasing him down."

"But she'd call and let us know. She hasn't. That's what has me so concerned."

He ran a hand through his dark hair. "Yeah, I get it. So, let's tell Bree and go to his house and see if he's there."

She nodded. "I'll see if Haley will go over to Maddy's home. I don't want to take Katie away from the other guests."

"No, we can handle this."

Olivia found Haley and Katie standing in the foyer talking. She explained the situation. Haley immediately grabbed her purse and keys. "I'm on it." She headed out the door. Olivia waved to Wade and he joined her. They followed Haley.

Maddy wasn't sure how many minutes passed while she and Quinn waited, listened, and watched. But he finally nudged her. "You go left, I'm going to go right."

"There's more coverage to the left."

"Exactly."

"Not to put down your excellent physical therapy progress, but how fast can you move?"

He squeezed her fingers. "Fast enough."

Still, she hesitated. "You go left, I'll go right. I'm faster."

"Not a chance."

"You're bigger, you need more coverage."

"Quit arguing, Maddy."

She recognized that tone, had certainly heard it often enough during his physical therapy sessions. The bad ones. She held back the snap she wanted to throw at him. "Fine. Don't run in a straight line. Zigzag your way through the trees."

"That was going to be my advice to you."

She breathed a low laugh that was more puff of air than anything. It definitely lacked humor. She wondered if she'd get the chance to find something to laugh about again. "Remember the map?" she asked.

"Yes, why?"

"If I'm going left and you're going right, we need a place to meet up."

He thought a moment. "Go back to the small clearing where the dogs were. It's sort of at the center and he won't expect us to double back, will he?"

"Probably not, but he's got pretty good tracking skills."

"We need to lose him for good."

She pulled the cap lower. "Or let him catch up to us."

"I like my idea better."

She drew in a deep breath. "All right, we'll try it your way. If you get yourself killed, I'm not going to be happy with you."

"Ditto."

He pointed. "Go."

She burst from the entrance of the cave and heard Quinn do the same. A thunk sounded behind her. She stopped, whirled, and hit the ground. Another bolt flew past. She sprang to her feet and took off again, bouncing from tree to tree. No more bolts came her way and she couldn't help pray she'd drawn the fire while Quinn got away.

A burst of fire along her upper thigh made her gasp, then stumble. She caught herself on the nearest tree trunk and swung around behind it. Then collapsed to the ground.

She pressed her hand against the wound and felt the sticky

wetness cover her fingers. Great. Her heart thudded as she listened for the hunter to come after her. She heard nothing but knew he was there, silently making his way toward her. To stay in one place invited death. She needed to move.

Tightening her jaw against the burning in her leg, she started to rise to her feet, but a sudden sharp pain in her lower back held her still.

"Well, well. Look who I found," the voice from the cement room purred.

Fear nearly shattered her and she trembled even as she tried to hide it. She clenched her fingers into fists and felt the blood drying on her hand make the action stiff. Her anger surfaced. She'd almost died once and it had only made her stronger. She wouldn't make it easy for him to kill her. "Why are you doing this? What did I ever do to you?"

"You were born, Maddy. And then you cheated death. Not everyone gets to do that."

Her practiced ear picked up some inflection in his voice, even through the fear that wanted to unbalance her. "Who was it you loved who wasn't able to cheat death?" she asked.

He inhaled sharply. The tip pressed harder against her lower back, and she felt her skin break. The trickle of blood seeped into the band of her sweatpants. She winced and her fear meter was off the chart, but she felt a slight surge of satisfaction about the fact that she'd scored with that shot in the dark.

"All I have to do is let the bolt go and you're finished," he hissed.

"Then what are you waiting for?" she gasped. "Do it."

He paused. She'd surprised him again. "Oh, I will. Just not now. There's a time to live and a time to die. Your time to die has not come yet because everything should be done in a fitting and orderly way. But soon, Maddy McKay, very soon."

The sharp pain in her lower back faded as the hunter whirled and raced away into the woods.

Heart racing, mind spinning that she was actually still alive, Maddy used the nearest tree trunk to brace herself while she stood and put weight on the wounded leg. She winced but the leg held. It was just a graze, a very painful graze.

Confused, yet nearly light-headed with relief, she sent up a prayer of thanksgiving that she'd been spared. She looked around and got her bearings, all the while being alert for any sound that interrupted the natural sounds around her, for any indication that the Chosen One had decided to return and kill her after all. She'd grown up hunting with her father. At least until the day she'd adamantly refused to shoot a living creature. He quit taking her after that, but she used the skills she learned during those few times she'd gone with him. She stayed still. Very still, and let her gaze roam. Left, right, behind her. Up to the treetops.

Where she paused. She narrowed her eyes and let them linger on an object wedged in the branches just out of reach. What was that? She let her gaze keep going, then finally dropped her eyes to the ground and waited. Listening.

Minutes passed and nothing happened. No hunter appeared, no more bolts winged in her direction, and she heard no more footsteps.

Disbelief held her suspended for a brief moment. For some reason he'd let her go.

She tugged the hat tighter against her skull and froze, her fingers still on the brim. The hat. Quinn's hat. He'd thought she was Quinn. He had plainly stated that they both would die, but he hadn't killed her when he had the chance. When there'd been no way for her to escape.

And yet he'd let her go. Why?

. . . everything should be done in a fitting and orderly way.
His words echoed.

He'd let her go because, for some strange reason, he wanted
to kill Quinn first.

Quinn had doubled back looking for Maddy when he realized
the hunter . . . or the Chosen One . . . had made her his target.
He'd heard the first bolt slam into a solid surface—probably
a tree—and the fact that it wasn't near him had him skidding
to a halt. He'd turned and run after Maddy but had lost her in
the trees. He stopped and knelt, trying to pick up her tracks.
Vegetation snapped and crunched to his left. He shifted to hide
behind the large bush in front of him.

And finally caught a glimpse of the man who had put this
nightmare into motion. A profile of him anyway. He had on a
vest over a short-sleeved shirt. He was tall and thin, but well-
muscled. He wore a Panama Jack hat with the brim pulled
low, the string dangling beneath a chin that held a five o'clock
shadow.

Quinn wished he could see the rest of the man's face, but the
hat blocked his view. The crossbow was in plain sight, though,
and ready to release its deadly bolt.

Quinn itched to jump the man and beat him into oblivion,
but caution held him back. He had to know where Maddy was.
The fact that the Chosen One didn't appear to be hunting her
but had changed his focus—most likely to find Quinn—worried
him. Before he took on the kidnapper, he had to know what
had happened to Maddy.

He stayed still, barely breathing as the hunter approached
the bush where Quinn hid. The man paused. Turned his head
slightly to the left away from Quinn. And started walking in that

direction. Quinn let out a low breath, the adrenaline rushing through him causing him to want to shake. He called on all of his emergency training and slowed his breathing, calmed his racing heart. Focus.

The Chosen One disappeared in the copse of trees just ahead and Quinn waited to make sure it wasn't some kind of trap. Had the man known Quinn had been hiding mere inches from him? Was he just toying with him? Had he walked off to draw Quinn out?

Quinn continued his wait and finally he could no longer hear the footsteps. Slowly, he rose from behind the bush, his legs aching from crouching in the position so long. He had to stretch them out before he trusted them to hold him. Fortunately, it looked like the man had left to search another area of the island. Quinn took off in a jog in the direction he thought Maddy might be.

As he followed the tracks left by the Chosen One, he couldn't help thinking about God. About why he was letting this happen. Why he'd once again decided to send Quinn's life into a tailspin.

Ten steps later, a hand reached out and grabbed his.

He spun, fist ready to slam into the nearest target, but he stopped when he saw Maddy leaning against a tree. A gasp escaped him when he spied the blood covering the side of her left thigh. "Maddy," he whispered.

"I'm okay," she said. "I didn't want to scare you by calling your name."

"So you grabbed my hand instead?"

She shrugged, then licked her lips. He pulled a water bottle from his front pocket. "Here, drink this while I take a look at your leg."

She took it. "Where'd you get this?"

"From our last meal. I grabbed the two we didn't drink, figuring we might need them later. I also snagged the loaf of bread. It's smooshed into one of my other pockets."

"Smooshed?"

"Sorry, my niece's favorite word these days." He shrugged and gave her a tight smile, knowing what she was doing. Small talk. Anything to keep them from thinking about what was waiting for them around the next corner. Or tree. "Thank goodness for cargo pants, huh?"

"Thank goodness." She twisted the top from the bottle and took a swig. "So how's Alyssa doing?"

"She's doing great."

"Really?"

"Really." He wiped the sweat from his eyes. "We have to think, Maddy. To stay focused."

"I know." He shot her a closer look and realized that even during the small talk, she'd been thinking, not avoiding the situation. Thinking and evaluating. Playing out scenarios in her head. Filing away some as possibilities and discarding others. Just like he was.

He dropped to his knees and pushed aside the torn fabric of her sweatpants. Mosquitos buzzed around him and he was already feeling the bites on his exposed skin. Birds sang in the trees and he could hear the ocean not too far away.

"Thanks." She tilted the water bottle to him in a silent toast and drank more.

"Yeah." Blood still seeped from the gash on her leg. "You've got a nasty cut there," he said. "Probably could use a couple of stitches."

"Let's hope I live long enough to get them then."

"Oh, you're going to live," he said softly. "We both are. There's no other option."

"Quinn, he had me trapped." Her hand came to rest on his shoulder. "He could have killed me."

He stilled and looked up. "What?"

"I knew he was tracking me, but I never heard him. He came up behind me and pressed the tip of the bolt into my back. I knew I was going to die." Her voice wobbled a bit on the last sentence and fury bubbled within him. As well as massive guilt. He should have been there with her.

He reached up and gripped her bloody fingers. "From now on we stay together."

"It was so weird," she said as though he hadn't spoken. "He said a few things, but there was one thing that stood out."

"What?"

"He said, 'Everything should be done in a fitting and orderly way.' I got the feeling that he wants to kill you first."

"Why?"

"I don't know."

The world around them went quiet and she tensed. He stood and moved in front of her. "He's back."

"Go," she whispered. "I don't care where, just go. But be careful. This place is probably rigged with all kinds of crazy stuff."

Quinn started walking and she followed behind, limping with each step. Quinn went slow, not wanting her to lose any more blood and not wanting to trigger any booby traps. "Keep your eyes down. I'm keeping mine up. Let's get to the ocean and see what we can see."

They walked, stepping carefully. Watching for wires, loosely covered ground, and anything else that might kill them. Fifteen minutes later, Maddy paused. "I hear the ocean," she said.

"Yeah, so do I." He kept walking.

She grabbed his arm and pulled him to an abrupt stop. "Don't move."

"What?"

"There."

He looked down to see a very faint trip wire attached to the two trees on either side of him. His stomach lurched. "Good catch, I didn't see it."

"Step over it."

He did and she followed. Soon, they came to the edge of the tree line. A beautiful sandy beach lay just ahead. And water. And . . . "Is that a boathouse?" he asked.

"Yes. You think there's a boat in there?" Excitement filled her voice.

"Only one way to find out."

"What if there's not?" she asked.

He could see another island not too far in the distance and pointed. "Then we'll go swimming. You up to it?"

He gripped her hand and she squeezed his fingers. "Let's go." She took another step. He heard a crunch, then the ground gave out beneath her.

[6]

A scream escaped her as she felt herself fall. Then come to a bone-jarring halt. Pain raced from her hand to her shoulder. Something snapped and a new level of hurt like she'd never felt before brought the blackness hovering. She held on to consciousness with a concentrated effort. But the pain . . .

Another cry welled and she bit it back. She looked up to find Quinn's white face hovering above hers. He lay flat on his stomach, his head hanging over the edge, his right hand clamped around her left. And his grip was slipping. "Keep your eyes on me, Maddy, and reach up with your other hand."

She found thinking nearly impossible through the haze of hurt. She started to look down.

"Maddy!"

Her gaze snapped back up.

"Don't look down, look at me and give me your other hand now."

To reach up with her right hand, she had to brace herself, and the waves of pain just kept coming. "I can't, Quinn. Just let me go and find a way off this island."

"Give me your hand!"

"I can't!"

"So you're all of a sudden a quitter? Doesn't sound like you, Maddy."

Anger flooded her, coming close to blocking the pain. "What do you know about how I sound? What do you know about me?"

"You want to get into this now? He probably heard your scream. We have to get out of here. Now give me your hand!" Sweat dripped from his forehead and the frantic demand in his voice spurred her.

Tears leaked from her eyes, flowed down her sweaty temples and into her hair, and whimpering gasps escaped her. But she dug deep within and grasped on to one last reserve of strength. "I'm only going to be able to do this one time, Quinn. Don't miss."

"I won't. Just do it!"

Maddy kicked out with her left foot and searched for a toe-hold. She found one in the dirt and flung her right hand up as she tried to stand. Fire shot through her arm, dizziness bordering the line of unconsciousness threatened. But he did it. Quinn caught her right wrist and the pressure on her left shoulder eased considerably, although the pain was still there. She could breathe again. Slowly, she felt herself being lifted out of the pit by her uninjured arm. She tried to help by walking up the dirt wall.

Finally, she was on the ground next to Quinn, her pulse pounding so hard she thought her chest might explode. And then feeling kicked in once again. She gasped. The *pain*. "My shoulder."

Quinn sat beside her, his gaze bouncing from the tree line to her and beyond. "I think it's dislocated. I'm going to have to set it for you. It'll be sore but feel a ton better than it does right now."

She shivered. Nausea swirled and she truly thought dying might be better than the pain of trying to survive. But Quinn was right. She wasn't a quitter. And she didn't want the psycho who was orchestrating all of this to get away with it. She had to live if only to catch him. She tightened her jaw—and her nerves. "Like you said. Just do it."

He moved over next to her and placed his hands on her shoulder. "Take a deep breath and count to three."

She sucked in. "One—" Another burst of blinding pain hit her as her shoulder slid into place and the sky blurred, then went dark.

Quinn carried Maddy back to the cave, as that was the only shelter he knew of on the island. The cement room didn't count. He wasn't going back there. With his back against the cave wall and his eyes on the entrance, he held her against him as the sun went down. He held her and thought about praying. If ever there was a time in his life he should pray, it would probably be now. And yet, even as the words wanted to form, he shut them off. When had God done anything for him?

Maddy stirred and he looked down at her. The half moon cast enough light so that the interior of the cave wasn't pitch black.

He sent Maddy into your life.

He didn't know where the thought came from but acknowledged its truth. He was very thankful for her. With her head resting on his thigh, her dark lashes against her cheeks, she looked innocent and frail. But he knew of her inner strength, her toughness. He was keenly aware of her intense love of justice and her determination to do her part to right the wrongs of the world. To make herself a roadblock to evil.

She was still out from the setting of her shoulder and she

needed the rest. He continued to keep tabs on her while watching the entrance, but the truth was, he didn't know how he would defend them if the Chosen One decided to show up with his deadly crossbow. Quinn supposed he would do the best he could and hope it was enough.

His arm throbbed and his mind spun. He should try to rest, but he knew he probably wouldn't sleep until he and Maddy were safe. Every time he closed his eyes, he saw her dangling over the edge of the hole in the ground.

A hole about ten feet deep.

With sharp spears buried halfway up the shaft. Razor-like blades just waiting to tear into vulnerable flesh. Maddy's flesh. The thought made him sick. If he hadn't had a grip on her hand when she stepped over the pit, she'd be dead at this moment.

And he'd be alive.

So was Maddy wrong? She said that the Chosen One spared her because he had to kill Quinn first. Something about everything being done in a fitting and orderly way. So "orderly" meant Quinn had to die first? But what if Maddy had fallen onto the spears at the bottom of that pit? How did that fit with what the Chosen One had told her?

He pressed his fingers to his burning eyes. His stomach rumbled. They'd have to find some food somewhere. He had the loaf of bread he'd snatched from the tray in the cement room, but it wasn't much and it wouldn't last long. He'd let Maddy sleep a few more minutes, then they'd slip out and—

A rustle outside the cave brought his head up. He gently eased Maddy's head from his leg and laid it on the ground. He grabbed the sharp stick he'd picked up from just outside the cave and crept toward the entrance.

A panting, a whimper, a shuffle.

And then a profile filled the entrance. Quinn let out a slow breath. The pit bull.

Quinn held still. He could see the shaft of the bolt still sticking out from the side of the animal. The dog padded slowly inside, then dropped to the ground with a huff and another whimper.

Gladness filled Quinn to know that he hadn't killed the dog. Then sadness took its place as he realized the animal would probably still die from his wound. He slowly approached. The dog raised his head but did nothing. Not even a growl.

Quinn continued his approach and finally stopped when he was within touching distance. And still the dog just watched him, his eyes reflecting his pain—his need for help.

Quinn held out a hand and slowly lowered it to the dog's head. A quivering sigh filled the cave. Quinn moved his hand down the dog's warm body until he reached the shaft of the bolt. He had to do something. He couldn't leave the animal like this.

"This might hurt, dude, but I'll pull it out if you let me." He knew the head of the bolt was slim, not arrow shaped. It shouldn't cause too much damage coming out. And it looked like it wasn't buried too deep, so maybe he hadn't hit anything major when he stabbed the poor thing. He closed his fingers around the wood and prepared himself to get bitten again.

But first . . .

He reached up and ripped off his other sleeve.

Then he placed his left hand on the dog's big head and pulled the bolt out.

A sharp yelp filled the cave and the animal gave a halfhearted snap at the hand holding him down, but that was the extent of his resistance. Quinn pressed the torn sleeve against the bleeding wound and held it.

"All right, dude . . ." He shook his head. "I guess I can't keep calling you Dude. How about . . . Watson? You like that? Yeah, so do I. That works." He stroked the dog's head. "Sorry, Watson, I don't know what else I can do for you."

Watson butted his head against Quinn's hand.

"Yeah, I'm hungry too."

He reached into his pocket and pulled out the loaf of bread that had managed to survive. It was in pretty bad shape—definitely smushed—but still edible. He pulled off a hunk and gave it to the dog. Watson swallowed it in one gulp. He'd save the rest for Maddy.

He stroked the dog's ears. "I promise I'll take you with me if we get out of this, okay?"

Watson licked his hand, then laid his head back on the cave floor. Quinn went back to Maddy's side and shook her good shoulder.

Her eyes went wide and she sat up. Looked around and shuddered. Her hand went to her shoulder. "What happened?"

"You passed out."

She winced. "Oh yeah. That hurt." She frowned. "You said to count to three."

"I never wait for three, I always go on one. You tense up when you know it's coming. Makes it worse."

"Good to know." She scowled, then smoothed her features, knocking his hat off her head in the process. She raked a hand through her hair, then rubbed her eyes. "So what's our—?" She looked past him and blinked. "Wait a minute. Is that the dog that attacked us?"

"That's Watson. We've become friends." He pulled the bread from his pocket. "Here, eat some."

She broke off a piece and passed the rest back to him. "You eat some too. What about Watson? I'm sure he's hungry."

He took a bite. "I gave him a bit."

"Good. Hopefully, we're not going to be here much longer."

He rose to his feet and walked to the entrance, staying out of the direct moonlight. She followed him. He glanced back at her and caught her trying to hide a wince as she held her injured arm up against her. "You need a sling."

"I need off this island."

"We're getting off. One way or another."

"You think Olivia and Katie and the rest are looking for us yet?"

"I sure hope so. Unfortunately, unless we can give them a clue how to find us, they're not going to."

She drew in a deep breath. "Yeah."

* * *

Olivia slammed a fist against her thigh as she surveyed Maddy's home. "Where did she go?" They'd tried the front door and the back. The garage was closed, and neither she nor Wade was tall enough to see in the windows that would give them a view into the area.

Wade sat in the driver's seat while he waited for Olivia to make up her mind what their next move was. Olivia appreciated his patience.

He scanned his phone. "Still no answer on our calls and texts. You don't think they ran off and got married or something, do you?" he asked.

Olivia snorted. "No."

"Yeah, I didn't really think so."

Olivia knew her husband wanted to believe something like that. Frankly, she did too. It was preferable to believing their friends were in trouble.

"Have you called Bree?" he asked.

Olivia nodded. "Yes. I called her from Katie's house just

before we left. She was on her way to the party when I caught her. She was late because of something with her sister but said she hasn't heard from Quinn and hadn't missed any calls from him."

"Not good."

"No, but she said she'd call around to some people she knows, including his family, and see if he's had any contact with them."

"I like that plan."

Her phone rang. "It's Haley." She pressed the button. "Did you find something?"

"Yes. Not Quinn or Maddy, but Quinn's puppy."

"And?

"I hate to say this, but it looks like Quinn hasn't been home all last night or today. The puppy is still in his carrier and he's messed in it. Poor little guy was frantic when I got here. Bree just walked in and is putting a BOLO out on both Quinn and Maddy."

Olivia's heart trembled. "Okay, search his place. Wade and I'll do the same here with Maddy's. I have a key."

"Question the neighbors too," Bree said. "I'll send someone over to help."

"Right." She looked around. "Most should be home by now. We know Quinn and Maddy had dinner last night. It's possible someone saw them leave—and noticed if they came home. Or not."

"We're on it," Bree said.

"Stay in touch if you find anything."

"Of course."

"Bree?"

"Yes?"

"I have to admit, I'm worried."

"And I have to admit I think you have a reason to worry."

"Talk to you soon."

⁙⁙⁙⁙⁙⁙⁙⁙⁙⁙⁙⁙⁙⁙⁙⁙⁙⁙⁙⁙⁙⁙⁙⁙⁙⁙⁙⁙

Maddy's entire body ached. Her shoulder throbbed, but at least she could move it if she was careful. That sling he mentioned would be nice. For now, she'd use her other arm to brace it as much as she could. "You think he'll expect us to move during the night?"

"Unfortunately, I have no idea what this guy expects, but I think it's time for us to go on the offensive."

She leaned forward. "I think you're right." She watched his hand move over the dog's head, calming, soothing. Gentle. He'd moved from the entrance of the cave to sit by the animal. She followed and let Watson sniff her fingers. He gave them a swipe with his tongue, then laid his head back on the floor. "I wonder where the retriever is."

"I don't know. I haven't seen him since our confrontation in the woods."

She drew in a deep breath. "You know, now that my brain is starting to work again, I've thought of a couple of things."

"What's that?"

"The map on the wall didn't have a house on it."

"I know."

"But that doesn't mean there's not one on this island. I mean, the dogs obviously belong to the guy who's doing this, right?"

"Yes."

"Then there's got to be a place where he's been living while he set all this up."

Quinn squinted and glanced around. "Excellent point."

"So, if we find that place, we can figure out who he is and what all this is about."

"And maybe a phone or something to call for help."

"Yes."

"All right then. You stay here with Watson while I climb to the top of this little mountain and look around. I want to see if I can find lights on anywhere."

"I'll come with you. I don't want to be separated again unless there's no alternative."

He hesitated for only a moment, then gave a slow nod. "Okay, that's probably the smart thing to do."

She glanced around. "He's got cameras set up out here. I saw one in a tree near where he nearly stuck the bolt in my back. I think he's watching us."

"Then why hasn't he killed us yet?"

"I don't know."

He stood and walked to the cave's entrance. "I can't see much out there. The moon is good, but I could trip a wire or something."

"I know. And it's possible he has night vision goggles."

"Yeah. I'd thought of that."

"Just wanted to make sure."

"Thanks."

"Anytime." She pressed a hand to his shoulder. "Are we going?"

"Yes."

"What about the dog?"

"Let's worry about us for now. If we can find a way off this island, we can take him with us."

And if they couldn't find a way off, it wouldn't matter. She got it.

He slipped out of the cave and nerves attacked her. The what-ifs started racing through her mind, and she had to put the mental brakes on those thoughts. If they wanted off the island, they'd have to take risks. She followed Quinn around the side of the cave to the sloping area next to it. He climbed and she followed, ignoring the pain and fatigue pulling at her. She considered herself in good shape, but she hurt. A lot. Her back, her leg, her shoulder. What she wouldn't give for some ibuprofen.

She tightened her jaw and kept her attention on the area, grateful for the bit of light the half moon provided, grateful to be able to still *feel* pain. It meant she was alive. At the top of the hill, she paused as she looked around and caught her breath. "I don't see anything," she whispered.

"I don't either." He looked up. Grabbed ahold of a branch and swung himself into the tree. "Stay put. I'll be right back."

"Be careful."

They kept their voices low, hushed, but she wasn't sure why. If the Chosen One was watching his cameras, he probably knew exactly where they were. She watched Quinn climb, then planted her back to the tree trunk and kept watch, listening for anything that didn't come from above.

And then even Quinn was silent. She waited, skin pebbling with goose bumps, though it wasn't cold. She figured it was probably around eighty degrees. A shiver wracked her and she wondered if she had a fever.

Then Quinn was coming down, the leaves swaying gently with his movements. He dropped to the ground beside her.

"You see anything?" she asked.

"Yes," he said with a thread of excitement in his voice.

"What?"

"Lights. And I think I know how to get there."

"Lead the way then."

He grasped her upper arm—the one attached to the uninjured shoulder. "Are you sure you're up to it?"

"I want off this island, Quinn. I'm up to it."

"All right. Let's go."

He took the lead and she stayed on his heels. By the light of the moon, he moved carefully, pausing every so often to stop and listen.

And sniff.

"Do you smell that?" she asked.

"Yeah." He breathed in. "Yes, I do."

"Is that what I think it is?" Of course it was. She'd smelled that odor more than once during her career as a special agent with the FBI.

"The smell of death," he murmured. Light-headedness hit her and she reached out to brace herself against a tree trunk. He turned and caught her arm. "You okay?"

"Yeah, just give me a minute." A roar overhead caught her attention and she looked up but could see nothing except some twinkling lights. "What's that?"

He'd stopped to look too. "Sounded like an airplane."

"That's what I thought."

He pressed the last bottle of water into her hand. He'd already twisted the top off. "Drink." She downed half of it and passed it back to him. He refused. "Finish it."

"No way. You can't get dehydrated. That won't help either of us."

He grunted. "Fine. I'll save it for you for later."

"We're not going to be here later. Drink it."

But he didn't. He tucked it back into whichever pocket had held it. "I don't think it's that much farther."

"How long has it been, do you think?"

"What?" he asked.

"How long have we been here?"

"I don't know. I'm not sure how long we were in the room. But I'd say we've been out here for a little over seven or eight hours maybe? Since sometime after lunch? If that was lunch."

She fell silent and he continued to lead the way. As he walked, she thought she could see better. "It's getting lighter. The lights from the house are helping."

"Yes, but do you notice something else?"

"The stench is growing stronger."

And then they were at the edge of the tree line. Maddy looked in the distance. A large house with blue vinyl siding and white trim sat in the middle of a plush green lawn. Spotlights illuminated it, lighting it up like Christmastime. She could hear the ocean lapping against the shore and figured they were at the front of the house. The back of it faced the water. "Look at that," she breathed. "And is that a runway?"

Quinn squeezed her hand. "I think so. I noticed a long lighted strip when I climbed the tree. I couldn't tell it was concrete from there. All I knew is that it stood out."

Excitement and hope stirred within her heart. "Then that means there's a plane somewhere."

"Probably how he gets on and off the island."

Lights blazed along the side of the concrete strip, lighting it and the area around it. "You think he's in there?"

"Well, I don't think he's out here." He looked up. "It's possible that might have been him in the plane that was overhead a few minutes ago."

"You might be right. We weren't supposed to get this far," she said. "We were supposed to be dead by now."

"Yes. Probably."

"But we're not and he knows it." She studied the innocent-looking structure in front of her. "If he has cameras out here, he probably has cameras rigged all over that house."

Quinn nodded. "Not to mention booby traps in case someone breaches the perimeter." He looked around. "There could be other people on this island, other buildings that we haven't seen."

"Could be."

"But for now, I'll settle for checking the house." He sniffed and grimaced. "And where is that smell coming from?"

She pulled the collar of her shirt up over her nose. "I don't know, but it's really bad over here."

He glanced around. He moved to the left, staying in the tree line. "Look." He pulled to an abrupt halt and she slammed into the back of him. He reached back to steady her and she saw what had caught his attention. The lights from the runway and the house had illuminated another discovery.

"Quinn, are those . . . ?" she whispered.

"Yes. I think so."

"Crosses." Small white crosses all in a perfectly straight line had been placed in the dirt one beside the other.

"Exactly." He moved closer. Carefully placing his steps as though waiting to step wrong and set something off.

She didn't blame him. She walked right behind him, staying in his footsteps.

"Ten of them," he said. "And they're numbered." Black numbers, one through ten, had been painted on them. A large mountain of dirt lay next to a shallow pit.

He moved to the edge and she followed him. He dropped to his knees and looked down.

She did the same and stared into what she realized was a grave filled with bodies in various stages of decomposition.

[7]

Maddy gasped and rocked back. "Quinn."

"I know."

"He didn't even bother to cover them up," she breathed.

He felt sick. He'd seen a lot during his years in law enforcement, but he had to admit this was the first mass grave he'd come across.

A branch snapped behind them and they spun at the same time. Only to find the dog had followed them. "Watson," he rasped. The dog trembled and he simply collapsed at the edge of the trees. Quinn went to him and scratched the animal's head. He felt hot and Quinn figured his wound was infected.

"I guess he didn't want to be left behind either," Maddy said softly.

"Guess not." Without thinking, he drew in a deep breath. Immediately regretted it and coughed. "All right, let's get away from here so we can breathe and figure out our next plan of action."

"I'm good with that." Together, they moved toward the house, silently watching the area around them. Watson heaved himself to his feet to follow, his steps slow, painful, determined to keep up.

Quinn's nerves drew his skin tight and he almost expected to feel the tip of a bolt slam into him. However, they made it to the edge of the property without snarling dogs attacking them or any weapons being fired in their direction. Or tripping any more booby traps.

"Be careful," she cautioned. "That could have been him who left in the plane, but he could have left behind help."

She stared at the house, and he knew she was evaluating the best way to get in, watching for any movement that might suggest someone was inside. When she was attacked and had her throat slit almost a year ago, it had damaged her confidence, thrown her off her game. As it would anyone. But he'd watched her come back from the brink of death to become the woman she was before the initial attack.

And now this. Since they'd awakened in the room, she'd let him take the lead for the most part, and he knew it was because she felt shaky in her fear, afraid to make the wrong decision. Scared she'd miss something and get them both killed.

Now, as he looked at her, he saw the old Maddy starting to emerge. She had a new fire in her eyes and her tight jaw said she'd come to some conclusion with her internal struggle. She also had flushed cheeks that he didn't think had to do with the heat. Fever? If so, she wasn't letting it hold her back.

"Okay," she whispered. "So, I see cameras on the exterior near the front door. Two on either side of the house."

"And probably more around on the back."

She breathed deep. "All right, so there's absolutely no way to approach the house without one of the cameras alerting him. Or whoever is in there."

"If someone is in there."

"And we need to find that out." She tapped her chin. "Well, here goes nothing."

She stood and started walking toward the house.

Quinn froze for half a second. "Maddy," he hissed. She ignored him and kept going. "Maddy . . ." She never turned. He was going to . . . what?

Follow her.

Biting his tongue on the lashing he'd like to let fly, he slipped up behind her as she led him straight up the front porch steps.

She reached for the knob, then paused. Stepped to the side with Quinn right behind her. She twisted the knob and pushed the door open.

Quinn's breath caught in his throat as he half expected bullets or a bolt to come flying out the opening.

Instead, the only thing moving was the island. The sounds, the animals, the ocean on the other side of the house. "All right then," he finally said, "that was dumb."

"But effective."

"True. Ready to go in?" he asked.

Before they could take a step, Quinn saw Watson out of the corner of his eye. The dog slowly crossed the yard, every step obviously painful for him. Quinn almost moved to help him but held still, his hand on the curve of Maddy's waist. Together, they watched the dog climb the steps and limp into the house. Heat radiated off Maddy and he realized his guess was right. She had a fever.

They followed behind Watson, then Maddy stepped ahead of him, rounding the door like she had a weapon in her hand and was ready to use it. Quinn wished she did. He stayed behind her, worried about her physical state as well as her mental one at this point. Once inside, Quinn shut the door behind them.

75

Watson went into the kitchen and slumped to the floor in front of the sink. "He's thirsty," she whispered. "So am I."

He pushed her to the floor. "Sit. I'll get you both something as soon as I know we're safe. I'm going to check the rest of the house. You stay put. Scream your head off if anyone comes in, understand?"

"Yeah." She licked her lips and he noticed the bright flush in her cheeks. He had to get help to the island ASAP. He checked the kitchen drawers and found a large knife. He pressed it into her hand. "Use this if necessary."

She looked at him with dulled eyes. "Haven't you heard you don't take a knife to a crossbow fight?"

He wondered how high her fever was. "No, that's a new one," he said. "Stay here."

She didn't answer and he moved fast to clear the rest of the house. It was a fairly large house with four bedrooms and four bathrooms, a bonus room, and an office that he'd be back to look at when he was finished making sure they were safe for the moment. "No booby traps," he whispered, "and no weapons." Frustration nipped at him. He wanted to feel the weight of a weapon in his hand so bad that he was close to going through withdrawal. He whirled to hurry back to the kitchen to find Maddy where he'd left her. Watson had stayed put too. "It's clear," he said. "But I couldn't find weapons of any kind."

"Guess the knife will have to do." She pushed herself to her feet, pain and misery written all over her face.

He went to her, took the knife from her hand, and set it on the counter. He then raided the kitchen pantry and found dog food, which he poured into the bowl next to the laundry room. Fresh water in the other bowl caught Watson's attention and he went to work on it.

Next Quinn opened the refrigerator and found water bottles.

The same kind their captor had served with their dinner in the cement room. He grabbed two and opened one. "Here, there's plenty more. Drink." She didn't argue with him. He opened the other one and finished it in several gulps. "All right, Maddy, let's find a way to call for help."

She swayed, but pushed away from the counter. "Show me where the phone is."

Instead of answering her, he swooped her into his arms. She laid her head against his shoulder and closed her eyes. He carried her to the office he'd cleared only moments before. His goal was the leather couch on the wall opposite the large desk. He gently placed her on the sofa and felt her forehead. Hot.

Her eyes fluttered and she tried to sit. "I'll help you search."

"No, I've got this. Just rest."

She flopped back and that worried him more than if she'd insisted she could help. He raced out of the office and down the hall, through the master bedroom and into the en suite bathroom. He opened the medicine cabinet he'd seen on his sweep and studied the bottles there. Prescription and several over-the-counter bottles. He pulled them out one by one, reading them. Noting the names on the prescription labels. He'd come back to those later.

Finally, after he was just about to give up, he found the ibuprofen. He doubled-checked to make sure the medicine was what the label said it was, then downed three. He bolted to the kitchen, grabbed another bottle of water from the refrigerator, then made his way back into the office. Maddy was still conscious, but her eyes fluttered as though she wanted to resist resting, sleeping.

He lifted her shoulders, careful of the sore one, and sat behind her. "Here."

"What?"

"Take this medicine, it'll make you feel better."

She blinked again and he helped her sit up a little farther.

After she swallowed three of the pills, he let her lie back down and then moved to the desk. No phone.

He started opening drawers and found files, papers, and other items, but no phone. He tried the file cabinet behind him. Locked.

"Wait, there were keys," he muttered. Which drawer was it? Top left.

He pulled it open and grabbed the ring of keys. He found the one he thought might fit and jammed it in the lock. Wonder of wonders, it opened on the first try. He pulled out the first drawer and his heart nearly stopped. A satellite phone.

He grabbed it and powered it on, then went back to sit beside Maddy. He could almost hear his adrenaline rushing through his veins. His heart thudded as he dialed his partner's number. "Come on, Bree, pick up."

Just about when he was going to give up hope and hang up, she answered. "Hello?"

He heard the caution in her voice and knew it was because she hadn't recognized the number. "Bree."

"Quinn!" Her shout made him wince. "Where are you?" she demanded. "Are you okay? Is Maddy with you? Olivia and Wade found a note resembling our serial killer's MO in Maddy's house."

"Slow down and listen. Yes, I'm fine. Maddy's with me and she's sick. I don't know where I am. We were kidnapped by a white male. Bald. And with a sick idea of fun and games. I need you to find a way to trace this satellite phone."

"I was just walking into the office when your call came through. Give me a minute to get to my computer." He heard her footsteps going at a fast walk. "Everyone's been so worried about you guys. We've been looking everywhere. Tried to trace your phones and came back empty."

"The guy who kidnapped us probably smashed them and then dumped them somewhere. I sure hope someone has Sherlock."

"I let him out in your yard earlier. He's fine."

Quinn breathed a sigh of relief. As much as he hated to admit it, he'd been worried about the little guy.

"All right," Bree said. "I'm at my desk, let me get the software pulled up." He heard the keyboard clicking in the background. "I've got the number you called from and it's in the system now. You better hope that thing has its GPS system turned on." He waited, impatience ripping through him. "And . . . there you are. I've got you."

"Where are we?"

"Off the coast of Key West. You're on an island called Hogan's House."

"That's the name on the medicine bottles. Hogan."

"What?"

"Have someone run the name Keith Hogan. Find out all you can about him. And send a chopper filled with a SWAT team. We might need to dispense with the guy if he's still on the island. Make that two choppers. Maddy needs a doctor." He glanced at his arm where Watson had torn the flesh. "And I probably do too. And a vet."

"A what?"

"A veterinarian. You know, an animal doctor."

"I know what a vet is, Holcombe. Why do you need one?"

"I have a new friend who needs some help, okay? Now quit asking questions and just do it." He thought he heard her mutter something under her breath about him being bossy, but he didn't care. She could mutter whatever she wanted as long as she got help on the way.

He glanced at Maddy's face. It didn't seem to be quite as flushed as before. Maybe the ibuprofen was working.

"Anything else?" she asked.

"Yeah, I need a crime scene unit, a forensic anthropologist, a medical examiner, and whoever else you can think of. We've got a mass grave with possibly ten bodies in it."

She gasped and fell silent.

"Bree?"

"Yeah, I've got it." Her voice shook slightly, then she cleared her throat. "I'm calculating the time it's going to take to get there. If I'm looking at the island right on this satellite program, it looks like there's room for at least two choppers to land at the same time. First we're going to get you and Maddy out of there and to the hospital in Key West."

"And Watson."

"What?"

"Watson. The reason for the vet."

"And the vet. Okay, I know a people doc and an animal doc who both owe me favors." Her fingers continued to fly over the keyboard. He could hear them. "All right," she said, "we should be there . . ." She sighed. "It's going to be at least two hours—maybe three. I'm going to contact the local authorities. They'll be able to get out there a lot faster."

"We'll be here."

"Putting it all together as we speak. I'm going to go run this by the captain and then I'll be out the door, heading to the chopper to pick up everyone. Looks like I'm going to be one of your pilots."

"Thanks, Bree."

"Can't wait to hear this story."

"Can't wait to tell it," he murmured. He hung up, and it was only then he noticed the note on the back of the phone.

Congratulations, you've won this round and have the honored privilege of advancing to the next. Now it gets a bit personal. Until we meet again, my friend . . .

[8]

The commotion woke her. For a moment, she was in full-blown panic, then felt the leather under her fingertips and paused, her heart slowing slightly. If she were still in the cave in the woods, she'd not be sleeping on leather.

Slowly her mind started working again. She felt her face and realized her fever had broken. A sheen of sweat covered her and she decided she simply wanted a shower. Then she tuned in to the noise. She sat up to find law enforcement officers everywhere. One spotted her and nudged the guy next to him. He left the room and she figured he was alerting someone to the fact that she was awake.

Her left arm was wrapped snug against her chest and her shoulder ached only a little. Aggravating, but not the blinding pain she'd had.

When she moved, something tugged at her thigh and she looked down to find the leg of her sweatpants cut away. A white bandage wrapped around her leg. She briefly mourned the loss of the jogging pants, as they'd been her favorite. Then again, she probably wouldn't have been able to wear them again without being reminded of the ordeal. With her good arm, she reached behind her and felt a bandage covering the wound on her lower back.

And finally it hit her. She was safe and she'd been medically attended to. She stood, her legs shaking. And then Quinn was at her side, one hand under her elbow, the other encased in a white bandage. Before she could ask what happened, he was pushing her back toward the sofa. "You need to sit back down."

"Actually, I need a bathroom."

"Ah." He stopped pushing and started tugging. Gently. He led her down the long hallway. "You're in luck. That was the first room I had them process for evidence so you can use it."

"So," she said. "They found us. We're actually still alive."

"They did and we are."

"How?"

"I discovered a satellite phone in the lunatic's office and got ahold of Bree. She's here somewhere. So are the Monroe County Sheriff's Office and the FBI."

"FBI?"

"It was a kidnapping, Maddy. Interstate. We're in Florida. Off the coast of Key West to be exact."

"Florida. Yeah, that makes sense. The island was very tropical." She closed her eyes for a moment. Then opened them. She shook her head. "My brain will kick in, in a moment."

He paused at a door and pointed. "There's a bathroom through there. It should have everything you need." When she glanced at his clean-shaven jaw, he rubbed his hand against his chin. "I've already raided it. Once the local officers got here and collected all the evidence from it, I slipped in and cleaned up. There's hot water and everything."

"So Miami's FBI Evidence Response Team has jurisdiction because it was an interstate kidnapping, right?"

"Yes, they've been called in and are on the way. Bree is going to represent South Carolina law enforcement involvement, so she'll be in close contact with the sheriff here. His name is Greg Danvers."

"Okay then. Who does this place belong to?"

"A guy by the name of Keith Hogan. But he's dead."

"Oh."

"While you were catching up on your sleep"—she punched him only a little gently in the stomach and he gave a low grunt— "I was gathering information. This place—the house and the island—is in probate. Hogan's wife died three years before he did, and now his heirs are battling it out to see who gets what. But before they can settle anything, they have to find a missing sibling who's been doing mission work in Africa for the last couple of years. No one's heard from her since before her father's death."

"She didn't come to the funeral?"

"Apparently not."

"So, the house has been sitting empty."

"That's what the family claims."

She looked around. "Doesn't feel like it's been empty very long."

"No. It's pretty obvious our attacker has been living here."

Her eyes went to his bandaged forearm where Watson had gotten ahold of him. "Who took care of us?"

"Bree flew a doctor in, along with a SWAT team I requested. They're covering the island as we speak. They didn't want to go with my assumption that he was long gone. Anyway, the doc checked you out, bandaged you up, and even gave you a shot of antibiotics. You took it like a champ. Never even flinched."

She rolled her eyes, then pressed a hand to the shoulder that hadn't been hurt in her fall. "So that's why this shoulder hurts now?"

"Guilty."

"How long have I been out?"

He shrugged. "About four hours."

"Right. Okay." She touched his smooth face. "You look awful. I'm guessing you didn't have the benefit of passing out?"

"That bad, huh?" He huffed a humorless laugh and gripped her fingers in a squeeze. "I can always count on you to keep me humble." But he hadn't taken offense. "No, I cleaned up, but I haven't slept." He touched her cheek with his free hand. "I will."

"When?"

"Soon."

She gave a short nod, still trying to process the fact that they were safe.

He nodded to the bedroom. "Bree brought you a change of clothes too. There's a small overnight bag with all kinds of things you females think you need."

"A toothbrush?"

"Yep."

She let out a small sigh. "Bless her."

"Go. You're safe. You're fine. We both are. Even Watson's going to make it."

"You're going to keep him, you know."

He shook his head, then gave a slight smile. "Yes, it certainly looks that way."

"I figured when you named him Watson, you would. What about the golden retriever? Have you seen him?"

"No, he hasn't shown up."

"You think the guy who did this took him with him?"

"Probably. He's evidence, especially if he's chipped."

"Watson," she said. "We'll need to check him."

"We will."

"All right. I'll see you in a few minutes." She stepped inside the room and started to shut the door behind her.

He stopped her and gestured to the sling holding her injured arm. "You can take that off to shower. It's got Velcro. I can help you get it back on when you're ready."

"Thanks."

Once she was alone, Maddy started toward the bathroom, then stopped and leaned against the wall. Slowly, she slid down it until she sat on the hardwood floor. Then she lowered her head and didn't try to stop the tears.

Seconds after the storm started, she felt hands on her shoulders and stiffened. She looked up to find Quinn staring down at her. She bowed her head again. "Go . . . away."

He slid down beside her. "Not a chance." His strong arms pulled her close and he pressed his lips to her head. "I've already had my meltdown. I figured you were due, so I waited."

He was absolutely right. She was definitely due. She cried into his chest and soaked his shirt. Finally, she caught her breath and stilled. Then sniffed and wiped her nose with her sleeve.

"You're never going to wear that shirt again, are you?" His breath whispered across her ear.

She hiccuped and sniffed again. "How'd you know?"

"You wiped your nose with it. You'd never do that if you intended to wear it again."

She gave a soft, shaky laugh, pulled the sling off, then let Quinn help her get the long-sleeved shirt over her head. She gave it a toss. "You're right. I never want to see these clothes again." In the short-sleeved shirt she still had on, she shivered, but warmth radiated from him and she soaked it up. "What kind?" she murmured against his chest.

"Huh?"

"What kind of meltdown?"

He cleared his throat. "Uh, well, you know. The guy kind."

She hiccupped a laugh. And remembered another reason she liked him so much. When she didn't want to smack him silly, she usually found herself laughing at him—and even *with* him sometimes. "What's a guy meltdown?"

He sighed. "You're going to make me tell you, aren't you?"

"No, I already know."

"Do not."

"Do too."

He reared back to look at her. "What is it then?"

"You punched a wall."

His brow shot up. "Huh."

"It's simply observation. Your hand wasn't hurt the last I remember." He held it up and looked at it. "Oh right." He sighed. "Yes, I punched a wall. Or three."

"So, did it help?"

He tried to flex his fingers and winced. "Naw. It was a dumb thing to do."

"But it helped."

He gave a low chuckle. "I can't get anything past you, can I? All right. Yes, it helped. It was still dumb, but at least I didn't break anything and it's not my gun hand."

"I think I like crying better. It doesn't hurt." She pressed a hand to her aching head. "At least not as much."

"Nope, crying makes you stuffy. I prefer pain."

She gave a little laugh, sighed, and started to pull back, then decided she liked where she was better and stayed put. "When have you ever cried, Quinn?"

"Why do you want to know?"

"'Cuz."

"I . . . don't remember."

"When you were a kid?"

"Yeah."

"What about when your sister died?"

He stiffened, then sighed. "I . . . no. No, I didn't."

She stilled, but didn't pull away to look at him. "Why not?" she murmured against his chest.

"I couldn't."

"You need to, then."

"Probably." He tapped her chin and stared down at her. "I cried when I thought you were going to die."

"You did? Why?"

"'Cuz," he mocked her gently. His eyes dropped to her lips and his head started to dip.

She frowned at him even as her heart picked up a beat. "Don't even think about it."

He paused and a gleam she'd never seen before entered his eyes. She could see him trying for an innocent face. "Think about what?"

"You know what." There was no way their first kiss was going to be this moment. As much as she didn't want to, she pushed away from him and stood. "I need to brush my teeth and take a shower. I'll see you in a little while."

A smile played at the corner of his lips, then he turned serious. He stood too and pressed a kiss to her forehead. "Want me to help you wash your hair?"

She blinked. "Uh . . . no. I can do it."

"Or I could help you." His eyes widened and he flushed. "Do it in the sink, I mean. I wasn't suggesting—"

She placed a finger on his lips. "I know, Quinn. But I'll manage. Thanks."

"All right then." He paused and placed another kiss on the top of her head. "I'm glad you're all right," he whispered.

She felt the tears threaten again. "Yeah," she whispered back. "I am too. I'm glad we're both still alive." She glanced at her bandaged thigh and gave him a tight smile. "And I've never been so glad to get stitches."

But she knew the person who'd done this was still out there, and until he was either behind bars or dead, she didn't think she'd ever be able to live without looking over her shoulder.

....

Quinn found the doctor who'd patched them up. He was in the office, talking to one of the special agents. They stood next to the couch Maddy had recently vacated.

The doctor was a young guy in his early thirties with a military buzz cut, blue eyes, and a dimple in his left cheek. He'd introduced himself as Joshua Ayers. Quinn had liked him instantly, and when he'd seen how respectful the man had been while treating the unconscious Maddy, his admiration had increased exponentially. Quinn touched the man's shoulder to get his attention. "Dr. Ayers, are you sure Maddy doesn't need a hospital?"

"It's Joshua." The doctor shook his head. "And no, she's a little dehydrated, but while her wounds were heading toward infection, the antibiotics should take care of that. There's no head trauma or internal injuries that I could see. Her shoulder's going to be sore for a while, but you did a great job getting it back in place. As long as the infection clears up soon, she should be fine." He tilted his head. "Now, if she starts spiking a fever, then she should see her doctor."

Quinn nodded. "Okay, thanks."

"Same with you and your arm."

"I'll keep an eye on it." He lifted a hand, then dropped it. "How did Bree convince you to fly all the way out here at the last minute?"

"Bree's brother, Jeff, is my best friend. I've known Bree since kindergarten."

"And you dropped everything to come?"

He shrugged. "Bree's like family. I'd do anything for her." He flashed a smile. "And she knows I'm a good doctor with an excellent partner who doesn't mind taking up the slack when I have to run to a friend's aid."

"Glad to hear it." Quinn took in the military haircut, the way the man carried himself, to the slight shadow in his eyes that hadn't faded since he'd arrived. "So where'd you serve?"

Joshua's lips flattened. "Afghanistan. Two tours as a medic, then I got out and opened my own practice."

"Thought so."

"It's what God had in mind for me. Not sure I agree with the way his plan played out, but looking back I can see some of his purposes."

"You believe that?"

Joshua raised a brow. "Sure. I wouldn't say it if I didn't believe it."

Quinn gave the man a slight smile. "Okay, good enough. Have you seen Bree?"

"Think she was outside meeting with some of the FBI agents. She doesn't have jurisdiction here, but that doesn't seem to matter to her."

He laughed. "No, it wouldn't."

"Sheriff Danvers is here too. I overheard him say that the crime scene unit is on the way. Along with a medical examiner. She was at another site, so they had to wait on her to finish and that took some time."

"Thanks." He shook the doctor's hand and walked out the front door to find Bree. He spotted her talking to a woman with an FBI vest on and a man he assumed was the sheriff.

Bree saw him and waved him over. "Hey, this is Special Agent Lydia Collins with the Miami FBI office. She's with ERT. This is Sheriff Greg Danvers with the Monroe County Sheriff's Office. Lydia was telling me that the sheriff here is a graduate of the FBI's National Academy. Lydia, Sheriff, this is Detective Quinn Holcombe, my partner."

Quinn shook hands with the sheriff and then the pretty blonde. She had her hair pulled back in a ponytail. Her green eyes were sharp and intense. The sheriff's tight jaw was rock hard, his brown eyes like granite. He had a feeling neither one of them missed a thing. "Glad you've got the training you have, Sheriff. I can see why they'd want you on this case. Nice to meet you both."

"Likewise," the special agent murmured. The sheriff nodded.

"Did Bree fill you in?" Quinn asked them.

Lydia nodded. "We've found the spear pits you told us about. There's one about every five yards around the perimeter of the island. It's amazing neither one of you fell into one."

Quinn felt himself pale. "We came really close to dying." He knew it, of course. He'd just lived through it, but saying the words out loud was like a punch in the stomach.

"Several times, it sounds like," Bree said. She reached out and squeezed his nonbandaged hand.

"Yes. Several times," he said. Quinn shook his head. He'd faced death before, simply due to the nature of his job. But never had he been the object of a deliberate, personal attempt to wipe him out. Even the act that had broken his legs and put him in the hospital and rehab for the past six months hadn't been targeting him specifically. He'd just gotten in the way. But this . . . this was personal.

"Hey."

He turned to find Maddy limping toward them. She'd dressed in a pair of khaki knit pants and a pink short-sleeved shirt.

She wore matching pink tennis shoes with white ankle socks. Her wet hair was pulled back into her perpetual ponytail. She carried her sling in her hand.

"Hey. What are you doing out here?" he asked.

"I want to be involved in this investigation every step of the way." She narrowed her eyes at him. "I want to catch this guy and I want to do it yesterday." She shot him a wry look. "If this is your serial killer, it looks like I'm going to be on your task force after all."

Quinn almost smiled to see the fire back in her. He had to admit he'd been worried she'd survived one terror-filled event only to let this one claim her spirit. He should have known better. Maddy was a fighter. The youngest of ten children, she'd had to be. "How did you manage to wash your hair with one hand?" he asked.

She gave a choked laugh. "You'd be surprised at what I can do when I put my mind to it. I managed."

Because that's what she did. Quinn shook his head. "Stubborn." She bit her lip. He figured it was to keep from sticking her tongue out at him. "This is Special Agent Lydia Collins and Sheriff Greg Danvers."

Maddy nodded, took a deep breath. "Nice to meet you."

They exchanged handshakes, then Lydia turned to Quinn. "We found that mass grave you saw."

Maddy tilted her head. She held her sling out to Quinn. "A little help, please?"

Once she had her arm immobilized once again, he turned to Lydia. "Lead the way."

Lydia walked to the edge of the woods where they'd found the grave and stopped when she reached the large hole in the ground. "I don't want to disturb anything until the medical examiner gets here. But I noticed something."

"What's that?"

"There are ten crosses."

"Yes."

"But, if you count the skulls, there appear to be only eight bodies."

[9]

Maddy flinched. Then let out a low sigh as she stared down at the poor individuals who had ended up dying so tragically.

The killer had laid them out one by one, side by side, on their backs with their hands crossed on their chests. At least that's what she thought. Some of the bones were missing, no doubt carried off by animals. But the most recent body, the one lying under cross number eight, was very much intact. Decomposing for sure, but . . . "This one isn't more than a couple of weeks old, I'm guessing."

She returned her attention to the other end of the line of bodies.

The victim lying at the foot of the first cross had obviously been the first to die if the decomp was anything to go by. Mostly bones, with some patches of soft tissue and hair, were all that was left. "Who was the first victim?"

"Jessica Maynard." Quinn placed his hands on his hips. "Twenty-eight years old, single, never married, no kids. It's so sad. She was so alone. Her parents are dead and she didn't appear to have any close friends. Just an introvert who kept to herself. Didn't hurt anyone and definitely didn't deserve to die like this. If that's her."

"Who reported her missing?"

"Her boss. When she didn't show up for work or call in on the second day, he got concerned and asked someone to check on her. By the fourth day, he filed a missing persons report."

"Poor thing," Maddy murmured. "And now she's died all alone as well."

"If that's her."

"Yes. If." She shifted for a closer look. "Who was the second victim?"

"Gerald Haynes."

"Who is he?"

Quinn raked a hand through his hair. "Haynes was an engineer. He was working on a pretty important project for his company. He'd come up with some kind of invention and had just turned in a prototype of the device. He disappeared that afternoon." Quinn shook his head. "He was going to take his family on vacation the next day. He never made it home from the office."

"That's odd that he's taking victims of both sexes. Most serial killers pick one or the other," Maddy said. She frowned. "And the third?"

"Kelly Masters. A new doctor who finished her degree in three years."

Lydia stared at him. "How do you remember all that off the top of your head? Do you have some kind of photographic memory?"

He shook his head without taking his eyes from the victims in the grave. "Have you ever had a case that haunted you day and night? A case that wouldn't leave you alone so you read the file over and over and over until you could practically quote it?"

"No."

He looked at her. "This serial killer was that case for me. When you have yours, you'll understand."

"Okay then." She paused. "I hope I never have that one, to be honest."

"I hope so too."

Maddy sighed. "We won't know for sure until they're identified, but it appears that they're lying in order of their deaths," she said. "Especially if the crosses and the numbers mean anything."

Quinn nodded. "I noticed that."

While Lydia snapped pictures, the sheriff watched them work, taking everything in. His eyes never stopped moving and she knew he was processing. She had a feeling he was a smart man who wasn't worried about other law enforcement stepping on his toes. He was comfortable in his role of sheriff and was humble enough to admit he was out of his league with this mass grave and a possible serial killer on the loose in his jurisdiction.

Maddy looked again at the victims and tried to distance herself from the fact that she was probably supposed to be lying under either the number nine cross or the number ten. Probably the number ten, since the killer had let her go in order to kill Quinn first. "Assuming all of the skulls are here and there aren't two bodies missing from those cleared spaces under the last two crosses, you were supposed to be number nine," she said.

She glanced at Quinn. His tight features said he was thinking the same. He reached over and gripped her hand. "I guess that makes you number ten."

"Story of my life. Literally," she muttered. Then gritted her teeth against the fury that wanted to take over. She couldn't let it. She had to keep her head—and her cool. She had to think, be smart.

The sheriff finally spoke. "You think this guy is your serial killer?"

Quinn pursed his lips. "I suspect it. Once we identify the bodies, we'll know for sure."

"It would explain why you couldn't find them," Maddy said.

"For sure. They disappear from South Carolina and wind up here. Why?"

"He's familiar with this place," Bree said. "He knows this area."

"But he also knows South Carolina," Maddy said. "He knows his victims, their routines—and the easiest way to snatch them," she murmured, her mind spinning, going where she didn't want it to go. But she would once again delve into the darkness if it meant catching the person responsible for trying to kill her and Quinn—the person who had already killed eight innocent people. "He's watched them, either one at a time or he bounced between them. Probably one at a time, making notes, taking pictures, planning their deaths to be on his timetable." She bit her lip. "Order is important to him." She looked at the crosses. "Numbers are important to him."

Quinn pursed his lips, his brow furrowed in thought. "Yes."

The sheriff lifted a brow. "What do the numbers mean?"

Maddy shook her head. "I'm not completely sure, of course, but I think it means they died in a certain order. Quinn was supposed to be number nine, I was supposed to be number ten—'because everything should be done in a fitting and orderly way.'" Sheriff Danvers frowned and Maddy shrugged. "That's what he said. He also lost someone close to him. Someone who wasn't able to 'cheat death.'"

"But who?" Quinn asked.

A helicopter thumped overhead and she looked up to see the Monroe County Sheriff's Office logo on the side. It would land on the runway far enough away not to disturb the crime scene. "That's the crime scene unit, I'm guessing."

Sheriff Danvers nodded. "That's them."

Bree backed away from the grave. "I'll show them where to come." She spun on her heel and went to meet the chopper.

Maddy studied the bodies again. "Three of the skulls I can see have holes in one side. I wonder if the other side of the skull is even there."

"Bullets?" Quinn asked.

"Probably crossbow bolts. The tips were very slender and very sharp. I can see it making a clean hole on one side before exiting out the other."

"So where are the bolts?"

Maddy grimaced. "He took them?"

"Must have."

She stepped back and frowned. "He's a good shot."

"And yet he missed us on several occasions," Quinn said.

"The first bolt went into the wall behind us."

"He didn't want to hit us at that point, he wanted to spur us on, make us run so he could enjoy the chase."

Maddy tilted her head, her mind whirling. The sheriff's attention was pinging back and forth between her and Quinn as they talked. "I wonder if he thought you'd grab the bolt," she said.

"You grabbed one of the bolts?" the sheriff asked.

"Yeah," Quinn said absently. "He probably thought about it, but didn't figure I could do much damage with it."

"Guess he inadvertently saved your life," Maddy said, then shrugged. "In a weird way."

"Very weird."

The sheriff blinked. "Do I dare ask?"

"Sheriff, can you come here a minute?" One of his deputies waved him over.

"Excuse me," he said and left Quinn and Maddy alone.

She shivered in the heat and clasped her arms. He gripped her biceps and pulled her close. "We're going to get him," he whispered in her ear.

"Yeah."

She stood there, her head on his chest, relishing the feeling of safety. Security. Unfortunately she knew it was going to be short-lived. "He's not finished with us, is he?"

"No. I'm afraid not."

He'd have to tell her about the note from the back of the satellite phone. Later. For the life of him, he couldn't imagine what this person thought he was doing. Why target him and Maddy? And if Quinn was supposed to die before Maddy, why had he gone after her first? He'd broken into her home and waited on her to get home. He'd knocked her out first. He'd *planned* to take her *first*.

Why? And who had helped him? Quinn thought about the "why." Could it be he thought it would be harder to get to Quinn? That he'd have to use Maddy to lure Quinn in?

Maybe.

And maybe once they knew for sure the identities of the people in the grave, he'd have a clearer picture of who the mastermind was behind all of this. And what did he mean about now it was going to get personal? It already felt mighty personal to Quinn.

"Lydia!" The special agent turned and Quinn followed her gaze. Another officer dressed in an FBI vest broke through the trees.

"What is it, Chris?" Lydia called.

Maddy raised a brow. "Special Agent Christopher Jordan,"

Quinn told her. He'd heard the man's name as he'd talked to the lead agent inside.

Chris motioned for them to follow him. "Come here, you've got to see this." He looked at Quinn. "You too, Detective Holcombe, since the whole serial killer thing started with you and your case."

Quinn tensed. Maddy placed a hand on his arm. "All right," he nodded. "I'm right behind you."

"Where are we going?" Maddy asked.

"I think it's the place where you were held before he let you out to hunt you," Chris said.

Maddy shuddered and Quinn reached for her hand.

Together, they retraced part of the route they'd taken on their flight from their "prison" to the main house. Maddy nearly vibrated with . . . something. Fear? Anger? From the corner of his eye, Quinn studied her features. Her jaw was set like a rock while a muscle pulsed in her check. Her eyes stared straight ahead and her nostrils flared with each breath.

With his good hand, he gripped her fingers. She didn't look at him and he knew she'd gone somewhere in her head. Somewhere that would allow her to cope, to go back to the place where they'd awakened and found themselves prisoners of a madman.

He had to admit he wanted off this island. His nerves had taken just about all they could take. Instead, he found himself facing the building he and Maddy had been released from only hours before. "What time is it?"

Lydia glanced at her phone. "Noon. Why?"

"Today is Sunday, right?"

"Yes."

"So, we were snatched around nine o'clock Friday night. It's noon on Sunday. So, a little over thirty-six hours."

Maddy nodded. "Such a short time to feel like a lifetime."

"Exactly."

She walked up to the door and put her finger into the hole left by the bolt Quinn had pulled out. "This is it." She stepped back.

Chris pointed to another door. "Let's go this way. I have something else to show you."

Maddy followed without a word. Quinn walked behind her, while Lydia pulled up the rear. Quinn watched the agent pull open a door that had a blackened square just above the handle.

"What happened?" Quinn asked.

"It had a code to get it open. We had to burn through the touch pad with a blow torch."

Maddy stepped inside and gasped. Quinn let his gaze fall on the opposite wall. His reaction echoed hers. Before them was a wall of pictures. Pictures of the missing victims and pictures of the two future victims.

Pictures of him and Maddy stared back at him.

He pointed. "That was the night he took us." They sat across from each other at the table in the restaurant. She had a half smile on her face. He looked angry. Below that picture was one of him alone, walking into the police station with Bree at his side. Next to that picture was Maddy coming out of the bodyguard agency. Several more pictures of him and Maddy going through their daily lives dotted the wall.

Maddy hadn't said a word since they'd arrived. She'd paled a few shades, but her lips had remained shut. "Maddy?" She cut her gaze to him. "You okay?"

"Yes. Are you?"

"I'm—" He shook his head. "I don't know, to be honest." Surprise flickered on her features and he shrugged. "That was some scary stuff. This makes it even more scary. I'm tired of scary."

"Yeah," she whispered. "I am too." She walked up to the wall, started to raise a hand, then looked back at Chris.

He nodded. "Already dusted for prints."

She turned and touched the picture of her and Quinn. "He's been watching us." She moved to the next picture. "For a while now. That was taken about three months ago, wasn't it?"

"And that's not all," Lydia said. She had a drawer pulled open and was pulling pictures from it. Quinn moved to look at them as she laid them out on the small desk.

He blew out a harsh breath. "Well, now we know." He looked at each person Lydia laid out. He recognized each face since he'd studied them enough over the last several months.

"Know what?" Maddy asked.

"It's definitely our serial killer." He met her eyes. "Welcome to the task force."

[10]

Maddy stood at the edge of the beach just out of reach of the waves that lapped at the shore. She yanked the band out of her hair and raked a hand through her air-dried strands before pulling it back once more. She wished she'd kept Quinn's cap. But she had other things to worry about than that silly ball cap. Like the fact that the SWAT team had swept the island and come up empty. The guy—the killer—was gone.

And now the bodies were patiently waiting for the medical examiner to arrive. They would be transported off the island to the morgue in Key West. Outwardly, she kept her expression still, calm, poised. Inwardly, her emotions raged. Those had been living, breathing people. They deserved justice. As far as she was concerned, they would *get* justice.

A noise caught her attention, and in a few minutes she could make out a small boat powered by a single engine zipping across the water toward the island. It looked like two people occupied the craft. As it drew closer, Maddy could see the lettering on the side. TABOR TRANSPORT AND FERRY SERVICE.

A few feet out, the captain cut the motor and pulled it up,

then used a paddle to steer the boat all the way into the sand, where he beached it. He hooked a ladder over the side, then, barefoot, hopped out. The water came to his ankles. He pointed to the front of the boat and his passenger nodded.

Maddy watched as a woman hefted a large bag, then climbed onto the seat, up over the bow, and dropped into the sand. She wore khaki shorts and a green shirt that identified her as with the Monroe County Office of the Medical Examiner. She had brown hair with a few gray streaks, pulled back in a ponytail. Her dark-rimmed glasses covered startling blue eyes. Those blue eyes snagged Maddy's gaze and she approached with an outstretched hand. "Hi."

"Hi."

"I'm Dr. Callie Forsythe, the ME for Monroe County. I got a call about a mass grave. Sorry it took me so long to get out here."

Maddy shook her hand. "I'm Maddy McKay. I can take you to the grave."

"What's your role here?"

Maddy blinked at the woman, unsure how to answer. Victim? Task force member? "Good question."

"Here ya go, Ms. Forsythe," the gray-headed man said to her. He handed her a clipboard. "Just need you to sign right here so I can bill yer office."

Callie signed and he added his signature, then ripped off the bottom page. He handed it to the woman, then set the clipboard back in the boat.

Maddy took note of the man who'd captained the boat out to the island. Long gray hair with a matching mustache and in need of a shave. Sunglasses covered his eyes. His skin glowed with a healthy tan and his hands looked strong and capable. She guessed he was in his early to midfifties, but it was hard to tell with the beard. He could be ten years older.

Sheriff Danvers stepped around the crime scene tape at the edge of the trees and walked down to the beach with an out-stretched hand. "Callie, good to see you. Still won't fly, huh?"

"Not a chance." She set her bag on the sand and stepped forward to shake his hand, then planted her hands on her slim hips.

The sheriff looked at the captain. "Thanks, Burt."

"Sure thing, Sheriff." Burt nodded. "Lemme know if you need anythin' else." He looked around, his attention on all the law enforcement. "What's going on out here? And what are those pits? I never seen them a'fore."

Maddy followed his gaze. Every five yards, there was a six-by-ten pit with spears at the bottom. They'd been methodically uncovered and marked with yellow crime scene tape. The memory of almost falling into one of them flashed and she sucked in a deep breath to keep the gasp from passing her lips.

"A crime scene," Sheriff Danvers said. "Keep it to yourself, will you?"

"Yeah, of course."

Maddy wondered if he really would, but the sheriff seemed to know the man fairly well.

"You need me to stick around?" Burt asked. "I don't mind." He glanced at his watch. "I got a ferry in about two hours, but happy to do what I can to help you between now an' then."

"I've got a question for you."

Burt crossed his arms. "What's that?"

"When was the last time you came out to this island?"

A tan hand reached up to stroke his long beard. "Well, I reckon it was a while back. I been ferrying nigh on to five years now. Keeps me busy and I don't have to think so much about . . . well, you know. I used to bring things out to Mr. Hogan, but then he died a couple a years ago, so . . ." He shrugged. "Two years, I guess?"

"You haven't been out here since Mr. Hogan died?"

"Nope."

"You notice anything going on over on this island while you were out on the water in between islands? A plane coming in or taking off?"

Another stroke of the beard. "Yeah. I mighta seen a plane a time or two. Just figured it was Hogan's kids coming to check on the place or something."

"What kind was it? Did you notice? And the color?"

"Aw, shoot, Sheriff, I think it was gray and blue. Don't know what kind it was. I'm not into planes much, other than using them to get from one place to the other."

"I understand." The sheriff nodded. "Thanks, Burt."

"Yep. You need anything else?"

"Not for now. I'll give you a call when the good doc is ready to leave."

Burt nodded. "A crime scene, huh?" He shook his head. "I don't get why God lets stuff like that happen. I don't guess I ever will."

"I know what you mean, Burt. Thanks for your help."

"I'll be back when you need me, then." He shoved his boat back into deeper water, climbed the ladder and pulled it in, then let the motor down. The engine revved and he was gone, soon to become a small speck as he headed back toward Key West. Maddy didn't bother listening as the sheriff filled in the medical examiner. She knew the details.

A hand came to rest on her shoulder and she spun, heart thudding. Quinn pulled his hand back and stood in the "I surrender" position. "Sorry."

Maddy placed a hand over her pounding heart. "No, I'm sorry. It's going to take a while to get over the jumpiness."

"I know. Are you ready to go? There's a chopper here that will take us home."

"Home. Yes. Home sounds good."

He placed a hand on the small of her back. "Are you going to stay with your parents for a while?"

She snorted a laugh. "No. Are you?"

He scowled. "Not likely."

They walked a few steps, then she stopped and looked up at him. "We almost died, Quinn."

"Yeah, but we didn't."

"I know and I don't know why."

He brushed a few wayward bangs back out of her eyes. "Where's your faith? Your trust in God?"

"It's still there, but I'm . . . questioning."

"What?"

"Just . . . stuff."

"I thought I was supposed to be the secretive one in this relationship."

"Relationship?" She looked at him. "What relationship?"

His mouth worked. "Well, that was a low blow."

She sighed. "Sorry. Again."

"No. You have every right to feel that way." He drew in a deep breath. "Maddy, I'm sorry, I—"

"Don't say anything, Quinn, okay? Now isn't the time to try to figure out what we are."

He fell silent and she almost felt bad for cutting him off, but the truth was, she was so mixed up inside that anything he said was just going to add to the clamor. She needed quiet. She needed peace. She needed someone to not be trying to kidnap or kill her. Just for a little while. Without looking at him, she reached for his hand and held it. He let her.

And together, they stood in silence, lost in their own thoughts. Separate. Yet not. Then he squeezed her fingers. "Let's go home."

"No," she said. "Let's go catch a killer."

[11]

Quinn sat next to Maddy in the five-seater private plane. Daniel Matthews piloted the Cirrus SR-22T, an upgrade from the plane he'd lost when his had been stolen, crashed, and burned approximately six months earlier. The man was confident in his ability to fly and Quinn knew he could relax for the next two hours or so. He looked out the window as the plane banked over the water and had to admit he wasn't sorry to leave the chaos behind. He had no idea how long the investigation on the island would take, but he'd be kept in the loop.

Watson lay at his feet, his wound cleaned, sewn up, and wrapped, thanks to the vet Bree had managed to fly out to the island. The dog had gotten his shot of antibiotics too.

Quinn looked over at Maddy. She had her eyes closed, and the farther they got from the island, the softer her features became. Quinn decided she had the right idea and shut his eyes too. Sleep was going to be hard to come by until the madman was caught.

Quinn jerked when the wheels touched down and he blinked in surprise that he'd actually slept the entire flight without dreaming about running for his life—or being crushed in a giant tin can.

Maddy still slept, her lips gently parted, breaths coming in even puffs.

Daniel taxied down the runway to the hangar, but left the plane just outside the building. Only when he pulled to a stop did Maddy open her eyes, blink, and come to instant alertness.

Quinn stared. "How do you do that?"

"What?"

"Sleep through everything including the landing, then wake up when you're supposed to?"

"Habit. Training. Whatever. I don't know, I just do."

"I have some special ops buddies who would envy that ability." He reached for his hat and stopped, clenched the fingers on his good hand into a fist, and sighed. "Rats."

"What is it?" Maddy asked.

"I left my hat on the island."

She frowned. "What's so special about that hat?"

"It's not the hat, it's who gave it to me."

"Oh. Who?"

"Stacy. Just before she died."

Sympathy and guilt flashed in her eyes. "Quinn, I'm so sorry. I think I left it in the cave."

He shrugged. "It's okay."

"No, it's not. I'm really sorry."

He reached out and cupped her cheek. "Maddy. It's okay. Really."

Then the doors opened and the subject was closed. Daniel exited the plane first, with Maddy right behind him. He held out a hand and she took it as she descended the steps.

Quinn liked Daniel's home. In an aviation neighborhood, the property was open and spacious. As was the house. Katie had made it a home for the three of them while waiting for her wedding date to finally arrive. She'd told Maddy she wanted a place she could move into as soon as the vows were said without worrying about redecorating. She and Daniel's niece Riley had apparently bonded even more over the experience. Daniel claimed he was close to taking out a second mortgage to pay for it all, but Quinn knew the man was loaded and could well afford the expense. Daniel's former sister-in-law, sister to his deceased first wife, still lived in the small apartment across from the main house. He admired the man for looking out for her.

Quinn saw his SUV parked in the drive and wondered how that had happened. Then the front door to Daniel's home opened and people streamed from it. Olivia, Katie, Haley, Wade, and Charlie, Olivia's brother. Olivia reached him first and hugged him. "We're so glad you two are okay."

Surprised, he hugged her back. "Thanks. We're kind of happy about it too."

Olivia moved to Maddy. "My friend, we're going to have to roll you in bubble wrap."

Maddy smiled, and over Olivia's shoulder, he saw the tears in her eyes.

And he was hit with a realization that nearly brought him to his knees. These people cared. These people had formed a tight-knit group who watched out for one another and took care of each other.

And they'd let him inside.

Actually, dragged him kicking and screaming inside, and he'd tried to push them away. He'd been rude and snide and acted like a two-year-old who hadn't gotten his way. Shame covered him and left him nearly breathless. "I'm sorry," he said. He cleared his throat. "I owe you all an apology."

The din of voices faded and they all turned to stare at him. Maddy frowned. He shrugged, feeling embarrassed, but wanting to set the record straight. "I've been a jerk. And . . . I'm sorry. Thanks for . . . everything."

Again the women hugged him with choruses of "We knew you'd come around." And "Well, if you were okay in Maddy's book, you were okay in ours." And then they were back to business as usual, wanting to hear the details. Katie waved them inside. "No sense in standing around out here while you two are still targets."

And with that simple sentence, reality crashed in and all sense of safety fled. They moved into the large living area.

He caught Maddy's eye again. Still she frowned and watched him with a pensive look. His heart thudded. Had he done something wrong by apologizing? Then her lips lifted slightly and her eyes grew soft. He blew out a relieved breath. She nodded and he tilted his head in response. Good, he was forgiven for his bad behavior. Now what? He didn't know. He just knew he didn't want Maddy upset with him. Or in danger. He stood at the window and looked out.

A car pulled into the drive and he recognized Bree's Camry. She'd flown one of the choppers back, so she'd made excellent time. Bree climbed out and headed up the front steps. He opened the door before she could knock and she stepped into the room. "Hi, everyone." They greeted her and she turned her attention to him. "I got you something."

"What's that?"

She pulled a phone from her pocket and handed it to him. "This and information. Your phone hasn't turned up yet. I had a spare, so had it programmed for you."

He took it and looked at it. Twelve missed calls. "Time to get back to it, I see. What kind of information?"

"We received another note."

Maddy flinched at Bree's announcement. Another note. And she hadn't even been home yet. Or checked in with her family. She wondered what they'd heard, or if they were trying to get ahold of her. Since everything had taken place in Florida, she wasn't too concerned about their hearing what had happened. She and Quinn had been found fast enough that Olivia and the others hadn't had to inform their families. Thank goodness.

She needed to replace her phone too. Or maybe it was somewhere in her house. She lifted a hand to her head. Her house. "My house is a crime scene."

Quinn paused in the act of listening to his voice mails and looked at her. "You're right." He turned to Bree. "Who's there?"

"Detectives Diego Gonzales and Julie Van Heerden."

He nodded. "A good team."

Although she was no longer sleepy, Maddy's wounds ached. Her thigh especially throbbed with an intensity that wanted to distract her. It seemed to be in competition with her shoulder. But she'd been hurt worse. Pain was irrelevant at this point. She was dead serious about catching this guy, and going on the offensive was the only option now. But where to start?

"Okay," she said. "Let me think." The room fell silent once again. All eyes turned on her. "What did this note say and how do you know it's from our guy?"

Bree pulled out her phone. "I took a picture of it. It came to the station with Quinn's name and address on it. Since it was the same kind of envelope as the serial killer's we've been trying to find, I went ahead and opened it." She looked at Quinn. "Sorry."

He waved a hand. "Go on."

"It said, 'Not many people manage to surprise me. You and Ms. McKay have. I lift my glass to you. Until we meet again.'"

Quinn paced to the mantel and back to the window. "All right. I think that's pretty straightforward. Just like the note on the phone."

"What note on the phone?" Maddy asked.

Quinn cleared his throat. "I might have left out that little detail."

She raised a brow and he told her about the note taped to the back of the satellite phone.

She shot him a dark look and he shrugged. "This is the first chance I've had to tell you and actually discuss what it might mean."

She sighed and waved a hand, indicating she'd let it go. "Fine. So why both notes?"

"In case I didn't find the phone and we found some other way off the island."

She blinked. "Like how?"

Quinn shrugged. "I don't know. Once CSU is finished with the island, they may have more information to share."

"True." She paused. "The plane. In the hangar next to the house."

Quinn drew in a deep breath. "Yes. If we'd found the plane, we could have used the radio on it—or flown out of there."

"Since when did you become a pilot?"

He shrugged. "I'm not officially, but Daniel's taught me a thing or two. I would have risked it to get off that island."

"And I would have gone with you," she muttered. "Okay, so, ignoring the note for now, what else do we know?" Before anyone else could respond, she held up one finger. "I'll tell you what we know. We know he's made this personal." A second finger joined the first. "He's educated."

"Yes," Quinn said. "I got that too. His voice didn't have a particular accent, but the way he talked was a giveaway."

"He used words like 'fortify' and the way he talked to us, like he was amused or above us."

"'My dear friends,'" Quinn murmured.

Maddy shuddered and dropped her hand. "Yes, he used that phrase. And another one. It's from something I've heard before, but I can't place it. I was going to google it when I got the chance."

"What?" Haley asked.

"Something like 'Everything should be done in a fitting and orderly way.' Do you recognize it?"

"I do," Katie said. "It's from the Bible."

Maddy blinked. "He's quoting Scripture to me?"

Katie pulled her phone and tapped on the screen. Maddy waited, knowing she was looking up the phrase. "First Corinthians 14:40, the NIV translation," Katie said.

"The Bible, huh? Guess he missed the part about 'Thou shalt not kill,'" Daniel said.

Maddy frowned. "All right. So he's familiar with Scripture. And if he picked that one, then he might be a little OCD as well. Considering the fact that he could have easily killed me, he let me go because I wasn't next on the list." She slid her eyes across the room to the man near the window. "Quinn was." He dipped his head in acknowledgment and Maddy slipped into profiler mode. "He's a planner. He makes lists and checks them off."

"Family man?" Quinn asked.

She thought about that. "Possibly. He didn't really reveal anything that would indicate that, but he did say something about me cheating death. I think he lost someone close to him and he's bitter about that. So, if I had to make an educated guess, yes, he's a family man."

"And you had something to do with him losing someone he loved?"

"Not specifically probably. But the fact that I came so close to dying and didn't might bug him somehow." She frowned. "The same thing happened to you, Quinn. You came really close to dying and survived."

He looked at Bree. "Check those eight people and see if there's something to that. See if any of them had a near-death experience."

Bree nodded.

"What else?" Katie asked.

Maddy closed her eyes and tried to replay those thirty-six hours at the mercy of a madman without letting the terror cloud her thinking. "He's methodical. He's . . ." She blew out a sigh and opened her eyes. "I don't know. I need to think about it for a little while longer."

"Sure," Katie said.

Maddy pulled the band out of her ponytail and let the dark waves fall around her shoulders.

"One other thing you can add to the list about this guy," Quinn said.

"What's that?"

"He's an adrenaline junkie. He made it so we had no choice but to give him his thrills. It was either run or get gassed. Who's going to stay and be gassed to death?" Maddy nodded. "And also," Quinn continued, "he shot the bolts to spur us on, not to kill us."

"He figured one of his little traps or something would get us."

"Exactly. There were most likely more that we didn't know about, didn't set off. His traps would cause death, but it would be slow and he'd be able to watch."

"And then fire the final shot, finishing the kill. He's a coward—and a bully," Maddy murmured.

Quinn gave a slow nod. "Which is why he had all the cameras. He needed to know when it was safe to approach. He's probably pretty skilled in some hand-to-hand combat because he did come after us on foot, but he made sure he had massive advantages in his little game."

"The more I think about it, the more it fits," Maddy murmured. "He kidnapped us in a way that would ensure he didn't have to face us, locked us in a room we couldn't get out of until he let us out . . ."

"But it was still pretty risky even doing what he did to take us," Quinn said.

"Risk he probably calculated," Katie said. "Because even though he sent the notes, did you really expect to be ambushed?"

"No." She rubbed her forehead. "And while it occurred to me he might have sent it, I really didn't think it was from him because it was different from his usual MO. There was no name on it, for one, and it didn't come through the mail. Plus the note cards were different sizes."

Quinn nodded. "Same here."

"And he most likely had help, minimizing said risk."

"He's tech-savvy. The room was well built with custom features. I imagine he did it himself."

"And as such, he would have had to purchase the materials from somewhere," Maddy said.

"And on that note, it looks like money isn't an issue. He's well set financially," Katie said.

Lizzie leaned forward. "Unless he stole the stuff."

Maddy shrugged. She didn't think so but knew it was an angle that needed investigating.

Bree nodded and made another notation in her phone. "I'll get on this. In the meantime," she said with a glance at Maddy, then Quinn, "you two shouldn't go anywhere alone."

Olivia nodded. "Definitely. Haley and Lizzie can take turns

staying with Maddy while Charlie and Katie will stay with Quinn."

Maddy frowned. "I don't think that's necessary. I mean, I know he got to me once, but that was a sneak attack, an ambush. I'm alert and on guard now. I'll be expecting him to try again, and when he does, I'll be ready."

"You still need someone to watch your back," Olivia said. "This guy appears to have unlimited resources at his disposal."

Maddy bit her lip on another protest. As much as she hated to admit it, she had to concede that her friend was probably right. She nodded. "Fine, thanks. Now, it's time for me to get a gun and a phone and then go home and check on my house."

"I'll get you a phone," Katie said. She glanced at Quinn. "Let's go."

Haley stood and nodded at Maddy. "I'm ready when you are."

[12]

The Chosen One chuckled as he poured himself a cup of coffee. He'd just come up from the weight room and felt energized. Working out helped him think. And he had a lot to think about.

He set the carafe back on the warmer, lifted the cup, and inhaled the steam. None of that instant stuff people used these days. Those little machines that made one cup at a time. Fake coffee. The Chosen One ground his own beans and brewed his coffee fresh.

He took a sip and felt his tension start to fade, even as he experienced a pang at the loss of the island. Ah well, he'd known the arrangement wasn't a permanent thing. It had served its purpose and now it was time to move on.

He heard the click of nails on the wood floor and turned to find Bandit in the doorway. The dog sat, tongue lolling. "Come here, girl."

She obeyed instantly, nudging up against his left leg, begging for an ear scratch. The Chosen One complied. She was lonely now. He'd hated to leave the pit bull behind, but it couldn't be helped. He'd had no attachment to the dog. The mongrel had simply been a guard dog that followed commands. Most especially the word "attack." Yes, a pity to leave him behind, as he and Bandit had gotten along and now she missed him. But the animal had done his job well, even though he'd been wounded at the hand of Holcombe.

And then the detective had done his best to help the creature. Interesting. Bandit walked to the door and waited expectantly. The Chosen One let her out. She looked around the yard and whined. "Go," he said. She did.

Maybe he'd find a way to get the other mutt back. Had he been left on the island? Surely he was still there. Unless the detective had taken him with him. He'd have to check the cameras and see.

A loud thud came from the second floor and he frowned.

Then the sound of a video game vibrated through the house and he shook his head. He walked to the intercom and pressed the button. "Turn that down, will you?"

Within seconds, the sounds muted to an acceptable decibel level. The Chosen One drew in a calming breath. Soon, his mission would be complete.

"What would you like for breakfast, sweetheart?"

He turned to see Leigh in the doorway, her salt-and-pepper hair falling softly around her shoulders. He smiled. "Glad to see you're up."

"Well, of course, Peanut's coming home today. I need to get things ready."

His jaw tightened and fury ripped through him, but he smiled through it. "Of course." He poured her a cup of coffee. "Why don't you take this into the sunroom and I'll join you in a moment?"

"But breakfast . . ."

"I'll have Dottie make it."

"Oh. I forgot she was here today. Yes, that'll make things easier." She took the cup from his fingers and turned to walk from the kitchen, through the den area, and into the connected sunroom.

When the Chosen One heard the sunroom door close, he released the rage and hurled his coffee cup across the room. He watched it shatter against the wall, his chest heaving as he battled for control. The dark coffee slowly dripped down to spatter against the floor.

Just like Quinn Holcombe had shattered his life, his family, and what should have been the Chosen One's entire future.

He couldn't take his eyes from the dripping dark liquid. It was a symbol. A sign. Of how Quinn's blood would spill against the floor. And then Maddy's. Soon. Very soon.

———

Quinn stepped into his home, his weapon held ready to use if necessary. A quick stop at the station had allowed him to arm himself again. He'd left Watson in the car for the moment. Once he made sure it was safe, he'd carry the animal in.

Quinn did a cursory survey of the open area, then moved down the hall toward the bedrooms. Katie followed him in.

She'd wanted to clear the place first, but Quinn assured her he could do it himself. She acquiesced, but he was glad she was at his back. It didn't take long to clear the sixteen-hundred-square-foot house and soon he was back in the den. He set the gun on the mantel and turned to find Katie sliding her weapon into her shoulder holster. "Thanks."

"Sure."

He noticed the empty dog crate. "Where's Sherlock?"

"I think they left him in your yard. They put his bowls and some food out there too."

"Good." He walked to the sliding glass door and found

Sherlock sunning himself on the deck. When the dog heard him, he popped to his feet and charged the door, skidding to a halt before he crashed into it. A black lab. All gangly limbs and slobber. What had Maddy and her friends been thinking?

He opened the door and Sherlock jumped on Quinn, quivering his delight at Quinn's return. Quinn scratched the animal's ears. "Sit."

The dog hesitated, then reluctantly obeyed. Quinn gave him another scratch and reached for the treats he kept on the mantel. He slipped two of them to Sherlock. "I'm going to get Watson and introduce the two."

"Two males. Good luck with that."

He'd thought about that. If the two dogs didn't get along, he'd find another home for Watson. The thought panged him for some reason. Katie followed him out the door, and he knew she was scanning the area, watching for anything that alarmed her. He was too. At the SUV, he found Watson in the back where he'd left him. The vet had cleared him to go home with prescription antibiotics and some pain meds.

Quinn picked up the hundred-pound dog with a grunt and carried him to the door. Katie opened it for him. "Thanks."

She shut it behind them. Quinn set Watson on the floor in front of the fireplace. Sherlock bounded over and the sniff fest began. Watson growled low in his throat and Sherlock dropped to the floor to stare at this new creature who'd invaded his territory. Fortunately, it looked like Sherlock was going to be willing to be the second in command. He dipped his head and belly crawled closer. Watson nudged him, then laid his head on the floor and closed his eyes.

Quinn let out a breath. "Well, guess that's that."

"They'll be friends. Sherlock is still such a puppy that they'll be all right."

"Yes." He shook his head. "Unbelievable."

"From zero to two?"

He laughed. "Exactly. What am I going to do with two dogs?"

"Love them. That's all they want from you."

He fell silent. Then slapped his hands to his knees. "Right. And now we need to find a killer."

"I think that may be easier said than done."

"It usually is, but that's not going to stop us. Not by a long shot." He ran a hand down the side of his face.

Katie nodded. "Then we'll get at it. After you sleep some."

"I'm not going to argue with you."

Katie raised a brow. "Now that's scary."

"Ha." He retreated to his bedroom and shut the door. Only then did it occur to him that he probably should check in with his family. He unclipped his phone from his belt and stared at the screen. Then again, why bother? He placed the phone on the nightstand, stretched across the bed, and closed his eyes. Then opened them. He needed to know Maddy was okay after walking back into her apartment. He shot Haley a text and waited.

From the kitchen, Maddy stared at the den area. She'd been dreading reentering the house from the moment she'd thought about it—and yet she'd hurried the process of stopping by her office to replace her weapon. Now she wished she'd made time to get another phone instead of waiting for Katie to bring a replacement.

Her gaze landed on the closet where *he*'d hidden. The crime scene team had been there and gone. At least they'd been courteous and cleaned up after themselves. Mostly.

"Did they find anything?" she asked Haley.

"Haven't heard. They're probably still processing everything."

"Of course. It's too soon."

She shivered and crossed her arms, then winced when she moved her shoulder wrong. Her wounds throbbed. She walked to the cabinet and found her bottle of ibuprofen. While a stronger medication would bring more relief, she didn't want to be drugged.

"Why don't you go lie down," Haley said. "I'll keep watch." She hefted a bag of M&Ms. "I'm prepared. Want some?"

Maddy forced a smile. "That's all right. And I'm not sleepy yet." Not a complete lie. She was tired. Exhausted, actually. But not ready to shut her eyes. It galled her to realize she was afraid too.

"I promise to wake you if anything new develops—or if you're dreaming things you'd rather not dream."

Maddy smiled. "You know me pretty well, don't you?"

Haley shrugged. "We're a lot alike."

"Yeah." Maddy sighed. "What do you know about Quinn?"

Surprise lit her friend's face. "That was random. You have anything specific you want to know about? I imagine you know more than just about anyone."

Frustration nipped at her. "That's what I figured."

"So why ask?"

Maddy groaned. "I don't know. He makes me crazy."

"You love him."

"Yes. Maybe." She wouldn't completely deny it, but she didn't have to like admitting she'd probably given her heart to a man who couldn't love her back—or wouldn't. But she wouldn't lie about her own feelings—if she even knew what they were. "At least I think I do."

"Love." Haley scowled and opened the bag of chocolate. She poured several into the palm of her hand and lifted them to her mouth to crunch and swallow. She pointed a finger at Maddy. "Don't mess with men and love."

"Why not?"

"Because they mess with yer mind, me friend."

Maddy narrowed her eyes. "And when you feel passionately about something, your Irish accent comes out in full force. Why does talking about love bring it out?"

Haley's scowl deepened. "We're not talking about me, we're talking about you, remember?"

"I'm willing to change the subject."

"Well, I'm not. Now go get in yer bed and get some rest."

Maddy smiled. Haley would share when she was good and ready and not a minute before. She'd always known there was more to Haley's story than she'd told. Now, she'd let slip there was probably a broken heart somewhere in her past.

The barely there smile slid from her lips. "How did he manage to get in my house?" she asked. "I know my alarm was armed because I had to disarm it when I came home."

"We're not sure. It's a fairly simple system yet good enough to keep most ne'er-do-wells out, but this guy seems to be a bit more sophisticated than your fly-by-night criminal."

"I would agree with that."

A knock on the door startled her and she reached for her weapon. Haley did the same. They took up a stance on either side of her door. Another knock. "Maddy? You in there?"

Maddy lowered her gun and ordered her heart to slow its crazy pounding. She twisted the knob and swung the door open to find Quinn and Katie on the doorstep. "What are you doing here?"

"Looking for you."

"You couldn't call?"

"I did. And I texted," Quinn said through his glower. He looked tired. Worn slap out. "I didn't get an answer."

"I don't have a phone yet."

"I know. That's why I tried Haley."

"Here." Katie handed her an iPhone box.

"Thanks." She opened the box and powered up the phone, then let her gaze bounce between Quinn and Katie.

"We tried your phone, Haley," Katie said as they stepped inside and shut the door. "Why didn't you answer either?"

Haley frowned and pulled her phone from the clip on her belt. She stared at the screen. "I don't have any indication that you called or texted." She tapped the screen. "But I don't have any indication of a signal either."

Quinn pulled out his phone. "Neither do I." He looked at Katie. "You?"

She checked her device. "Nope."

Maddy frowned. "What's going on?"

Quinn looked around. "Something's blocking the signal."

"But what?"

"He planted something," Maddy said softly. Her jaw tightened.

Katie narrowed her eyes. "Okay, I can see why you would immediately jump to that conclusion. We'll go with that for the moment. Assuming it's not some cell tower mishap, then where did he plant it?"

"Tear the place apart and let's find it," Maddy said flatly.

"I'll see how far I can walk from your house to get a signal and I'll check with the company to find out if there's something going on in the area," Katie said. "Give me that phone back. I'll program it while I'm out there and have a signal. You don't need to be without a phone another second. Keep your weapons on hand."

Maddy turned the new phone back over. Katie slipped back out the door and Maddy turned her attention to the closet that had been cracked when she'd first walked into the house the night she was attacked. She opened the door and pushed aside the jackets she had hanging there. She checked corners, the shelf, every square inch. "It's clean," she called out.

She straightened and shut the door. When she turned, she noticed the others doing the same to the rest of her home. Maddy curled her fingers into fists at her side, then let out a slow breath and relaxed, flexed her fingers, and refused to let the anger take over. She had to keep her cool. Look at this like a job. An attempt on her life had been made and now it was her job to protect herself while investigating the incident. With detached professionalism. Like she was any other client.

Right.

She looked around, trying to figure out where someone might have planted a cell signal blocker. Her eyes landed on her mantel and she stared at the row of pictures. Maddy walked over to stand in front of them, momentarily distracted.

"What is it?" Haley asked, coming up beside her.

"I'm not sure." Maddy picked up the third picture from the left and held it. Stared at it. Her unit. Her friends. Her team. All dead except her. "I cheated death," she whispered. She turned to Haley. "I thought he was talking about when that maniac attacked me and slit my throat." She touched the area. A habit she'd almost kicked except in times of extreme stress. She lowered her hand. "But what if he's talking about something else?"

Quinn rested a hand on her shoulder. "Like what?"

"You know why I left the FBI, right?"

"Yes. It was a sting operation turned ambush, right?"

Haley joined her to look down at the picture. Memories swept over Maddy, and she desperately wanted to push them away, but she couldn't. "It was supposed to be low key. A simple warehouse raid to rescue trafficked illegals and arrest those who were the perpetrators." She pressed her fingers against her lips to keep them from trembling. "There were twelve of us. Six from my squad. Six from another squad."

"And you backed out at the last minute," Quinn murmured.

She nodded. "I had food poisoning. I was so sick I could barely lift my head. I knew there was no way I could be on that raid, so I called in." She sighed. "After it was all over, I was in shock, but I went back to work two days later. No one came right out and accused me of being the mole, but it was in everyone's eyes."

"Surely not everyone's," Quinn said.

"Well, okay. There were some who knew me well enough to know I'd never do anything like that, but the others . . ." She set the picture back on the mantel and turned around. "You know the one that hurt the most? My boss. Andrew Williams. He turned his back on me and that almost killed me."

Quinn frowned. "Why's that?"

"I looked up to him. He recruited me. He was my squad supervisor for two years, then he moved on to headquarters. About the time I qualified and became an agent, he was a field supervisor. He made me believe in myself, that I could do the job."

"Let me guess," Katie said. "He didn't stand behind you when you were accused."

"Yeah. I know he was going through a tough time, but that was no excuse to abandon me like he did." Maddy rubbed a palm on her thigh and blinked as though to wipe away the memory.

"What kind of tough time?" Quinn asked.

"His wife was suing for divorce. She'd had enough and was doing everything in her power to make sure he had no contact with her kids."

"Ouch, that's rough," Haley said. "I can see why he'd be a little distracted when it came to the job."

"A little, but it wasn't just that, it was like he believed I was guilty." Maddy ran a hand over her hair and let the memories, the feelings, sweep through her. "Like I would actually do something like that. When I asked him how he could think I would, he said, 'If Chloe can do what she's doing to me, then I have no kind of judgment when it comes to what people are and are not capable of. I don't want to believe it, but when the evidence slaps you in the face, what else is one to do?'"

Quinn grunted. "Harsh."

"Well, not only was he having to deal with his marriage imploding, he was dealing with the investigation into the deaths of eleven agents, questioning his judgment, and all that. He was completely wiped, emotionally, physically, in every way possible." She spread her hands and looked away for a moment, the memories almost too much to bear. "Anyway, after he made it plain that *he* didn't trust me, almost no one wanted to work with me. I made people nervous. They wondered if I was going to have them killed next." Bitterness welled and she had to make an effort to shove it down. She'd moved on and made a good life for herself.

"There was no evidence," Haley said.

"Of course not. Not real evidence anyway. Circumstantial, but nothing that the DA or US Attorney would pursue." Maddy gave a rueful smile and shook her head. "They even checked my story of being in the hospital. Only the fact that I was severely dehydrated and hooked up to an IV saved me from being outright arrested, I'm sure." The memories brought the kind of tension she'd hoped not to feel again. "But the fact that they never could find a motive for anyone else to set up the ambush was the deciding factor in some agents' minds." She gave a short laugh. "Of course, they couldn't come up with a motive for me either. That didn't matter, though."

"So you quit," Quinn said.

"Well, not right away, but yes, eventually." And it still galled her that she'd done it. "My . . . father convinced me it was the right thing to do."

Quinn's brow rose. "Wait a minute, you never told me that."

She shrugged, already regretting admitting it. "That's a story in itself and not relevant to the whole point I'm making."

"Which is," Haley said, "that the attack could be related to this incident in your past."

"Yes."

Quinn stared at her a moment longer, as though wondering what else she hadn't told him. Well, he could wonder. His indignation was misplaced. Like the pot calling the kettle black. He hadn't completely opened up to her either and she was tired of the roller coaster. She kept his gaze without blinking. He finally shook his head. "We'll need to investigate each dead agent's family. See if there's anyone with the desire and ability to pull this off."

"I know each one of those agents' families," Maddy said. "None of them would do anything like this."

"You're too close," Haley said. "You know as well as the rest of us, when people get pushed beyond their limits, they're capable of just about anything."

"But this?" Maddy sighed. She stared at the picture again. "Hilary Barron." She ran a finger over her dead friend's face. "She was a mother with young children—two boys ages ten and fourteen. Her husband was devastated. He lost it for a while."

"We'll check him first."

"He's an accountant over on Academy Street," Maddy said. "His name is Arthur Barron."

"Anyone else who might need to be a priority?"

She sighed. "I don't know. Paul Curtis maybe. He's Darnell's twin brother. He tracked me down at the office about three weeks after the ambush and said if he found out I had anything to do with Darnell's death, he'd come after me and make me suffer."

"That's a pretty direct threat."

"Yes, and I took it seriously, but I also knew he wouldn't find anything—unless someone was deliberately trying to set me up to take the fall—because I had nothing to do with it." She shook her head. "I should be dead so many times over now."

"And yet you're not."

"Just means God's got a reason for keeping ya here," Haley said quietly. "I, for one, am glad."

Maddy shot her a weak smile. "I am too."

"Who else?"

She sighed and studied the picture. "Trey Ballentine. His dad was Special Forces twenty years ago. He would have the ability to carry out something like this. He wouldn't, but he has the ability."

"Along with loyal friends who might help him?"

She shrugged. "I don't know. Like I said, I don't see it, but I suppose it's possible."

Quinn tapped the screen on his phone and gave a growl. "I can't send this. We need to find that blocker." They went on the hunt once again.

And came up empty.

Maddy threw her hands up. "Maybe it's outside."

Haley nodded. "That makes sense. I'll check. You two stay inside in case he's watching with a rifle at his shoulder."

Haley opened the door, and over Haley's shoulder, Maddy saw Katie on the doorstep. "I had to walk quite a ways to get a signal. Bad news: there's nothing's wrong with any cell tower around here," she said. "Good news: I got your phone working using the same number you had."

"Thanks." Maddy took the device and Haley stepped around her. "Katie and I'll check out here for any signal-blocking device. Be back in a minute."

Haley shut the door behind them.

Quinn sat on the sofa and stared at her. Maddy stared back and resisted the urge to squirm. "What?"

"Why did your dad encourage you to quit?"

She sighed. "You can probably figure it out."

"He's law enforcement."

"Yes. He knew that until it was proven that I had nothing to do with those agents' deaths, I would be the bad apple in the bunch. I'd be shunned."

"Why hasn't anything been proven, do you think? Why hasn't the person been caught?"

"I don't know. I've lost sleep thinking about it for sure, but I just can't put my finger on any one person other than the group we were after. The problem is, there was no concrete evidence of who tipped them off. Nothing." She rubbed her cheeks, then tilted her head. "And frankly, there was some circumstantial evidence that suggested I could have been the one to set it up."

He frowned and leaned forward. "Like what?"

"Someone sent pictures of me meeting with the main guy we were after." She shrugged. "We looked friendly, but I was undercover. I was supposed to be friendly. Andrew said he knew this and threw the pictures in the trash. Someone dug them out and posted them in the break room."

He spread his hands. "Why?"

"I don't know. Not for sure."

"And you're not trying to figure it out?"

She shook her head. "I did for a while, but for now . . ."

He frowned. "You said you were up for a promotion at the time."

"I was."

"So who benefited by making you look bad?"

She laughed, but there wasn't any humor in it. "Don't you think I've gone through all of that? Asked myself that question?"

"And?"

Tension tightened her shoulders even while frustration ate at her. She wished she'd nipped this conversation in the bud a few sentences back. "Like I said, I don't know for sure."

"But you have a theory."

"Yeah," she bit out. "I have a theory."

"So what is it? Why are you making me drag this out of you?"

The door opened and Katie stepped inside. She took one look at them and stopped. "Should we come back later?"

"No," Maddy said, "we were just discussing something."

"A theory," Quinn said.

"Oo-kay."

Haley stepped around Katie and held out her gloved hand. A small dark box sat in her palm. "Found it."

"Where?"

"Strapped to the trunk of a tree. It took some searching, but I finally caught a glimpse of it." She paused. "You know, I bet this guy is pretty tall. I'm five nine and had to stretch to grab it."

"He was tall," Quinn said. "But I was looking at him from a crouch in the jungle, so . . ." He shrugged.

Maddy pressed a hand to her head. "My phone worked the night he grabbed us," she said. "You texted me and I got the message."

"So when did he plant the device?" Quinn said.

Maddy shrugged. "It had to be recent."

Haley tapped her phone. "I'll see if I can track the serial number."

"So, he left the island," Quinn said. "He wouldn't have had to file a flight plan or anything. There are plenty of private airstrips around here that he could have used. I would say there's no sense wasting time even trying to track him from that angle, but if we send out a message to those airstrips, maybe we'll get lucky. Let's ask Bree to canvass the airpark neighborhoods and see if anyone landed within the time frame we have. And if there are any cameras that recorded said landings."

"That's a long shot, a needle in the haystack," Maddy said. "I can't even describe the plane."

"Regardless," Quinn said, "he had plenty of time to get here and plant that before we arrived back in town. I'm just not sure the reason behind it." He caught her eye. "Unless he's planning to strike here once again."

"I wouldn't put it past him, but he has to know that we'll take precautions, have people watching our backs." She shook her head. "He's like a terrorist. He wants to instill fear and . . . be a bully. Or get revenge for a perceived wrong." Maddy shut her eyes against the forming headache. "I don't know. I'm exhausted and I can't think right now."

Quinn nodded. "I'm there with you." He looked up at Katie and Haley. "If you'll bring Bree in on this and update her, she'll get everything going on our end."

Katie pulled her phone out. "I'll call her. Why don't you two get some rest? We can pick this back up once you're clear-headed again."

Maddy rested a hand on Quinn's forearm. "Take the guest bedroom. It'll be easier on Katie and Haley if we stay together. They can take turns sleeping and guarding."

"Are you sure?" Quinn asked. "I don't want to invade your space."

She smiled. "I'm sure." She pointed down the hall. "Last door on the right. The bathroom is an en suite. It's clean and ready for use, including a razor, toothbrush, and paste. There are some men's sweatpants and T-shirts in the closet." At his raised brow, she snorted. "One of my brothers is a frequent visitor. You're about the same size. Have at it."

Still, he hesitated. "I need to make arrangements for the dogs." He pulled his phone out. "Let me see if I can get my neighbor to run by and let them out." Within minutes, he was nodding. "JD's going to take care of them today and tomorrow. After that, if I need to board them, I will."

Haley looked at Katie. "I'll take first watch."

"And I'll call Bree." She bounced her gaze between Maddy and Quinn. "You two get some rest, and by the time you're up, maybe we'll have some news."

Maddy nodded. "Thanks, guys. See you in a few hours." She pointed toward the bedroom at the end of the hall. "Go," she said to Quinn.

He held up his hands in surrender. "I'm going, I'm going."

And he did. He disappeared into the room and shut the door. Maddy stood for a moment, trying to think, and finally decided it wasn't worth the effort. "See you in a few." She walked to her bedroom and collapsed on the bed. She sighed. "Now what, God?"

[13]

Quinn opened his eyes and stared at Maddy's ceiling while his nose appreciated the scent of strong coffee wafting his way.

He showered and dressed in the clothes he'd had on the day before, then walked into the kitchen to find Maddy at the stove. When she heard his footsteps, she turned. Faint circles shadowed her eyes.

"Did you sleep at all?" he asked.

She tried to smile at him, but he saw the weariness behind it. He moved closer and caught a whiff of lavender. He didn't know if it was from her soap or her fabric softener. He did know he liked it.

"A bit," she said. "How about you?"

"Best in a while." He narrowed his eyes. "Nightmares?"

"Hmm. Maybe one about being chased by a madman through a jungle," she muttered and turned back to flip the bacon.

He rested his hands on her shoulders. "I wish you'd come and woken me when you had the nightmare."

Her head drooped and he massaged her neck and shoulders.

134

Then she straightened and scooped the bacon to drain on the paper-towel-covered plate next to the stove. "It wouldn't have mattered, Quinn. No sense in both of us losing sleep." She tilted her head. "You didn't have any nightmares. Why?"

"Not this time. I was too tired to dream, I think."

She nodded and picked up the platter of eggs and bacon and set it on the table. "Breakfast is served. Help yourself, I nibbled while I cooked."

He snagged a slice of the bacon. "Where are Haley and Katie?"

"Keeping an eye on the place."

Quinn served himself plenty of eggs, bacon, and toast, then took a seat at the table.

Maddy's cell phone rang and she snatched it from the counter. "Hello?"

At her gasp, he looked up.

The longer she listened, the paler she got. "Okay, um . . . which hospital?" Quinn straightened. She nodded. "Okay, okay, Mom, I can be on the way in about ten minutes." She hung up. "Eat fast."

"What happened?"

"My sister Gina was just taken to Baptist Hospital. She was riding her bike and a car hit her, then sped off. I have to go to the hospital. She's not just my sister, she's my best friend."

Quinn raked a hand through his hair. "I know."

The door opened and Haley stepped inside. "Everything is all clear."

Quinn quickly explained the situation while he wolfed down the rest of his breakfast. Haley snagged some and then texted Katie. Maddy fixed Katie a plate, then disappeared back into her bedroom.

By the time she reemerged ten minutes later, the food was

gone and he and Haley were waiting by the door. Haley opened it. "Katie's checking the car."

Quinn's jaw tightened. Checking for explosives. They waited another few minutes.

"Clear!" Katie's call triggered their exodus from the house. Moving as one unit, they loaded into the SUV with Katie behind the wheel. Haley took the passenger front seat after she made sure Maddy and Quinn were in. Quinn buckled up and Maddy did the same. Worry stamped clearly on her face, Maddy stared out the window, her eyes bouncing between the mirrors she could see.

Quinn, too, watched. He didn't see anyone, but that didn't mean no one was there. It was a tense ride to the hospital, and he, for one, was pleasantly surprised when they pulled to the Emergency Department door without incident. Katie exited and held the back door while Quinn stepped out of the vehicle. Maddy slid across the seat to follow him.

"Do you know which room she's in?"

"No." She headed for the person behind the desk. "Gina McKay, she was brought in a little while ago."

"Maddy?"

Maddy spun and Quinn looked to his left to see Maddy's mother, Faith McKay, coming toward her. The woman's eyes were red-rimmed and her cheeks blotchy. She was in her early sixties, trim and healthy. But her eyes, the same sapphire blue as Maddy's, revealed her grief—and fury.

Maddy hurried to her mother and grasped her hands. "Is Gina going to be okay?"

"The doctor thinks she will be. She has a broken femur and a head injury and is still in surgery. Your father was wearing a hole in the tile so I convinced him to come down and get some coffee."

Maddy's muscles tightened even more right before his eyes. Her gaze darted. "Where is he?"

"In the restroom. I was just waiting when I saw you come in." Faith swiped a tear that escaped.

Maddy pulled her mother close and hugged her. "Have they caught the guy yet?"

"No. There were plenty of witnesses, though, so hopefully one of them will have something helpful to share." She motioned to Maddy's arm in the sling. "What happened to you?"

"An accident. I dislocated my shoulder, but it'll be fine in a couple of weeks." Quinn watched Katie subtly stay in the background. He didn't think Maddy's mother had noticed her yet.

"Goodness." Faith patted Maddy's nonwounded shoulder, then gave Quinn a shaky smile. "Hi, Quinn."

He hugged her. He'd met Maddy's parents on several occasions and liked them, although he thought Maddy's father, Harold, was a bit of a hardhead. "Hi. I'm so sorry."

"I am too. We'll catch the guy." Faith's fingers fisted at her side. "If it was an accident, that's tragic enough, but to run, that's not only criminal, it's cowardly."

"*If?*" Maddy asked. "You think there's a possibility it could have been deliberate?"

Faith dabbed at her eyes again. "I don't want to think so, but someone said she was riding her bike on the sidewalk and that the car waited until she was off the sidewalk and in front of an alley. The witness said the car sped up and went right for her. Another said he'd seen the car pass by twice before swerving to hit her."

"That's crazy! Why? Who?"

The door to the café opened and Maddy's sister Lindsey stepped out with four cups of coffee in a drink holder. She jerked to a stop when she saw Maddy, and if the cups hadn't had lids, the coffee would have been everywhere. Then she lifted her chin and approached the small group. Maddy looked up to see her and froze. Then smiled, a forced baring of her teeth that made Quinn raise a brow. He wondered what the story was there.

Maddy nodded. "Hi, Linds."

"Mads."

Then Maddy focused her attention back on her mother and Lindsey stood to the side, awkwardly holding the drinks.

Faith held clasped hands to her chest as though to pray. "Gina's a lawyer," she was saying. "She's working a pretty high-profile case right now against that Russian mafia head. We're thinking someone from that family went after her."

"Then she needs round-the-clock care," Maddy said. "Protection."

"I'll arrange this one for you, if you like," Quinn said.

Maddy's mother bit her lip. "I have people I could call, but yes, if you'll take care of it, I'll let you do it. Just until we find out for sure what's going on."

Maddy avoided her mother's eyes. Katie stepped forward. "Hi, Mrs. McKay."

"Katie? Goodness, child, I didn't see you standing there." The two women hugged.

Katie stepped back. "All of our resources are tapped at the moment." She shot a tight smile at Quinn. "Whatever you can do would be appreciated.

Quinn pulled his phone from his clip just as a man in his early sixties came out of the men's restroom. Tall, still in good physical shape, he ran a hand through his head of gray hair and stopped when he saw Maddy and her mother. "What's she doing here?"

"I called her, Harold. Be nice."

"Hi, Dad," Maddy said.

Quinn heard the underlying tension in the two words, the hope that Maddy's father would lower his walls and just love her. Quinn wanted to wrap an arm around her shoulders, protect her from the man who'd helped bring her into this world.

Her father sighed. "Hi." And that was it. No hug, no asking how she was, no mention of her arm that was in the sling. Maddy's parents knew nothing of what had happened to them on the island and that was the way she planned to keep it, Quinn knew. Harold nodded to Quinn with a bit more warmth and reached out to shake his hand. "Quinn, good to see you."

Quinn wouldn't lie and say the same. His anger over the man's treatment of Maddy was very much on the surface at the moment. He did shake hands, though. For Maddy's sake. "Sorry it has to be under these circumstances." Harold's jaw tensed and Quinn tightened his fingers around his phone to squelch the urge to punch the man for his lack of faith in his daughter. "I'll get protection lined up for Gina."

"Thank you, Quinn," Faith said.

With both of Maddy's parents retired from law enforcement, he knew there wouldn't be any shortage of volunteers to protect one of their children.

He stepped to the side and saw the chapel sign over the door. He motioned to Maddy that he was going in and she nodded. With the phone pressed to his ear, he waited for Bree to pick up.

"Standish."

"Hey, I need you to round up about four or five officers who don't mind volunteering or earning a little extra money."

"What's up?"

He told her and she promised to take care of it.

When he hung up, he stood still and noticed the detail of the small, quiet room. The lights were low and soft music filled the area. He recognized the song as "Amazing Grace." The door opened and closed behind him and he took note of the man who entered and slipped into the back pew. There was another man kneeling in front of the large cross at the altar. The cross glowed, thanks to the light placed strategically in front of it. It could have been a gaudy thing, but surprisingly it wasn't. Instead, it just seemed peaceful. Quinn pressed his fingers against his tired eyes. When was the last time he'd felt peace? He couldn't remember, but knew his restless soul craved it.

He drew in a deep breath and thought about approaching the God he'd given up on long ago. There was so much pain and suffering in the world. It wasn't right. It didn't seem to him that a just God, a loving God, would even allow it. At least not a God who was actually in control of things.

He shook his head. He wasn't here to get all spiritual. He started to turn toward the door. A sharp pain in his lower back made him gasp. "Just stay right there, Detective."

Quinn froze. He recognized the gravelly voice. "You."

"Oh yes, me. I'm very happy you decided to come along for the ride. I rather figured you would since you stayed with Maddy last night."

"You ran down Maddy's sister."

"Well, I really needed you two to get away from those bodyguard friends of yours. It's quite vexing to have them around all the time. And, like I told you, this little adventure needed a personal touch for you and Maddy."

Quinn's heart rate kicked into high gear. "Why are you doing this?"

"You're a smart guy, Detective, you'll figure it out eventually. If you live long enough."

"Unlike you, I don't really care for games. Why don't you just tell me?"

"Where's the fun in that? Now sit."

Quinn's mind raced. He rolled his fingers into fists. His gun was in his shoulder holster, but he wasn't sure he could get it before the guy plunged the knife into his back.

"Detective, I said sit."

Quinn slowly sank onto the pew. The sharp point moved to the back of his neck and he heard the man settle in the pew behind him. "Now that I have your attention, I must say I'm most impressed that you managed to survive the island. No one has ever done that."

"So you said. We found the mass grave."

"Yes."

"Were there more than eight victims or do we have them all?"

There was a slight hesitation before the man chuckled. "I don't suppose there's any harm in telling you that fact. You found them all."

"And Maddy and I were supposed to be numbers nine and ten."

"Hmm. Supposed to be. And will be at some point. But you are providing a most interesting and thrilling chase."

"Glad to oblige," Quinn said through gritted teeth.

"So now we're on to the next phase of the game."

"Which is? Oh right, making it personal."

The door opened and two ladies entered. Quinn stiffened.

"No, no, Detective. Don't do anything to put them in jeopardy. Let's just sit here and talk until they leave."

"What if someone else comes in?"

"We might be sitting here a long time."

"And if I get up and walk out?"

"Then an innocent one will die."

Quinn drew in a breath through his nose and let it out of his mouth while he scrambled for an idea of how to catch this guy. "You enjoy killing innocents, don't you?"

"And you enjoy letting the guilty go free."

"What are you talking about?"

"You have a beautiful family."

Everything within Quinn went still. "What do you know about my family?" The man was talking in circles. Probably on purpose, to keep Quinn off guard. He'd roll with it while he decided on the best course of action.

"More than you would like, I'm sure. I know that pretty little Alyssa goes to Peabody Elementary. And her brother, JJ, goes to the preschool just up the road. I know their mother, your sister, Stacy, killed herself a little over three years ago, when JJ was just an infant. What was the story? The gun went off accidentally when she and you were planning to go on a hunting trip?"

"How do you know those details? Who have you been talking to?" Chills skittered up and down his spine. Dread filled him. This killer knew about his niece and nephew, their names and where they went to school. Most especially, he knew about his sister. And since, by Quinn's father's orders, they hadn't told anyone the true story of Stacy's death, the fact that this man knew she had killed herself just took this attack to a whole new personal level.

"I've been talking to a lot of people. And while you may have told one story to your family and friends, the police know the truth. As does the autopsy report."

How had he gotten his hands on that? Quinn's muscles trembled from the tension. "What. Do. You. Want."

"I want justice," he said. "I want you to have your judgment day. I want you to suffer the way I've suffered." The knife pressed harder. "You're in an appropriate place to say your prayers. Pray hard, Quinn. Alyssa and her little friends need your prayers."

"What have you done?"

"I've just responded to my calling. And I've heightened the stakes of the game. Let's see if you can get to the next level on this one."

Maddy pushed open the door to the chapel and stepped inside. A sense of peace swept over her. Her sister was still in surgery, but she was alive and expected to recover in time. She'd seen Quinn's pensive look, the conflicted emotion on his face as he slipped into the chapel, and decided to leave him alone for some private time.

But when he continued to stay, she couldn't resist checking on him. She could see two men just ahead of her, one behind the other. Two ladies to her right at the front knelt in prayer.

"Quinn?" she whispered. "Are you in here?"

Her voice was a little louder than she'd intended and it seemed to echo through the small chapel. The two women looked around with frowns. And then the men in front of her moved. She heard a curse.

"Maddy, run! He's here!"

She couldn't see Quinn, but the man who'd been sitting behind him fled toward the altar. For a moment her blood froze even as her feet reacted. She raced toward the fleeing figure and bolted past Quinn, who'd rolled under the pew and now shot to his feet.

"Are you all right?" she asked.

"Yes, but that's him."

Maddy whipped past the altar and pushed aside the black curtain only to face a steel door. She pressed the handle and heard Quinn scrambling after her. He flung the curtain away as Maddy pushed the door open. They rushed into the hallway to find it teeming with people, patients and medical staff alike.

Quinn spun to the right, then left. Maddy did the same. The hallway held door after door.

"Too many choices," she muttered. "He couldn't have gone far this fast." She tried one and found it locked. Then another. "All locked."

"There are too many people. He had on a white lab coat. He's blended right in."

"We need the security cams." She hurried toward the nearest staff person.

Quinn followed, dialing his phone. "He won't have shown his face."

"I know, but we've got to try . . . Ma'am, where's the security office?"

The nurse looked up. "It's on the ground floor, A-wing all the way to the end of the hall." She frowned. "Is everything all right?"

"It will be," Maddy said. She bit her lip and looked back over her shoulder toward the door to the surgical suite where her sister lay. "Let's go."

Quinn looked up from his phone. "What about your sister?"

"She's still in surgery. Mom's going to text me when she's out."

Together, they headed down the hall in the direction the nurse had indicated. Maddy heard Quinn barking an explanation of what was going on. "We'll need to question everyone who worked on that floor." He caught her eyes as he continued to speak into his phone. "The two ladies in the chapel. We need to get them. They would have seen the whole thing. The man who attacked us, he came in behind me and sat in the back pew. I can describe what I saw of him and I should be able to recognize him in a lineup. Thanks, Bree." He hung up, and knocked on the door.

A man in his early forties opened it. "Help you?"

Quinn flashed his badge. "I'm Detective Quinn Holcombe. I need to see security footage of the chapel and the area around it."

"What's this about?"

"There's a killer in your hospital and I'm trying to track him down."

The man paled. "Right this way." He settled in the nearest chair with Quinn and Maddy standing behind him. "I need to put our staff on alert. Who are we looking for?"

"Let's see if we can get a picture and you can send it out to them. But for now, we're looking for a guy who's bald, tall, and white. Not very helpful, I know, but if you could have security watch the exits, I'm going to have extra officers sent over to help look as well. He'll probably be gone by that point, but we have to try."

The officer quickly made the requests for added security while Quinn called Bree. Then the officer turned to his computer and pulled up the footage at the time Quinn specified, then zoomed in on the back door of the chapel. While they watched, the officer looked up at them. "I'm John."

"I'm Maddy." Maddy massaged her sore shoulder and watched the chapel door open. A man in a white medical jacket exited. He tugged his collar, patted his hairless head, swiped a key card on one of the doors Maddy had tried to open, stepped inside, and shut the door. Maddy appeared next, then Quinn. They'd missed him by mere seconds.

They disappeared off camera, the door opened, and the man walked in the direction of the exit. The officer clicked keys, changing cameras to keep track of the killer.

"He's gone," Quinn said. "But check whose key card he used."

John again went back to the keyboard. He looked up. "The

card belongs to Wilson Brown, he's part of our maintenance crew."

"And where is Mr. Brown now?"

John consulted his computer again. "He's working today, but we'll have to track him down. I've got his cell number right here."

Quinn nodded. "We'll call him in a minute. I need a better angle of our guy's face."

"Let me see what I can do." More key tapping by John. "This is him going into the chapel, but he kept his head averted."

"Of course he did," Maddy muttered.

John managed to get a partial side view and Quinn pursed his lips. "It's not good enough," Quinn said, "but we'll run it through the facial recognition software. Maybe we'll get lucky. Send a copy of the video to my email address." He gave it and John sent it while they stood there.

Maddy touched his shoulder. "Thanks, John."

"Of course." He grabbed the handset from the base of the phone. "Let me see if I can get Mr. Brown." Within seconds, he looked up. "Yes, Mr. Brown, this is security. Do you have your badge with you? Uh huh. All right. We'll have to issue you another one. Please stop by as soon as possible." He hung up. "He said he hasn't seen it since he stopped at the cafeteria for breakfast. He set it on his tray and noticed it missing just after he left. He thought he might have thrown it away. The kitchen staff looked, but didn't find it. Mr. Brown didn't want to report it missing until later. Another maintenance worker has been helping him out as far as getting him access into different areas." He rubbed his eyes. "I've deactivated the card so whoever has it won't be able to use it further. Anything else I can do?"

"Yeah," Maddy said. "Pray."

Quinn's eyes flashed. "Pray," he whispered, grabbed his phone, and started punching keys.

Maddy frowned. "What is it?"

"Something he said about my niece, Alyssa."

"What?"

He pressed the phone to his ear. "That she and her friends needed prayers."

She gasped. "He's going to do something at her school?"

"I don't know." He paced two steps, then back. "Or he's already done something." He paused, listened. Then looked her in the eye. "The phones at the school are down."

Maddy's phone buzzed. She glanced at the screen. "And my sister's out of surgery."

"I've got to get to the school."

"Call the cops and tell them to get over there," she said. "I'm coming with you."

"What about Gina?" he asked as they headed toward the exit.

"She's not going to wake up for a while. And she's probably safer without me in the vicinity. Katie has the keys to the SUV."

"Let's go."

[14]

Quinn bolted from the vehicle as soon as Katie pulled to a stop in front of the elementary school. Officers were already on the scene. Quinn flashed his badge and stopped one of the officers. "Who's the lead?"

"Lieutenant Grayson." He pointed to a large African American man standing beside a command vehicle. At least six feet three inches tall with a bald head and a "get it done" expression. "That's him."

"Thanks." Quinn knew Ben. He liked the man and had a high level of respect for him and his work ethic. Quinn hurried over with the ladies on his heels. "Ben."

Ben turned, his agitated expression clearing when he spotted Quinn. "Holcombe. Heard you were off the clock for a few days."

"I'm back on. There was a specific threat against my niece and her friends." He pointed to the front door. "And that's where they are. Why aren't you evacuating?"

Ben frowned. "They should be coming out at any moment. I had to go to the door and actually go inside to request the principal's ear. The phones are down." He waved his cell phone. "And so is this. Do you know what we're dealing with here?"

"No. But bring in the bomb squad and the dogs. And radios. As you've noticed, the cell signal's been blocked." As he spoke, the doors opened and children and teachers streamed from the building in a calm and orderly fashion. "They need to move faster."

"The principal didn't want to tell them it was the real deal," Ben said. "He wanted to handle it like a drill."

Quinn groaned. "That may just get them all killed. They need to move faster and farther away," he insisted.

"Yeah, I'll agree with you on that. What makes you think it's a bomb?"

"Intuition."

"So you don't have an actual 'I'm going to blow up the building' statement."

Quinn heaved a sigh of impatience tinged with fear and ran a hand over his hair. "No, not that. But I don't need that. I'm learning this guy and I *know* there's a bomb in there."

"When they see all of us out here, they're going to realize it's something more than just a drill anyway," Maddy said.

She was right. No sooner had the words left her lips than he saw teachers and students pointing. Quinn knew Alyssa's teacher by sight and looked for her. Unbeknownst to his parents, he'd run a background check on Alyssa's and JJ's teachers when they started school. And he'd done it every year since. One couldn't be too careful when it came to protecting the children.

When he couldn't spot the woman, he frowned. But there were students evacuating all around the property, not just the area he could see. He moved closer, letting his gaze roam from student to student.

Quinn's phone buzzed. He glanced at the screen and froze.

You worked fast. But not fast enough. Have you found Alyssa yet? I hope she enjoys fireworks.

"Ben!"

The lieutenant spun at his yell, a harsh frown on his face. Quinn held up his phone. "It's a bomb. Get them out of there!"

"How do you know?" Ben yelled back.

"He texted me."

"There's no signal. How could he text you?"

Quinn stared at his phone, then rushed over to shove it in Ben's face.

"I don't know. I just know he did. Now get those people away from that building. I'm going to find my niece." He raced toward the school with Maddy on his heels. Ben's harsh demand that he get himself back there bounced off his brain. All he could think about was getting to Alyssa and making sure every child was out of the building. He didn't know how much time he had, he couldn't think about that. "Everyone move! Get away from the building. This is *not* a drill!"

The teachers went from looking bored to shocked to frantic as his words registered. "Go, kids. Follow Mr. Dunbar's class. Go across the street and stay together," he heard one order. Similar commands went out. The children started moving, running.

He snagged the arm of the nearest teacher. "Where are the fourth-grade classes? Where would they go for safety during a bomb threat?" There were multiple classes of the same grade, and they were generally all in the same vicinity of the building.

She blanched at his question but pointed. "Around the back of the building. They would head to the little convenience store that's through the small section of woods. There's a path."

"Thanks."

She nodded and spun to race after her quick-moving class.

An explosion rocked the ground beneath him and he went to his knees. Screams filled the air and Quinn watched the smoke and debris billow upward from the back of the building.

Maddy had followed at a short distance. Quinn was completely focused on finding his niece and she didn't blame him. But the explosion sent her to the ground. She landed on her wounded arm and a cry of pain escaped her. Then she scrambled to her feet to find Quinn doing the same.

He reached for her. "Are you all right?"

"Yes. Are you?"

He shook his head. "Ears are ringing. I've got to find Alyssa." His eyes betrayed his fear.

She grabbed his hand. "Trust that the teachers got her out, Quinn. There could be more explosions coming."

"It's not that. I need to make sure she's here and not with that madman. If I wait until everything calms down and he's got her, the trail is just that much colder. What if he snatched her, knowing I'd come looking for her?"

Comprehension dawned. "Of course. But—"

"What would you do if it was one of your nieces?"

She grimaced, then nodded. "All right, let's go."

"No way. Not you."

"I'm not letting you go alone. So do you want to stand here and argue or go find your niece before another bomb goes off?"

She thought she heard him growl, then he spun on his heel and headed for the back of the building. Maddy went after him. Now that there was a confirmed explosive, she knew every precaution would be taken to make sure no lives were lost in the rescue/recovery effort. Her heart clenched. Had everyone made it out? She stayed right with Quinn, trying not to imagine if some children had still been in that part of the building. "Please, God," she whispered. "Don't let anyone die."

He veered off for the woods in the direction the other teacher had indicated. They easily found the trail and Quinn hurried down it. Within seconds, they were in the parking lot of the convenience store.

Students were huddled together, pale and shaken, scared. Some were crying and holding one another. Others simply stared in the direction of the school. Maddy found her heart breaking for their terror and her anger boiled. She so wanted to catch the monster responsible for all of this. News crews pulled to the curb as she scanned the faces for a little familiar one.

"How did they get here so fast?" he muttered.

Maddy pursed her lips. "There's no way someone called." She looked at her phone. "I still don't have a signal even this far away."

"Alyssa?" Quinn spun in a circle. "I don't see her."

He looked at the nearest child. "Where's Alyssa Green?"

The little girl's eyes went wide and she backed up a step. "I don't know."

Maddy pushed Quinn out of the way. "You're scaring her."

"Sorry." He stepped back, then dropped to his knees in front of the child and showed her his badge. "I didn't mean to scare you, honey. I'm looking for my niece. Do you know Alyssa Green?"

"Yes."

"Did she come out of the building with you?"

"No. She wasn't in the class when we came out."

Quinn's eyes shut and Maddy saw a ripple pass through him. She leaned over. "Where is she, sweetheart?"

"Who are you? Why are you talking to her?"

Maddy turned to find a woman in her early thirties hovering behind them. Dark hair framed her face, making her already pale complexion look positively ghostly. "I'm the substitute teacher." She wrung her hands. "You shouldn't be talking to the children."

Quinn showed his badge again. "I need to know where Alyssa Green is."

The woman raised a hand to her mouth and twisted her head in all directions. "I . . . I don't know. I just . . . this is my first day subbing and I'm just following the rules. I don't know the children yet."

"Who would know her?"

"Her." Maddy followed the woman's pointing finger. "She's one of the other fourth-grade teachers."

Quinn moved to the woman and she turned. He flashed his badge. "I'm looking for Alyssa Green. Is she here?"

"I saw her this morning just before school started. She should be with her class."

"She's not here," Quinn whispered.

"Oh wait," the teacher said. "She takes speech, right?"

He paused. "Yes. She's working on a lisp. Why?"

"It's possible she was with the speech teacher when we had to evacuate. I think she has it at the same time as one of my students."

"How do I find out for sure?"

She raised a hand to her head as though trying to force her brain to work. "The speech teacher, Mrs. Bolin. She's here, but I have no idea where." She glanced at the row of too-quiet children. "Ginger, the little girl in the blue shirt, she's the one who has speech with Alyssa."

Quinn's gaze followed her pointing finger. "And Ginger is here, but Alyssa is not."

Maddy could feel his rising fear for his niece. She had to admit she was starting to feel a bit panicked herself.

A woman raced past her, followed by a man in a suit. "Krissy!"

"Patrick!"

"Elly!"

So not only had the news crews arrived, but so had parents. They streamed as one to the children, terror written on their faces.

"You can't just take her, I need to see ID, please," one teacher hollered. Children rushed to their parents, grabbing them around their waists. But still no sign of Alyssa.

"He's got her," Quinn said, his voice low and hoarse.

"You don't know that," Maddy said. "Ask Ginger where she is and we'll find her."

Quinn turned in a circle. "In this chaos?" He lifted his phone. "I'm going to text Katie and Haley Alyssa's picture and tell them to search for her," he told Maddy.

"That would be a great idea if there was a signal."

He froze for a second, then put his phone away. His thoughtful look captured her attention.

"What is it?" she asked.

"He texted me."

"What?"

"There wasn't a signal, but I got his text."

She bit her lip. "He can control it. He can turn it off and on at will."

"Right, and it's off at this moment, so that means we search some more," he said.

"Quinn!"

He spun and blanched. "Mom?"

Quinn's mother pushed around the nearest officer and raced toward him, sick fear twisting her normally composed and still young-looking features. "Where's Alyssa?"

"I don't know, Mom. What are you doing here?"

"What do you mean? I came to get Alyssa, of course." She pressed her fingers to her eyes. "We need to find her."

He gripped her bicep. "How did you hear about this?"

"I got a text that said there was a bomb at the school and that Alyssa was in danger. Where is she?"

"I don't know, I'm working on it. Stay put while I see what I can find out."

He walked over to the dark-eyed nine-year-old and, not wanting to make the same mistake he'd made with her classmate, squatted in front of her. "Hi, honey."

"Hi."

He showed her his badge. "I'm a policeman and everything's going to be all right."

"Are you sure?"

"Pretty sure. I'm looking for my niece, though. Alyssa."

Ginger's eyes widened and she nodded. "We have speech together."

Quinn heard her say the word as "togever." "I know. Can you tell me where she is? Was she with you in class today?"

"Yes, she was there. We played a game."

"So, where is she now?"

She shrugged her small shoulder. "I don't know. I left before she did. Mrs. Bolin wanted to talk to her a little extra."

Quinn dropped his head and thought. "Okay, if you look out Mrs. Bolin's window, what do you see?"

"The playground."

"Great. Thanks, Ginger."

Her sweet brown eyes searched his. "Is Alyssa okay?"

"Yes, she's fine." *She'd better be. Please, let her be fine.* He wasn't sure if God would still hear his prayers, not after the things he'd hurled at the Almighty after his sister's death. But if God was so inclined to forgive and forget, Quinn had hopes that he'd hear his prayer and spare a little girl's life.

Maddy pointed. "The playground is that way. Let's head over there."

He raced back toward the building with Maddy right behind him. Smoke choked him and debris lay in his path. But no more explosions had gone off. The bomb squad would have the robots in the building. Then the guys in the suits with the bomb-sniffing dogs would take over to clear the building.

At the playground, he stopped and looked around, saw several groups of children hovering at a safe distance from the building. He hurried toward them, his eyes roving, touching on each little face. A few had some scrapes and scratches, but they were alive.

Finally, he came to the one he was looking for. "Alyssa!"

Her gaze snapped to his and she gave him a brilliant smile. "Uncle Quinn!" She ran toward him, ignoring the protest of the nearby teacher. She launched herself into his arms and he hugged her, breathing in her sweet vanilla scent. She leaned back. "What are you doing here?"

"I came to make sure you were okay. Why weren't you with your class?"

"I was in the hall on the way back to my room when the alarm went off. Mrs. Fraley told me to come with her. She's the kindergarten teacher."

Quinn's lungs finally felt free to operate at full capacity again. "Grandma's here looking for you too."

The woman who must be Mrs. Fraley approached. "Who are you?"

"I'm her uncle."

She eyed him suspiciously. Her fear and shock at the happenings of the day were stamped on her pretty features. "All right."

Alyssa gripped his hand. "Grandma's worried about me, huh?"

"Yes, she is."

"So text her and tell her I'm fine."

Quinn looked at his phone. Still no signal. "My phone's not working right now. I want you to come with me, though, okay?"

"You have to have permission to take me." She pointed to Mrs. Fraley, who frowned at him.

"I'm on the list to pick her up," he told the teacher, "so it should be all right."

"Could I see your ID?"

"Sure." He pulled out his wallet and showed her his detective badge, then his driver's license.

Mrs. Fraley looked at Alyssa, then back at Quinn. "I'm sure it's fine, but I just don't have access to the list with the names on it."

"I know."

She nodded. "The parents and children I know, I don't mind sending them, but I don't know you."

"I understand that." He appreciated her caution. More than she knew.

"Is there anyone here who can vouch for you?" she asked.

"I can vouch for him, Mrs. Fraley," Alyssa said. "He's my favorite uncle."

Mrs. Fraley tapped her iPad. "And this thing is worthless. I can't bring anything up. I guess the explosion knocked out the Wi-Fi."

"It's fine, Mrs. Fraley, Alyssa can go with him."

Quinn turned to find Maddy standing next to Ed Harmon, principal of the school. The man was in his late forties, with dark hair and a harried expression. Quinn's gaze met Maddy's.

She shrugged. "I spotted him checking on everyone, explained the situation with Alyssa, and hustled him over here."

Mrs. Fraley nodded. "Thank you. I just can't be responsible for letting a child go with someone I shouldn't."

"You did the right thing," Quinn said. "Good job." He swung his niece into his arms. "Now, let's get out of here so everyone else can do their jobs."

[15]

The Chosen One sat at the desk in his South Carolina rental home and watched the seven television monitors he'd had mounted on the wall across the room. He ignored the two computers in front of him and kept his eyes trained on the action playing out on the screens. He couldn't help the surge of satisfaction at seeing his handiwork on the local news channel. He figured it would be picked up nationally as well, but for now, the local would do. He hadn't heard if there'd been any casualties due to his bomb, but then again, he didn't really care. He'd thought he'd given them enough time to get out, but if Quinn hadn't acted fast enough and a few children had to die to fulfill his destiny, then so be it.

He flipped the news off and picked up the remote to the video game. The game was almost ready to be released. It would be the best one yet. And it was by far his favorite. Ashley had started the design and now that she was dead, he would finish it.

He flipped another switch and the monitor to his far left changed from the news to a black screen. The Chosen One pressed play and the video footage began. With detached interest, he watched the scenes play out in front of him.

Then began to type the code on the keyboard.

:::

Tuesday morning, Maddy paced the conference room of the Elite Guardians headquarters. Her leg and shoulder twinged with each step, reminding her of the seriousness of her mission now. Not that she'd forgotten and needed the reminder.

Quinn had stayed with his family last night and was now on his way over. Katie had read him the riot act about putting his life in danger at the school, but Maddy knew that underneath all the right words, the woman would have done the same thing, had it been one of her nieces. So Katie had stayed with him, insisting on being the extra set of eyes he needed.

Quinn stepped inside the office and Maddy motioned him over to the coffee machine. Katie had dropped him at the door and would soon be here as well. Quinn stepped up beside her and she poured him a cup of coffee, added two creams and a heaping spoonful of sugar. He took it from her with a sigh. "Thanks."

"How did it go last night?"

"It was all right. Mom and Dad were full of questions—and accusations."

She winced. "Accusations? I'm sorry."

He shrugged. "Yeah. Having Alyssa in danger really shook them. It brought up a lot of ugly stuff from the past with my sister. Not that the two are related, but still, the ugliness was there."

"Want to share?"

"They've never forgiven me for my sister's death." His voice was low to keep the others in the room from hearing it.

"Why would they blame you for that? I thought she died from an accidental gunshot wound when she was hunting."

"No, she didn't. I just let Dad convince me to let people believe that."

"Oh . . . I see."

"She was sick, Maddy. Mentally sick, not physically. And when I say mentally, I don't mean that in a derogatory way, I mean she was clinically depressed. And had been since she was a teenager. Her best friend was killed in a car wreck, and Stacy—she just never seemed to deal with it, to get past it." He stared at the wall a moment.

Maddy saw Katie enter and start to walk toward her and the coffee machine. She held up a finger asking her to wait. Katie raised a brow, but fell back with a slight nod.

"I see. Sort of. So she had a mental illness and you guys were hunting . . . ?"

"We weren't hunting. She committed suicide."

Maddy gasped.

His eyes met hers. "It's a long story. I don't want to get into it here." His eyes searched hers. "But I'll tell you soon."

She gave a hesitant nod. "Okay, then."

He ran a finger down her cheek, then went to take a seat at the conference table. Maddy filled another cup with coffee and grabbed a creamer. She turned and surveyed the room, absently noting that they were all there, ready to pitch in with ideas and thoughts on the case. They had their iPads and phones ready to do research.

The team sat around the conference table. Quinn pointed to the chair next to him, and she walked over to sit in it, her brain still processing his stunning revelation even as she calmly passed Katie her coffee and cream. Olivia sat to Maddy's left, Katie and Haley on either end, and Charlie and Lizzie opposite her. "Charlie, Lizzie, glad you guys could be in on this," she said.

"Wouldn't want to be anywhere else," Charlie said.

"Yeah," Lizzie agreed. "We take care of our own."

Maddy swallowed the emotional lump of appreciation that wanted to clog her throat, ignored the pain in her shoulder, and tapped the screen of her iPad to bring up the notes app. The wireless keyboard connected and she was ready to go. "Okay, let's go through everything we have."

Quinn leaned forward in his chair. "We've gotten ahold of the owners of the island." He swiped the screen of his iPad. "Bree talked to Keith Hogan's son earlier this morning and sent me a transcript of the conversation." He looked up. "I'm going to give you the abridged version. Basically, there are three heirs. One lives in Alaska, one in Minnesota, and one is a missionary with a remote tribe somewhere in the bush of Africa. They can't get ahold of her so everything is being held up in probate. The brother has hired someone to go in and find her, but he hasn't heard back from the investigator yet. From what Bree's been able to determine, neither the brother in Alaska nor the sister in Minnesota had anything to do with the island. They want to sell it."

"Which is why they've been keeping it up," Haley said.

"Right. Only the person they hired as caretaker said the family had canceled his services almost six months ago."

Maddy frowned. "Let me guess. When you ran that by the family, they didn't know what you were talking about and thought the place was being taken care of as always."

"Exactly," Quinn said.

"What about the payments? Wouldn't the caretaker be suspicious when the payments kept coming?" Lizzie said.

"Right, but the guy whose services were canceled said the

payments stopped just like they were supposed to. He said he usually got a check mailed to his home address around the first of the month."

"So where was the money going?"

"That's easy," Quinn said. "All our killer had to do was simply watch the mailbox a couple of days a month and grab the check when it came. And by cashing it, he avoided any red flags."

"So, let's check banks and find out where these checks were cashed," Katie said.

Quinn nodded. "Already got Bree working on that."

"What about the facial recognition from the guy at the hospital?" Maddy asked Olivia.

"I talked to Detective Van Heerden and she said that it was too fuzzy to get a hit."

"Of course. What about the bodies in the grave. Any word from the Florida medical examiner?" Haley asked.

"Yes," Quinn said. "Fortunately, with the pictures that were found on the island and the information already in the system, the ME was able to get a positive match for all eight victims via DNA and dental records. They're the eight people who each had a note for them sent to the police station, then disappeared. The notes have been compared and are all from the same stock." He looked at Maddy. "The notes we received were from different stock and were even written in a different hand."

She nodded. "He didn't want to tip us off."

"I don't know. I mean, he knows I'm familiar with the intimate details of the case. Maybe he *did* want to tip us off."

"But why?"

"Because it ups the stakes."

Maddy bit her lip. "Yes, I can see that. Then again, I think he had no choice but to send the notes."

Quinn raised a brow and leaned forward, placing his elbows on the table. "What do you mean?"

"He's got a disorder," she said. "He's OCD. He *had* to send the notes. He could make them different enough for us to wonder, maybe even be slightly suspicious, but *because* they were different, he rightly assumed that we wouldn't connect them to him or the other victims. But we *had* to have a note because all the others did too."

Quinn went silent, staring at the floor.

Maddy touched his shoulder. "What is it?"

He shook his head. "My sister was OCD. She struggled with it most of her life. I never understood it. When I was a teenager, I used to tease her about it." He sighed. "It really upset her when I made fun of her. I wish I'd known how bad of a disorder it could be, how it can affect people mentally."

She squeezed his shoulder. "I'm sure she understood later as an adult that you were just a kid and didn't realize you shouldn't tease her about that kind of thing."

"Yeah. Maybe."

The others had fallen silent, but Quinn didn't seem to notice. Or care. Maddy looked at her iPad. "So go through the victims in the order of their disappearance. The autopsies are still going on as we speak, so we'll see if their position in the grave matches the order they disappeared," Maddy said. She looked up. "But it will. Victim number one . . ."

"Jessica Maynard," Quinn said. "She disappeared six months ago. Twenty-eight years old, single, never married, no kids. No family—her parents are dead—no close friends. Reported missing by her boss. A forensic anthropologist was flown in to work with her and a couple of the other more decomposed bodies."

"And victim number two?" Haley asked.

"Gerald Haynes, an engineer, reported missing by his wife.

Victim number three was Kelly Masters. She'd just completed her medical degree and was headed to do her internship. Her parents reported her missing."

"Number four?" Katie murmured.

"Richard Tate. He was unemployed, but was a volunteer for the Protect the Earth Foundation. Number five was Grace Howell. She was active in her church and everyone loved her. Interesting thing about her was that she was a victim of a mugging while on vacation at Myrtle Beach. They caught the guy and he came up for parole last year. She spoke at his hearing and convinced them that he should be allowed another chance at making something of his life."

"Does he have an alibi for her disappearance?" Katie asked.

"Yes. Airtight. He was in a meeting with his parole officer, then the two went out and had lunch after."

Maddy pursed her lips and thought. "So, like her name, she extended him grace. She sounds like a lovely person. Why would someone want to kill her?"

Quinn shook his head. "Evil does everything it can to destroy good."

"So who was number six?" Olivia asked.

"Number six was Dr. Anthony Little. He specialized in in-vitro procedures. And number seven was a priest."

"Seriously?" Haley said. "A priest?"

"Yes, a very much loved one too. Father Timothy Grant. He was one of the more recent victims. And while he had been shot with a crossbow bolt in his head like the others, one of the MEs said he probably had a heart attack and died. He said heart disease was evident."

"Poor thing," Katie murmured. She shuddered and looked at Maddy. "I can't imagine the terror."

Maddy dropped her eyes. "It was bad, Katie. Just leave it at that." Then she raised her head and looked around. "But we survived it and we're going to get this guy."

Under the table she felt Quinn's warm fingers wrap around hers. She drew in a steadying breath and shoved the remembered terror away. "How many medical examiners do they have working on the bodies?"

Quinn looked at the iPad. "Three. And they're working around the clock. I think they're almost finished. Of course, it'll take a while for all of the results to come back, but I know Sheriff Danvers is really pushing for this to be top priority." He waved the iPad. "He's emailing me as he learns things."

Maddy nodded. "Good, I'm glad he's willing to do that. So. Who was number eight?"

Quinn released her hand and his attention went back to his iPad. "Number eight. Asher Kirby. He was a newlywed who'd just moved to Columbia to start his own business. It opened two weeks before he disappeared. Bree's looking into why he moved, what type of business he opened, and all that. We're hoping there's a connection to the death of someone close to the offender. We're doing that with everyone, of course, but so far nothing's jumped out at us."

Maddy pursed her lips. "And we were supposed to be numbers nine and ten."

"That's what it looks like."

"And all of them were killed in a specific order." She sighed. "Do we have any background on them that would connect them to any cases Quinn or I handled in the past?"

Haley tapped her chin. "I thought about that. We've been working overtime trying to find any connections, not only between the victims, but any connection between you and Quinn as well. So far we've come up empty."

Maddy stared at her fingers. "This man calls himself the Cho-

166

sen One. He quoted Scripture while he had a bolt positioned at my back that could have killed me. What does that indicate to you?"

Haley shrugged. "A religious fanatic?"

Maddy leaned forward, her brain spinning. "Maybe. But we've already decided he's smart, methodical. Possibly OCD. He doesn't make a move without thinking about it. Planning. The victims were all chosen for a reason." She met Quinn's gaze. "And so were the numbered crosses. The numbers mean something. More than just the next victim in the line."

"Biblical numerology?" Quinn murmured. "Is it a stretch?"

"Let's find out. What does 'one' mean?" Maddy asked.

Katie tapped her iPad. "According to this website—and I can cross-reference later to make sure—number one in the Bible denotes absolute singleness."

"That would fit with the first victim," Quinn said. "All alone, no family, no parents, et cetera."

"Two?" Maddy asked.

"Symbolizes witness and support," Katie said.

Quinn frowned. "Now that one confuses me. He was an engineer. But the number indicates that he was a witness to something. Or maybe he supported someone that the killer didn't like?"

"I'm not seeing anything more about him. I've got his obituary here and he left behind a wife and two daughters." Katie swiped to another page. "No arrest records, no articles in the paper about anything other than him taking the job at BroCorp, Inc., as one of the head engineers four years ago." She shrugged. "We might have to do more research to figure that one out. Let's go on to number three. That number signifies completion or perfection, and unity."

"What do we know about the third victim again?" Maddy ran her fingers through her hair. "I can't keep them straight."

"I'll type up a list and send it to you," Katie said. "I was keeping notes while we were talking about them a minute ago. Victim number three was a doctor."

"Who would think a doctor would signify perfection or unity?" Maddy said.

"It also signifies completion. She'd just completed her medical degree."

Maddy nodded. "All right, that would fit."

"And wait a minute. Here's an article about her in the local paper." Katie looked up. "She got her degree in three years. She was brilliant apparently."

"That definitely fits," Quinn said.

Katie snapped her fingers. "I've got number four."

"Tell us." Maddy rubbed her arms and Quinn figured she'd left her jacket in the car.

Quinn got up and turned the air down. She shot him a smile of thanks. It struck him that he liked noticing the little things about her. He liked taking care of her. When she'd let him.

"Number four in the Bible relates to the earth," Katie said. "The fourth victim was a volunteer for the Protect the Earth Foundation."

Quinn slid back into his chair. "We're on to something."

"Number five is a number associated with grace. Like when Jesus multiplied five loaves of barley to feed the five thousand. And there were five Levitical offerings." Katie looked up from her iPad. "The victim's name was Grace."

"And she's the one who extended grace to the man who attacked her," Maddy whispered. She pressed her fingers to her eyes. "I don't believe this. And the number six?"

"Number six is the number of man: Adam and Eve were created on the sixth day."

Maddy stood and paced to the refrigerator in the corner of

the room. She opened it and pulled out a Coke and turned to face the others. "And the sixth victim was a doctor, an in-vitro specialist."

"Creating man. So to speak," Quinn said.

"And seven?" Charlie asked.

Katie glanced at her iPad. "Seven refers to the number of God. It means divine perfection or completeness."

"And our seventh victim was a priest." Maddy returned to her seat.

"Yes. Bree's been busy," Quinn said. "She noted that he was a man who had no scandal attached to his name, no complaints from his parishioners, nothing. Everyone loved him. He was going to retire next year."

"Spiritual perfection," Maddy said. "At least the appearance of it. He was still human, which automatically gives him the sinful nature, but to all who looked from the outside in, I can see why it would appear that he was perfect."

"And number eight signifies new beginnings."

Lizzie sighed. "The newlywed."

Olivia pressed a hand to her head and looked around the table. "With the new business in a new city. Several new beginnings." Her gaze landed on Quinn. "And that brings us to number nine."

"Yes," Katie said. She looked up from her iPad. "The number of judgment."

Maddy frowned. "What do you need to be judged for?"

He snorted and rose to pace. He really didn't want to get into this, but sighed. "A lot."

[16]

Maddy stared at him. "We'll come back to that, but now your note kind of makes sense."

"Yes. Judgment day is coming."

"What about ten?" she asked.

Katie consulted her iPad once again. "The number of divine perfection. Or perfection of divine order."

Maddy frowned. "What? I thought that was seven."

She shrugged. "They're related, but ten has more to do with a divine order than anything."

"Well, I'm not perfect in any sense of the word. And I'm not sure about the divine order thing."

Quinn shook his head and realization dawned as he looked at her. "Think about it," he said. "The number ten."

It hit her. "Ahh," she said. "I'm the tenth child of a tenth child," she said.

Quinn looked back down at his iPad. "Noah was the tenth generation from Adam. Abraham was the tenth generation from Shem. Then you have the Ten Commandments. God said the

Northern Kingdom was to be formed from ten tribes. There are ten clauses in the Lord's Prayer—"

"There were the ten plagues on Egypt," Maddy said.

"And so on."

Maddy sighed and massaged her temples. A headache was forming and her leg and shoulder throbbed in time with her heartbeat. "So now we know why I'm number ten." She looked at Quinn. "And why you have to die before me."

"Yeah, wouldn't want to mess up his plan or anything." The sarcasm rolled effortlessly from his lips.

She gave him a faint smile. "Did any of the victims cheat death in some way? He seemed perturbed that I managed to do so. More than once."

Quinn ran his finger over the screen of the tablet, then tapped. "Yes. One was in a car wreck at the age of sixteen and walked away without a scratch while his two passengers were killed."

"Who was that?"

"The second victim."

"So maybe he was a witness to the crash? He's the only one we haven't figured out. Why was he number two?"

"That could be it, but I still want to do some digging."

"Who else?"

"Victim number one. She suffered a brain aneurism when she was fourteen and went into a coma. The doctors did emergency surgery and she lived without any brain damage. She was considered a walking miracle." He sat back and crossed his arms. "And that's it. Nothing in the other six victims' pasts that would indicate they cheated death."

"Then that's not the connection," Maddy said. She looked at Quinn. "What about your letting the guilty go?"

"Bree's still looking into that one." He shook his head. "I've worked a lot of cases. I've arrested people, questioned them, and then had to let them go because of a lack of evidence, only to turn around and arrest them again once we had the evidence in hand."

"Any one case stand out?"

His jaw went tight. "Possibly."

"Quinn?"

"Twenty-year-old Ashley Gorman. She'd been married about a year when she disappeared from her home here in South Carolina where she lived with her husband, Brad. She got a full ride to the University of South Carolina, so her husband moved up here to be with her. Well, technically, he was here to be with her. What he was really doing was staying in South Carolina on the weekends and staying in Sarasota during the week, as he was still working there some. Anyway, Ashley went to take the trash out one morning and no one ever heard from her again. Guess where she was from originally?"

"Florida?" Katie asked.

"Sarasota."

"Who's—what? Wait a minute," Maddy said. "I know her name. I know that case."

"She was the victim of a serial killer. His last victim." Quinn shut his eyes as though trying not to remember. When he opened his eyes, Maddy gasped at the torment there. And then it was gone. Hidden behind that hard mask she was so familiar with.

"Tell us," she said. But she didn't need to hear it. Every single detail was suddenly front and center in her mind.

Quinn stood and paced to the window, only he stood to the side and not in front of it. At least he was being careful. He looked back at them. "This guy was brutal. Really messed up. I'll spare you all the details, but we had a pretty good lead that it was him, so my former partner and I arrested him. Then the

DA said we didn't have enough evidence, the lead wasn't reliable, and it was all circumstantial. So I had to cut him loose."

"Ugh." Charlie grimaced.

"Yeah," Quinn muttered.

"So," Maddy said, "this could be about someone who loved her wanting to get back at you because you let her killer go after you had him off the streets. Before he killed Ashley Gorman."

Quinn shrugged. "Could be. There are other cases too, of course, but that's the biggest one with the biggest consequence for letting a guilty person go free." He looked at Maddy. "But why make you a part of it? You had nothing to do with that case."

"Actually, I did," she said slowly. "That was what, six years ago? I was still with the FBI at that point."

"Six, almost seven." He frowned. "I don't remember you on that case."

She nodded. "I was on it. The task force was huge. I was behind the scenes working on his profile. You and I never came into contact." She forced herself to think about the case. She locked her gaze on his. "He kidnapped the girls, flew them out to a wooded remote mountain area, and hunted them," she whispered.

"Then raped and killed them when he caught them, then returned their mutilated bodies to their families," Quinn finished. "It haunts me to think what those parents went through when they opened their doors to look down and see—" His throat convulsed and she thought she saw tears in his eyes before he lowered his lashes.

The room fell silent. Maddy swept her chair back and stood again. Her stomach rolled and she thought she might be sick. She remembered that case only too well now. Details she'd worked hard to shove out of her mind. She'd gotten into that killer's head and didn't think she'd ever be able to get out. And she didn't want to go back there. Didn't want the memories floating to the surface. She blinked and paced to the nearest window, then back to stand near her chair. She couldn't sit just yet.

"How do you know it's not your serial killer come back to continue his work?" Charlie asked breaking the thick silence.

"He's dead," Quinn said. "He was killed in a prison riot about four years ago."

Charlie nodded. "Guess it makes it a little hard for it to be him then."

"So *our* guy is a copycat," Maddy said. Just saying it left a bad taste in her mouth.

"Of a sort," Quinn said. "He kidnaps his victims and hunts them. That part I know. I don't think he had sexual assault in mind, but it will be good to know what the ME finds in her examination of the bodies we found. At least the ones that were still . . . examinable. And he buried them in the same place."

"It sounds like it could be someone who loved Ashley who's behind the attempts on your lives," Katie said. "What about her husband? Her parents? A sibling?"

Quinn nodded. "I wouldn't mind questioning them. Let's track them down and see what they have to say." He pursed his lips and picked up his iPad. "I want to get a look at everyone. Let's just see what their driver's license pictures look like." A few more taps and he had what he wanted. "Okay, Ashley's husband, Brad Gorman. Six feet one inch tall, dark brown hair and blue eyes, dark tan—" Quinn's eyes widened.

"What?" Maddy asked.

"He's in Key West now. Coincidence?" He squinted at the photo and shook his head. "I don't know. If he shaved his head and put on a big hat, it could be him, I guess."

"What about her father?" Maddy asked.

Quinn tapped again, then his eyes widened again. "Leonard Nance, aka Robert Tabor. Moved from Sarasota to Key West about six years ago. Short salt-and-pepper hair, six feet two inches, fifty-six years old, green eyes, dark tan. Gold-rimmed glasses. Huh."

"What?" Haley said.

"He kind of looks familiar."

Maddy moved to look over his shoulder. "Let me see." He held the iPad up so she could see. "You're right, he does look familiar. Where do we know him from?"

"He could just resemble someone we know." He shrugged. "Or it may be we're just remembering him from the trial."

Maddy mulled it over. "Maybe."

Quinn typed and hit enter. "Ashley's brother changed his name and moved too. Different address in Key West, though." He punched in a number on his phone. "I'm going to call this in, let the FBI know there might be a connection."

Maddy took a seat and the team sat quietly, listening to Quinn explain their theory and give them the names.

He disconnected and heaved a sigh. "It's a pretty thin thread, connecting the family to this after all these years, but it's all we've got to work with right now."

"So where do we go from here?" Maddy said. "What's the next step in finding this guy?"

Quinn ran a hand through his hair. "I go back to work." He looked at Maddy. "You stay under the radar."

Her eyes widened. "Really? Stay under the radar while you go back to work? Shall I lace up my corset too?"

He smirked, then turned serious. "I'll have a partner watching my back at all times."

Katie snorted, Olivia chuckled, and Haley rolled her eyes. "I guess we're all just chopped liver, eh?" Haley asked.

Quinn flushed. "That's not what I meant."

Maddy leaned forward, her hands pressing hard against the table in an effort to keep her tone civil. "Sometimes having someone watching your back means nothing, and you know that as well as I do. If he wants to get to you, it's very likely your partner will just become collateral damage."

Quinn froze for a split second. "Bree is trained." He hesitated again. "But I'll let her make that call."

Maddy gave a light snort. "Actually, I'm probably pretty safe. You're the one who has to die first, remember?"

"But he doesn't mind kidnapping out of order, remember?"

She grimaced and tamped down the desire to stick her tongue out at him. "So, what's better? Stay in hiding and hope we figure out who this psycho is or go about our daily lives and draw him out?"

Olivia stood. "I think you both need to stay under the radar." Quinn frowned at her and Maddy raised a brow. Olivia shrugged. "This guy isn't playing around. I think until we get the information back from Florida about the crime scene—the island—you need to lay low. He's already come after you in the hospital, which was something he set up. He wanted you there and he got you there."

"Yes, he did," Maddy said. "Very effectively."

"He also wanted you out at the school where Alyssa was. And he got you there."

No one said anything.

"So," Olivia continued, "instead of playing his game right now, you need to lay low and wait this out for now."

Maddy tugged at her ponytail and frowned. "I don't like that."

"But I think we need to do it," Quinn said.

Maddy jerked. "What?"

He nodded. "Olivia's right. We need the results from the investigation before we know which way to go with this. Let's give them a couple of days. I've already told my boss what was going on, and he said to do whatever it was I had to do to keep myself and my family safe."

Maddy let her gaze fall on each face around the table. They all agreed. She could see it. She drew in a deep breath and gave a slow nod. "All right."

"And by lying low, I mean heading to a change of scenery," Quinn said.

Maddy pursed her lips "Where?"

"Florida," Quinn said.

She narrowed her eyes. "Florida, huh?"

Quinn nodded. "Key West, to be exact."

Katie sputtered. "That's your idea of lying low?"

"You want to continue investigating from there," Maddy said, ignoring her friend.

"I do. I want to question those people closest to Ashley and I want extensive checks into their whereabouts during our abductions. I also want to know if any of them have been going from Florida to South Carolina on a regular basis."

"I'm game for that." She pulled her phone from the clip on her belt and looked at it. "I'm not worried about him being able to track our phones. They're special government-issued devices."

Quinn nodded. "I've got one too." He grinned at Olivia. "Besides, if we're not here, chances are good that he won't try anything with our families or friends."

Olivia frowned at him for a long moment, then conceded. "I guess I can't argue with that twisted logic."

"So is there anything we're missing?" Maddy asked. "Any way that he can figure out where we are?"

They fell silent for a moment. "If there's anything, I can't think of it," Quinn finally said. "The only way he's been able to keep up with us to this point is because he knows our schedules, our homes, our routes to and from work, our families. He can find us simply by showing up at one of those locations and waiting."

Maddy grimaced. "Yeah. But how did he get our cell numbers?"

"I've wondered that myself," Quinn said. "Mine's pretty simple to get. All someone has to do is call the station and say they need to get in touch with me about a case. I give out cards with the number on it." He shrugged.

"I suppose mine wouldn't be that difficult either," Maddy murmured. She sighed. "I guess we need to pack bags."

"So, you're determined to do this?" Katie asked.

Maddy nodded. "Yes. I can't just sit around waiting for this guy to strike again. I need to do this."

"All right, then. Daniel can fly you," Katie said. "As far as we know, we weren't followed here. I don't think it's wise for either of you to go home. Let's just go shopping for whatever you might need."

"I like new clothes," Maddy said. "And I need to make a phone call." She looked at Katie. "You get ahold of Daniel and I'll make my call." She shook her head. "Florida, huh? I guess there are advantages to knowing a guy who's good at flying under the radar."

Quinn buckled the seat belt and leaned back in the seat. Maddy's tight-lipped, cloudy expression concerned him. "You okay?"

"Peachy."

"All righty, then."

She sighed. "Sorry. Maybe I should have said snappy."

"Does that phone call you made just before we climbed aboard have anything to do with your sunny disposition?"

"Everything."

"Want to share?"

She sighed. "I'd rather just forget it, but . . ."

"But?"

Her lips twisted into a rueful smile. "I suppose I can't expect you to share what's going on with you and not do the same."

"Exactly."

"I called my mother to check on my sister, but my dad answered her phone."

"Ah. I know there's tension between you, but you've never said what happened."

"He's a retired cop. Almost my whole family is involved in law enforcement in some way. Cops, lawyers, forensics, something. It was ingrained in us from birth."

"Yeah, you've mentioned that before."

"He blames me for what happened while I was with the FBI. I think he honestly believes I was the mole—or that I know who was."

"What?" Quinn stared at her, truly shocked that her father could believe such a thing. "Obviously, he doesn't know you at all."

Tears gathered and she blinked them away when Daniel opened the cockpit door and climbed in. "Everyone ready?" he asked.

"Ready," Quinn said.

"I'm not filing a flight plan. No sense in leaving a trail to follow. Visibility is good. We'll be flying low and landing on a private airstrip behind the police department."

"Thanks, Daniel."

"My pleasure." He settled the headphones over his ears and powered up the engine.

Maddy reached for Quinn's hand and he curled his fingers around hers. He squeezed. "And?"

"My dad said something like 'what goes around comes around.'"

Outrage filled him and he had to bite his tongue to keep his first words from escaping. He took a deep breath. "Meaning he thinks you deserve to be tortured and killed by a serial killer?"

She winced. "I don't think he meant it quite that way. I might not have given him every detail, just that things had gone south with my job and I was going to have to disappear for a while."

He shook his head. "Almost everything is taking place in Florida, so he wouldn't necessarily hear the details. I'm sure the hospital kept it as quiet as they could about having a killer in the building."

"Right. And I'd like to keep it that way."

"How's your sister?"

"She'll be all right. There's a guard on her door, but it's the others I'm worried about. This guy ran my sister down in the street." She shook her head. "Who's to say he won't go after someone else in my family?"

"Did you mention that to your father?"

"Yes."

"And what did he say to that?" Quinn asked softly.

She grimaced. "That he would make sure everything was taken care of and he didn't need my help to do so. In fact, it was probably better if I just stayed away."

"Ouch."

"Yeah. But I can't really blame him for feeling that way."

Quinn grunted. "I can."

A short silence fell between them and Quinn continued to hold her hand. He just couldn't fathom how someone, especially Maddy's own father, could think her guilty of such a vile act as feeding information to the ones who killed her fellow agents and friends. "It had to be an inside job."

She pursed her lips and looked at him out of the corner of her eye. "Yes, I think so."

"Has anything else happened since then?"

"No. Not since I left. At least nothing that points to being related to the incident I was involved in."

"Which rather supports the fact that you might have had something to do with the ambush."

"Yes."

"You've got to figure out who was behind it."

"I would love to know who was behind it, but it was fully investigated. Nothing was proven. There was only the circum-stantial evidence."

"You're not a quitter, Maddy. You need to fight back on this."

She looked away and swallowed. Daniel was involved in his own conversation up front. Quinn just realized they were in the air, cruising smoothly beneath the clouds. He'd been so wrapped up in his and Maddy's discussion he hadn't even noticed taking off. Said a lot for Daniel's skills too.

"I'm not a quitter, I'll agree with that, but I can't . . . I won't press the matter too hard right now."

"Maddy—"

"My sister got the promotion."

He paused. "What?"

"Lindsey, my sister. We worked on different squads but were up for the same promotion. She got it when things went wrong for me. My family is only just recovering from everything I put them through. I won't be a part of any investigation that might—"

"That might what? Expose your sister as a killer?"

Maddy closed her eyes and leaned her head back against the headrest. "She wasn't behind it."

She obviously wanted to end the discussion. Quinn wasn't quite so ready. "Why? Because she's your sister? Maddy, if she had any part in that, she needs to be removed from her position. Shoot, she needs to be in prison."

"If I thought she was directly behind the ambush," Maddy said, "I would agree with you. But I don't. I think she let everything play out, saw where the investigation was going, and didn't do anything to stop me from taking the fall. If she even could have done anything. However, I do think she took full advantage of the situation to further her own career. But she's not a killer."

"Then there's one still out there."

She rolled her head to the side to look at him. "But no one else believes that except . . ."

"Except who?"

"My partner's wife, Kristy Newman. She was a police officer and a friend. She told me at his funeral that she knows I'd never do such a thing and that she was going to find out who was behind her husband's death."

"And did she?"

"I don't know. She called me and wanted to meet me. She said she found something, but she never showed up to the meeting. I called her and asked her why she stood me up and she said she was wrong, that she was dropping it and for me to let it go as well."

Quinn sat up straight and shot her a ferocious frown. "And that doesn't raise any red flags for you?"

"Yes, of course. A whole field of them."

"And you just let it go?"

"No, I went to her house. She threw me out and told me not to come back. A week later she was dead."

"Maddy . . ."

"I know."

"So, you're done?"

"No . . ." She hesitated, then shrugged. "Not exactly, but I don't have the contacts, the trust, in that office anymore. If I start making more waves, I can't predict what will happen or who else will die."

"What if someone else made some waves?"

"Then I have no control over that, but whoever does the wave-making better watch his back, because this person—or persons—doesn't want to be caught."

Quinn studied her. "You have someone looking into it."

She raised a brow. "What makes you say that?"

"Because you wouldn't just let him get away with it."

She nodded. "Yes, someone's looking into it. And has been." She held his gaze, then let a sigh slip out. "But you have to understand, it's been almost four years. There's no hard evidence anywhere. Whoever is behind it knows how to cover his—or her—tracks. And whatever Kristy found, she hid." She raked a hand through her hair. "I don't know where to find it. If there even was an *it*."

"Maybe you or the person working behind the scenes for you is just looking in the wrong place."

"Maybe." She glanced out of the window. "But truthfully, my first priority is our current situation. We need to stop him before he stops us."

[17]

Where were they? The Chosen One paced the floor of his rental. Unbelievable. He'd lost them. How was that even possible? He'd been monitoring them, had placed trackers on their vehicles. But they'd been removed. He should have known they'd sweep the cars before every ride. He couldn't track their cell phones. At least not yet. They were more sophisticated than he'd counted on. He could get the software that would allow him to hack their systems, but for now, he was going to have to think it out, be smart and logical.

He'd gone to the Elite Guardians headquarters and found it mostly empty. Just the receptionist, who'd been most unhelpful. If he'd had a number to match to her, he would have taken delight in killing her.

But he didn't. He couldn't just randomly kill someone. The killing had to be approved beforehand, and it was only permissible if it was to further the mission. And the receptionist was not on the list. He grunted. She should be.

So he'd left. Angry, but with the knowledge that his God would show him what to do next. Where to go next.

Who to kill next.

And how he would soon be able to return to his normal life once his mission was over. Until then, he'd keep his ears and eyes open, and he knew it wouldn't be long until he discovered their whereabouts once again.

Sheriff Danvers walked toward the plane with his hand outstretched. Maddy and Quinn shook it, then followed him across the landing strip and into the back of the Monroe County Sheriff's Office. Maddy swiped the sweat from her upper lip with the edge of her sleeve. "I will never complain about the humidity in Columbia again."

Sheriff Danvers laughed. "This is nothing. Stick around for July and August."

She grimaced. "No thanks."

He led them down a hallway and stopped to open a door with his name on it. "Come on in and have a seat."

Once they were settled, the sheriff placed water bottles in front of them, then took a seat behind his desk. Maddy leaned forward and clasped her hands in front of her, anxious to hear what he had to say. "Any word from the lab on the evidence you and the crime scene unit collected from the island?"

He sighed. "Yes, we've gotten a few preliminary reports." He rummaged through the stack of files on his desk and pulled one to open in front of him. "All right. In the house, we found quite a few hairs, fibers, fingerprints, et cetera. They'll run everything through the systems, IAFIS, CODIS, et cetera, and see if there's a hit."

"What else?"

"All those photographs were matched to the victims of the serial killer you've been after."

Quinn sat back with a sigh. "I'm not surprised."

"Any word from the medical examiner?" Maddy asked.

"As I've already told you, she and the other MEs we've brought in have been working around the clock. They matched up all of the victims. Dental records and DNA. That's all they've had time for up to this point, but they're working as fast as they can." He flipped the page. "In the meantime, the island was booby trapped. You two missed a few."

"Like what?" Maddy asked.

"Poisonous darts. One of the crime scene investigators tripped it. Fortunately, he was on his knees looking at something when he sprung it. The dart went right over him and embedded itself in one of the trees behind him."

Maddy shuddered. "What kind of poison?"

"It's actually snake venom. The kind that makes you violently sick and causes you to bleed to death from the inside out. It's a slow, painful death."

"The kind of death he seems to prefer," Quinn muttered.

"Because he wants to be the one to finish you off," Maddy said. "With a bolt through the brain."

"What a coward," Danvers said.

"Yes, but a smart coward."

The sheriff eyed them. "What have you two figured out?"

Maddy shifted in her chair, then sipped her water. "We found out he's got a religious background that's influencing his actions. He's using biblical numerology to choose his victims. What's your email address? Quinn can send you what we've come up with so far."

The sheriff told him and Quinn sent the information from his phone.

"Thanks," Sheriff Danvers said.

Quinn nodded. "What about Keith Hogan's family? Anything there?"

"Naw, they're still looking for their sister in the wilds of Africa. Nothing's changed as far as that's concerned. On another note, I've been going back and forth with Bree Standish."

"My partner," Quinn said.

"Smart woman. She found out that the checks that were supposed to be payment for upkeep on the house were cashed here on Key West at the First State Bank of the Florida Keys. We're going through security footage to see if we can snag a facial of the person who cashed them."

"That would help a lot," Maddy said.

"All right, well, it's not much, but we're getting there, I promise. We'll catch this guy."

Quinn blew out a breath. "Well, the good thing is, he's probably not going to kill anyone else."

"Why's that?"

"Because I'm number nine."

Maddy scowled. "Didn't stop him from running down my sister."

Well, there is that, but he didn't kill her, did he?"

"Could have."

"But he didn't."

She huffed. "Quinn, he blew up your niece's school."

"Okay, yes, there's that." Quinn narrowed his eyes. "But the only reason he did that was to get us to come running. It worked. Only now he knows our families are protected. I don't think he'll go after them again."

"What if you're wrong?" Danvers asked.

He scowled. "Then I hope the people protecting them will do their jobs."

The sheriff stood. "How about I take you two to the hotel where you'll be staying?"

"I need a rental," Quinn said. "We'll want to have our own transportation. We want to go talk to Brad Gorman."

"Ashley Gorman's husband?"

"Yes."

"Why? The FBI already talked to him, I believe, after your team reported a potential tie-in to his wife's murder. They met with the rest of the family too. I can show you a copy of the report."

Quinn shrugged. "I need a face-to-face with Brad. He has an alibi, but anyone can fabricate that. I want to speak to him, get a feel for him."

The sheriff nodded. "I understand. You can talk to him. He's usually down at the marina where the ferries come and go. He helps out Burt when they're shorthanded."

"Great," Maddy said. "We'll head that way, then grab a bite to eat. Any restaurant recommendations?"

Sheriff Danvers nodded. "If you're going to be at the marina anyway, you'll want to try the Flying Fish Restaurant. It's small and local and you'll need a reservation because it's always packed. As for the car, I'll get one of my deputies to drop off one of our official vehicles at the hotel in about thirty minutes. I need to see what's available and get it cleaned and gassed up for you."

"That's awfully generous of you."

The man smiled, but it was a tense one. "Whatever I can do to help. If I have a killer in my jurisdiction, I want him found. The more people looking, the better off we are."

Quinn threw his suitcase on the bed and eyed the connecting door. He opened it just as Maddy opened hers. Her head came to just below his chin and he noted that it would be real easy

188

to pull her close. Instead, he cleared his throat and motioned her to the sitting area. She crossed the room and dropped onto the couch. "Nice hotel."

Quinn nodded. "Might as well have a nice place to stay while we track down a killer."

"I'm all about that."

"What else are you all about?" He pulled the chair up opposite her and sat facing her.

She tilted her head. "What do you mean?"

"Is there an 'us,' Maddy?"

She blinked and her eyes went wide. "Whoa. That was random."

"Sorry, it's been on my mind." He rubbed his palms on his thighs and realized he was nervous.

She studied him, her eyes searching his, as though trying to read his deepest secrets. "Do you want there to be an 'us'?"

"Yes." Quinn was surprised at his lack of hesitation but didn't regret the instant answer. She simply stared at him, looking as stunned as he felt. "I mean, we've gone through a lot together."

"We have." She nodded.

He took her hand. "And I care about you."

"I care about you too. I don't think that's ever been in question." She hesitated.

"What?" he asked. "You want to say something else and you stopped."

"I don't want to make you mad by asking something too personal."

He swallowed. "Ask me. I won't get mad."

She bit her lip, then seemed to make up her mind. "What about God, Quinn? Where are you with him?"

He raised a brow. "That's not what I thought you might ask." He pursed his lips. "God and I have a complicated relationship."

"Tell me."

Her soft voice soothed him. He wanted to tell her. Share with her. "I guess it's just that after everything that happened with Stacy, I got mad at him. I don't like feeling this way about him, but I'm hesitant to trust him anymore. Especially with people I love."

"Because he let her die?"

"Yeah."

"I can see how you would feel that way, but that's not how God works. He can handle your anger, but he wants you to have peace. To let go of the bitterness. To keep trusting him even when you don't want to or when you doubt. Have faith that he is who he says he is."

"Is that how you deal with what happened to you? The injustice of a false accusation? You just let it go and trust him?"

"Yes. I'm not saying that I don't still get mad when I think about it, because I do. But good has come from it. I never thought I'd be able to say that a few years ago, but now"—she shrugged—"I can."

"I just don't know if I can do that, Maddy."

"You can."

The absolute assurance in her voice intrigued him. "How?"

"One day at a time. Pray about it."

"Praying means I have to talk to him."

A low chuckle escaped her. "Yes. Exactly. And the more you talk to him, truly talk to him, the harder it is to hold on to the anger."

"*You're* easy to talk to."

"I care about you, I want to listen, to help. So does he. Even so much more than I."

He let a long pause linger as he thought about it, then nodded. "Okay, maybe I'll try it."

"Good."

"Not making any promises, though."

"Fine."

And that was that. He dropped his gaze.

No, it wasn't. He had to force himself to be open with her. He'd be the first to admit that wearing his emotions on his sleeve made him antsier than a crook in a room full of cops.

"Go ahead," she said. "Say it."

She read him so easily it was scary. "I've never been good at relationships. Maybe that's why I have a hard time with God."

"How many relationships have you had?"

He laughed, but there was no humor in it. "Since college graduation? Not that many. A couple. And trust me, I wasn't any good at it."

"Why do you think that is?"

Now her calm façade reminded him of the couple of visits he'd had to make to the department psychiatrist. It was starting to annoy him. "I just lost the ability to trust people, I think, so I stopped trying."

"Kind of like you stopped trusting God?"

"Yes."

"I can understand that."

He moved to sit beside her on the couch and pulled her against him. She rested her head on his chest and he relished the feel of her in his arms. Definitely better than visiting the psychiatrist. "I know. You're the one person who actually can. And that's nice."

"Yes, it is. And your mind knows that. But . . ."

"But what?"

"What about your heart?"

She met his gaze and his pulse picked up speed. "I think my heart is working on lining up in agreement with my head."

"Working on it?"

"Yeah."

A slight smile lifted the corners of her mouth and he simply lowered his head a few inches to cover her lips with his. Finally. He breathed a soft sigh and settled in to kiss her with all the emotion he had in him. She didn't protest. At all. In fact, she kissed him back eagerly, shifting and lifting her hands to bury them in his hair. He lost track of time, of the fact that he even was in the universe, because he finally had Maddy where he wanted her. In his arms, his lips on hers and their hearts thudding against one another.

At least until she pulled back, her cheeks flushed and eyes glittering. "I think it's time I go to my room—or we go talk to Brad Gorman, then get something to eat," she said.

He wanted to object, to go back to kissing her. Instead, he cleared his throat. "Yes, that might be a wise idea. An interview then food sounds good."

"I want to freshen up a bit. Give me fifteen minutes?"

"Yes. Of course."

She started for her room.

"That's it?" he asked.

Maddy turned. "What's it?"

"That. We kiss and you're just going to go freshen up?"

"Am I supposed to do something else?"

He was stumped. He didn't know how to answer her. Or what he even expected. What did one do after sharing such an amazing kiss? "Well, shouldn't we at least talk about it?" Quinn truly could not believe those words just came out of his mouth. He ran from discussions like this, he didn't *instigate* them.

Maddy tilted her head, and he was willing to swear she was laughing at him, even though her lips weren't smiling and her eyes were dark and serious. "What's to talk about? It was a good first kiss, Quinn. Now I'm going to get ready, okay?"

"Uh . . . yes. Okay then." She made it to the door and had just stepped into her room and—he couldn't help it. "Just good? Not great?"

The door shut and he heard her laughter come from the other side. Against his will, his own lips tugged upward. "That was *not* a good first kiss," he muttered. "It was a *phenomenal* first kiss."

Maddy leaned against the shut door and placed a hand over her racing heart. It had taken all of her bureau training not to puddle on the floor at Quinn's feet and spill her emotions all over them. Now she understood the meaning of the phrase "to go weak in the knees." Never again would she laugh if someone said that. She'd just experienced it and she had to admit it had knocked her for a loop. She didn't need to freshen up, she just needed some time to get herself together.

She drew in a steadying breath and grabbed the overnight bag Katie had purchased and packed for her. "Oh my, Quinn Holcombe, what you do to me and my emotions."

He loved her, she knew he did, but he still hadn't said the words. Then again, she hadn't either. And didn't know if she ever would. Sadness wanted to step in and she refused to let it.

Her phone rang. She grabbed it. "Hello?"

"Hey, this is Nel, how are you doing?"

Special Agent Nel Tarrington and one of Maddy's best friends from her days with the FBI—and the one person next to Quinn whom she trusted implicitly. "Hey, Nel, what's up?"

"You have a minute?"

"Yes."

"So, after I got your text, I started snooping around again."

"You found something." She'd texted Nel after her and Quinn's conversation in the plane. She wasn't quite as laid back as she'd come across about clearing her name and didn't figure it would hurt to touch base with Nel.

"I think so, but I also think your sister is keeping a close eye on me."

Her sister. "Why does Lindsey feel like she needs to keep an eye on you?"

"I don't know. Maybe because she knows we're friends? And maybe because she caught me in your partner's old office?"

"Ah. Yeah, that might do it. What were you doing in there? You wouldn't find anything in there at this point."

"Actually, I wasn't sure. That room hasn't been used as an office since you quit. They turned it into a storage area. Loads of boxes of files and junk."

"What? Why? Surely they need that for office space."

"Yeah, another office would be nice, but the powers that be had other plans. So, I went in and started going through your partner's old desk. His wife cleaned out his personal things after he was killed, of course, but I don't think it's been touched since that day."

Maddy's heart beat an anxious rhythm. "And?"

"Unfortunately nothing much, but Lindsey interrupted me. I told her I was looking for a cold case file that was supposed to be in that office. She offered to help find it. Fortunately, I'd already looked one up that I knew was in there and we found it together."

"Okay."

"Anyway, long story short, with the desk a long shot—and a bust—I decided the only way I was going to find out anything was to do things the old-fashioned way. I made a list of friends and acquaintances and started going door-to-door. It paid off. I found out that his wife, Kristy, had a safe-deposit box."

"You found that out from who?"

"Her mother. She even gave me the key when I told her it's possible her daughter's death wasn't an accident."

Maddy sank to the bed. Could this four-year nightmare be close to being over? "Can you get a judge to give you access to the box?"

"I think so. I'm still working on him, but I think he'll crack before too long. Especially if I can convince him he'll be the hero in the story and get some serious positive media attention."

"Judge Timmons."

"Yeah."

She glanced at her watch. "That's great news, Nel, wonderful progress."

"Hey, you okay? You've been awfully quiet lately."

"I'm fine, just a lot going on. We'll have lunch sometime and I'll fill you in." After she beat a killer at his own game. "I've got to go, but we'll talk later, all right?"

"Sure. Take care."

Maddy returned to the bathroom and dragged the brush through her hair, then pulled the strands back up into her standard ponytail. She brushed her teeth, then stared at herself in the mirror. While the hope that her name could soon be cleared raced through her, so did the anticipation of spending the evening with Quinn.

Makeup?

No way. Then he'd know she was dressing up for him.

But so what? Why shouldn't he know? He knew how she felt about him.

So why bother with makeup?

She groaned and grabbed the bag. She hadn't asked for much,

but had put the request in when Katie asked her about cosmetics. Five minutes later, she studied her handiwork. A dab of eyeliner, a smidgeon of mascara, and a glossy pink color on her lips. Okay, so she looked good. She turned on her heel and went to knock on the adjoining door. It opened almost instantly.

Quinn's eyes widened, then narrowed. Then he smiled. A pleased smile. She shouldn't have put on the makeup. She resisted the urge to punch him. "Ready?"

"I am. You look beautiful."

She flushed and it made her mad. She ignored the heat in her cheeks and smiled. "Thanks."

"I called Brad Gorman's cell phone and he didn't answer. Next I tried the KEY WEST TRANSPORT AND FERRY SERVICE and got someone named Nathan Truett. He said Brad was out on a run but would be back around eight o'clock."

"Good. That means we can eat first. I'm starving."

"I know. I could hear your stomach growling while you were *freshening up*."

She wrinkled her nose at him. "You could not."

He grinned and the sight nearly took her breath away. Then it was gone. When was the last time she'd seen him do that? She couldn't remember, but it made her long to see it again. "Anyway," he said, oblivious to the palpitations he'd just inflicted on her heart, "I mapped the directions to the restaurant Danvers recommended. It's a seafood place right on the water next to the ferry. Our reservations are in fifteen minutes."

"Sounds wonderful. Let's go."

He took her hand and opened the door. He checked the hall with an intensity that reminded her that this was no ordinary date. Her tension returned. She hated it. Hated the reason for it.

"There's no way he could know we're here, right?" she asked softly.

"I don't see how." Quinn slipped an arm around her shoulder. "But we'll watch each other's backs. Deal?"

"Deal."

Together they walked to the county car and Quinn slid behind the wheel while Maddy buckled up in the passenger seat. She was hungry. Hungry for food, but hungry for the ability to believe Quinn when he said he wanted there to be an "us"—a relationship. One that was more than friends. One that was a forever kind of deal. But her heart was troubled as well. He might want a relationship with her, but something was holding him back. Something that wouldn't allow him to let himself go when it came to committing to her.

Quinn punched the restaurant into the vehicle's GPS and Maddy went back to her thoughts even while she admired his profile from the corner of her eye.

For the past couple of years he'd seemed perfectly content to simply be best friends. And she had felt the same way until about a year and a half ago when her heart had decided she wanted more. But he hadn't been ready for that, so she'd kept her feelings hidden, trying to be content to wait him out.

It had been a struggle for sure, but even as she'd prayed for guidance, she'd never gotten the green light from God to leave him and move on—or to accept the couple of offers for dates from other men. And then she'd lost her temper in the restaurant and it seemed to have opened his eyes. Maybe she should have done that a year ago.

Then again, if he wasn't ready, he wasn't ready. And she had to be at peace with that.

Somehow.

Quinn's phone buzzed. He looked at the screen and then Maddy. "It's Sheriff Danvers."

"Go ahead and answer it."

He hit the button on his hands-free device. "Hello, Holcombe here." He listened, then went still. "I see. All right, thank you. Keep us updated." He hung up.

"What is it?" Maddy asked, tension curling through her.

"They found another body on the island."

•••

The Chosen One laughed as he landed his plane back on Florida soil. It had been only a matter of hours before he'd located Quinn and Maddy and took off in his plane to return to Florida. He'd been on the phone with one of his business partners and they'd mentioned seeing the cop and his girlfriend checking in to the hotel. So, Maddy and Quinn had gone looking for him on his turf. How nice. Well, he certainly didn't want to disappoint them. He climbed out of the cockpit and headed to find the nearest drink and ask a few questions. It wouldn't be long before he'd know exactly where they were.

[18]

Quinn finished his lobster and leaned back in the chair, still thinking about Danvers's bombshell. "Another body," he said.

"Yes, I know."

His eyes traveled the restaurant, taking note of the faces of the patrons. He was antsy, itchy. Maddy's restlessness indicated she felt the same. "Do you want to go back to the island?" he asked. "Be a part of the investigation? After all, we're part of the task force—or we would be if we weren't staying under the radar."

She rolled her eyes. "We are so not under the radar. We might as well have flown in here with 'searching for a serial killer' stamped on the side of the plane for all the subtle we've been." She took a sip of her water and waved a hand. "Let's just wait to hear back from the sheriff about who the body is. As for the task force, I think taking a sabbatical was the wise thing to do."

"He said the body was buried well. One of the cadaver dogs found it."

"If he had the dogs out there, he was looking for more bodies."

"Yes. And he found one."

She absently scanned the pictures over the bar, and a familiar face below them caught her attention. "Is that Burt?"

"Who?"

"The ferry pilot." She nodded toward the bar. "The guy near the end of the bar."

Quinn turned to look. "Yeah, I think so." The man's eyes collided with his. Burt's gray head bobbed and he hesitated, then said something to the young man next to him. The younger man shrugged and turned back to nurse his drink. Burt glanced at the door, then stood and walked over.

He switched his beer bottle to his left hand so he could shake Quinn's hand with his right. "Surprised to see you folks back here. Figured you'd be home recovering from your terrible ordeal. How are you doing after all that?"

Quinn grimaced at the smell of alcohol on the man's breath, but didn't say anything. His blue eyes seemed clear enough.

"We're hanging in there," Maddy said. "Thanks."

"How'd you find this little hole in the wall? Not many visitors know about it."

"Sheriff Danvers recommended it," Quinn said.

"Oh yeah, it's a favorite of his, for sure. We eat out here three or four times a week." He aimed his bottle toward the back. "Bernard owns the place and the sheriff is real good about sending new business his way."

"I'm sure new business turns into repeat customers. My meal was outstanding," Quinn said.

"You know it." He glanced at the gold watch on his tanned arm. "So, you folks here to help find out who kidnapped you?"

Maddy drew in a breath and Quinn's shoulders tensed. "Something like that, but we'd appreciate it if you'd keep that quiet. We don't need the press getting wind of it."

"Sure, sure. If there's a crime on one of the islands, I'm

usually the one who carts the medical examiner out there. She don't fly, you know."

"I seem to remember hearing that," Maddy said.

Burt shrugged. "I can keep my mouth shut. Better for business that way. Sheriff appreciates it too."

"Thanks, Burt."

"You bet. Well, I got to go. I got a ferry to pick up."

Quinn lifted a brow. "Hope you're going to sober up first."

Burt laughed. "I'm not drunk. This is the only one I've had. I'm fine. Hey, you ever need a ride to any of the islands, give me a call." He pulled a tattered card from his pocket and handed it to Maddy.

"Thanks," she said. "We'll keep that in mind."

"Glad to see you folks are doing well." He shot Quinn a thin smile. "Still trying to figure out who I am, aren't you?"

Quinn leaned back. "Yes. Want to help me out?"

"I think I'll let you stew on it." He waved to someone behind the counter, then headed out the door. The young man he'd been with followed him, with a long sideways look at Quinn and Maddy.

"Interesting character," Quinn said as he watched the two go.

"How old do you think he is?" Maddy asked. "The older guy, I mean."

Quinn shrugged. "I don't know. Could be anywhere between forty and sixty." He pursed his lips. "He knows me from somewhere. And I have to admit, he looks familiar."

"But you don't know him."

"Apparently I'm supposed to, but . . ."

"Quit thinking about it. It'll come to you."

"Hmm. Maybe . . ." He let his gaze linger on the door until it was firmly shut. "I wonder who the younger fellow was."

She shrugged and picked up her glass. "So . . . ," she said.

"So . . . ," Quinn mimicked.

"Who do you think the body could be?"

"It could be anyone. There's no sense in speculating."

"Maybe the killer's partner who suddenly got a conscience?"

"Maddy . . ."

She waved a hand. "I know. I shouldn't do that to myself, but I really want to know."

"Why?"

"Because if there's another body, that means there's another number. And if that's the case, our entire theory about the numbers matching up with the bodies is completely wrong."

He grimaced. "Good point. Maybe." He took a sip of his drink and waited until the waitress cleared the plates from the table before he leaned forward. "I don't think we're wrong."

"I don't either, but I can't think who else he could have killed."

"Maybe he didn't."

She blinked. "Huh?"

"Maybe that body doesn't have a thing to do with the guy who killed the others. Maybe he didn't even know it was buried there."

She massaged her temples, then looked him in the eye. "You're right."

"What?"

"There's no sense in wasting brain power on this when we have nothing to go on. We need to wait for Sheriff Danvers to get an ID on the body and take it from there."

"Exactly. You want dessert?"

She groaned. "No, I'm stuffed. Thanks." She reached for her purse.

"I've got it."

"I can pay for mine. Katie even loaded me down with cash so we don't leave a credit card trail." She took a sip of water.

"I've got dinner. You can buy me breakfast."

She nearly choked on her water. "Breakfast is free at the hotel, you goon."

He shot her a smile and laid four twenties on the table. "Well, let's continue this as we walk over to talk to Brad Gorman. I'm ready to see what he has to say."

She nodded.

"Then we can go swimming."

"Swimming?"

He nodded "In the hotel pool."

"Why?"

"Why not?"

She scowled. "Last time you recommended a swim, I nearly fell into a spear pit and you pulled my shoulder out of the socket." She absently brought a hand up to massage the sore area.

"Hey," he protested. "I fixed your shoulder."

She glared at him, but he could see the mirth underneath the fierce look. "You cheated. You told me to count to three."

He shook his head and slid out of the booth. "I'm not going to hear the end of that, am I?"

"Nope."

As they walked from the restaurant to the building that sported the sign KEY WEST TRANSPORT AND FERRY SERVICE, Maddy relished the closeness she felt with Quinn. She savored it, completely let herself enjoy it, because she just had a feeling it was fleeting.

She also appreciated the fact that she could verbally spar with him. It helped put everything in perspective. If anyone else dared to joke about what had happened to them on the island, she'd probably punch them. But with Quinn, she could do that. Strangely enough, it actually helped lessen the terror. Slightly.

They stepped into the building and Maddy glanced around. Fishing tackle, Key West souvenirs, a picture-covered wall, snacks, and a drink machine were the highlights. Simple and efficient.

"Help you folks?"

Quinn walked to the counter. "I'm Quinn Holcombe. This is Maddy McKay. We were told we could find Brad Gorman here."

"Yeah. I'm Nathan, we spoke on the phone."

Quinn held out a hand and Nathan hesitated, then shook it. Maddy smiled and nodded.

"Brad should be back anytime," Nathan said. "He's been ferrying back and forth out to Hoskins Island for a birthday party. I think he's on his last leg back now."

"Thanks."

Nathan gestured toward the chairs lining the wall. Seats for guests waiting on a boat, Maddy supposed. At the moment, they were empty. "Feel free to wait," he said. "I'll let Brad know you're here." He disappeared into the back.

Maddy walked over to the wall covered in pictures. "Hey, Quinn, come here."

"What is it?" He stepped up behind her and she could feel his body heat warming her back.

She cleared her throat. "See anyone that looks familiar?"

"That's Ashley Gorman," he said.

"In every single picture with a lot of different men." Nothing too suggestive, but some of the pictures could be questionable. "So, if that was your wife in those pictures, would you be real happy with her?"

Quinn stepped closer and gave a grunt. "No, I'd be having a little chat with her, that's for sure." He continued his surveillance of the wall. "It's a tribute to her, a memorial."

"Brad and Nathan are there, as well as Leonard Nance. I would expect to see Brad, but that's Nathan driving the boat, with Ashley in the passenger seat there."

"So at some point in the past, Brad worked for Leonard too. Look." She pointed to the picture that displayed the front of the building. "I can't read the sign on it, but it's not this place. All of these pictures are taken at a different marina."

"Sarasota," Quinn said. "That's where they lived before Ashley died. Her father, Leonard Nance, owned the marina, and Ashley worked there during her summers and then again during her college years when she was home." He paced in front of the wall, his brow furrowed. "So, Brad and Nathan knew each other before moving to Key West." He pointed to a heavyset young man. "See that guy there? That's Ashley's brother, Jacob Nance. I remember him from the trial." He rubbed his chin. "They were in business together in Sarasota. So when Ashley was killed, chances are good that they all simply packed up and moved here."

"But why?"

"Probably the media. Maybe the memories were just too much."

"So where's Leonard these days?"

"Good question. Bree said it was taking longer to find information on the Nances because of the name change."

She continued to study the pictures. "Looks awesome, doesn't it? I mean, I would imagine that would be a paradise on earth for a teen. Living on the boats and water all summer."

"Looks like the adults didn't mind it so much either. Brad must still enjoy it."

"Well, who wouldn't? I'm ready to sign up as a volunteer. But why would Burt let Brad put up this memorial to Ashley?"

"Next time we see him, let's ask." Quinn continued to stare

at the pictures, then let out a low sigh. "Looks like an ideal life, doesn't it?"

"The perfect one, from all appearances." Maddy said. "And then Ashley went off to school in South Carolina," she murmured.

"Went off to school and didn't come home," a voice said from behind them.

Maddy turned to see a young man in his early thirties. He wore a muscle shirt that emphasized his strong arms and an almost perfect physique. She winced. And she thought she was in good shape. "Brad?"

"Yeah." He wiped his hands on a rag and laid it on the counter. He had a duffle bag over his left shoulder and he let it slide to the floor with a thud. "What do you people want?"

"I'm Maddy McKay and this is Quinn Holcombe."

"I know who you are. Saw the story on the news. I'm surprised you'd come back here after the awful experience you had on the island."

"We had some unfinished business to take care of," Quinn said.

Brad motioned them toward the chairs. "Unfinished business like arresting guilty people, then letting them go?" He dropped into the nearest one, and when his eyes locked on her and Quinn, Maddy shuddered at the hate in them. Then he blinked and it was gone.

"Just an FYI," Quinn said, "I didn't let him go. At least not without orders from the higher-ups."

"You arrested him too soon, didn't have the evidence you needed to keep him. That's sloppy police work, Detective."

Quinn sighed and Maddy felt sorry for him. There was always more to the story than the victim's loved one knew, but it didn't stop them from feeling justified in casting blame. "Look," Quinn said, "I did my job, but I'm not here to debate that. Someone tried to kill us. Was it you?"

Maddy blinked at the direct question. Quinn had obviously opted for the blunt approach.

Brad let out a sharp laugh. "What? Are you serious? You think I was the one who kidnapped you and took you out to the island?" He shook his head. "Why would I do that?"

"Revenge. After all, I let a guilty killer go and his last victim was your wife."

Brad nodded, then looked at the wall. "No, it wasn't me, but if I ever meet the guy who did, I'll want to shake his hand." He sneered, then shook his head. "I've already answered all the questions the FBI and Sheriff Danvers threw at me. And I'll answer yours if you want, but you're barking up the wrong tree."

Quinn gave a slow nod. "What are you doing working here? Thought you were some kind of video game programmer working with Ashley's brother."

Brad shrugged. "I do both. I like the water and I like boats. This lets me be around both. And Burt needs my help when there's a particularly busy week or something. So it works out."

Maddy looked at the wall of pictures. "Ashley liked it too."

"Yes."

"Looks like she liked a lot of things," Quinn said.

Brad narrowed his eyes. "What do you mean by that?"

"Was she cheating on you?"

Brad stood, the burning hate back in his eyes. Maddy slid her hand over her weapon in a subtle move. "No, she wasn't cheating on me. We're done here." He walked away without another word or a backward glance.

She let her hand fall away. "Smooth, Quinn, real smooth."

"Come on, Maddy, you know as well as I do that taking the

blunt approach sometimes makes people angry enough to say things they later regret . . . but we find very helpful."

"I know. I'm just not sure it was the right approach with him."

Quinn shrugged. "It gave me some information."

"What's that?"

"I'm going to go with my gut and say he's not behind all this. Then again, I could be wrong."

"Well, if you're wrong, I am too. I got the same feeling."

"Our killer is smart. He's used to playing things close to the vest. Brad didn't make any effort to hide his hatred. He's not a subtle guy. I guess I don't see him as the killer."

"Unless he's just playing us. He's sure got enough anger to power him through." She paused. "And he's sure got the muscles for it."

He looked down at her and frowned. "What?"

"Just saying he looks strong enough to cart you over his shoulder once you were knocked unconscious, without any help at all."

Quinn's frown deepened. "You think?"

"Yeah. I think."

He lifted an arm. "I've got muscles. I've never caught you noticing *my* muscles."

Maddy gave a low laugh. "Trust me, Quinn, I've noticed." And she had.

"Really?" He straightened and puffed his chest out a bit. A giggle slipped from her. She just couldn't help it. He looked so pleased. Then he grabbed her hand and pulled her toward the door. "Come on."

"Where are we going?"

"Swimming at the hotel."

"What, now? Why?"

"So I can show off my muscles."

Maddy laughed. Truly laughed for the first time in a very long time.

She was still smiling ten minutes later when Quinn pulled into the hotel parking lot. They walked into the hotel together and came to a stop when they spotted Sheriff Danvers sitting in the lobby.

Maddy's smile slid into a frown. "Hello, Sheriff, is something wrong?"

"No, just have some more information I thought I'd share with you."

She and Quinn exchanged a glance. "About the other body you found?" Quinn asked.

"No." The sheriff waved a hand. "They're still working on him. It'll be a while until we know anything about that one. And I say 'him' but don't know that for a fact. Could be a woman, for all I know."

"Let's go up to my room and you can fill us in," Quinn said.

The sheriff snagged an apple from the check-in desk and motioned toward the elevator.

Once in Quinn's room, they sat around the table and the sheriff pulled out his iPad. He swiped the screen. "That hair that was found at the house. It was long and gray."

Maddy straightened. "Burt has long gray hair. Could he have something to do with this?"

Danvers laughed. "Who? Burt? No way. At least he wouldn't have been my first pick." He frowned. "I mean, I'll have the lab check it against his, but he's not the only long-haired gray dude around town. We've got plenty. Especially some of the homeless."

"No homeless person put this together. The person who's behind all this has resources and money at his disposal." Quinn frowned and Maddy knew her expression matched his. "So, what does that hair tell us?"

Danvers sighed. "Nothing really, but it was a development, so thought I'd share it. We're still interviewing people on the other islands about what they might have seen, but so far they haven't been terribly helpful."

Maddy groaned. "Great."

He raised a finger. "However, there is something that caught my attention."

"What's that?" Quinn said.

"When I questioned one of the residents of the island nearest to Hogan's, she said she saw Burt on his boat heading for the island. Said she saw him pull into the boathouse, but that was it."

"And she didn't find that odd for Burt to be pulling his boat into a boathouse of an unoccupied island?" Maddy asked.

"No, she said she figured he was just doing an errand for someone, but the only reason she noticed him is because he buzzed right by her dock. She waved and he waved back." He shrugged. "The neighbors—if you can call them that, spread out like they are—know that this island is in probate and that the Hogan family hired someone to take care of it. Seeing activity over there wouldn't set off any real alarms."

"Okay," Maddy said, "then you need to ask Burt about why he was over here just a couple of weeks ago when I think I remember him saying he hadn't been on the island for at least a couple of years."

"I've got that on my to-do list, trust me."

"We just saw him tonight, you know," Maddy murmured.

"At the restaurant?"

"Yes."

The sheriff nodded. "He's a regular. He's in there just about every day since it's right there next to his business."

"Seems like a harmless fellow," Quinn said, "but then some

LYNETTE EASON

of the most dangerous men on earth come across that way. I've arrested some of them."

"I know what you mean," the sheriff said. He tapped a text and then set his phone aside. "I've got a deputy tracking Burt down now. We'll bring him in and see what he's got to say for himself." The sheriff stood. "In the meantime, I know you're trying to lay low. Unfortunately, Burt knows you're here now." He sighed. "He wasn't on my radar when I sent you out to the Flying Fish Restaurant." He pursed his lips and shook his head. "Truthfully, I can't imagine Burt having anything to do with any of this serial killer business. He's had a rough time of it, sure, drinks a little now and then, but I've known him about six years and he's been nothing but helpful, knows how to keep his mouth shut, and dotes on his wife and son." He shrugged. "But you need to watch your backs now that he's aware of your presence here. We don't need to take any chances."

"Well, Brad Gorman and the other worker, Nathan Truett, know we're here too, so we're not exactly off the grid anymore anyway. We had a little chat with Brad."

The sheriff paused. "Did you get anything more out of him?"

"Just that he hates me," Quinn murmured. "He definitely blames me for his wife's death."

"Yeah. He does. He's never hidden that. Her entire family blames you, actually."

"Right," Quinn said softly.

"Don't let it get you down. It's not your fault and you know it. Sometimes it's just the way the system works—or doesn't. I'll let you know what comes back on the hair."

"Thanks." Quinn paused. "Hey, who is Burt anyway?"

"What do you mean?"

"He just looks so familiar and I can't place him. When I

211

asked him about it, he said he'd let me stew on it. And then we saw all these picture with Leonard, Nathan, and Brad that were from Sarasota. Just seems odd they all moved here, and Brad and Nathan work at a marina business that Burt owns. What's the connection there? Can you shed any light?"

The sheriff blinked. "I thought you knew and that's why you're so interested in investigating him."

"Knew what?"

Danvers leaned back, looking slightly stunned. "You really don't know."

"Know what?" Maddy almost yelled.

"He and his family used to live in Sarasota, but a little over six years ago, they legally changed their names and moved down here to Key West—"

"What's his full name?" Quinn's eyes shot daggers.

"Burt Tabor is Leonard Nance."

Maddy drew in a shocked breath. "Robert Tabor! Ashley Gorman's *father*?"

"Yes. I'm sorry. It never occurred to me that you didn't know who he was."

"How were we to know?" Quinn asked. "He changed his name, his appearance, everything."

"Like I said, I'm sorry I made that assumption." The sheriff shook his head. "The media wouldn't leave them alone. If you ask the people in Sarasota what happened to them, they just shake their heads and whisper about the Witness Protection program. Truth is, they just wanted to get away from the memories that haunted them. So, they—and their son's best friend, Nathan, who didn't change his name—moved down here, opened up the transport business, and have lived quiet, unassuming lives—for the most part." He sighed. "Burt spilled the story one night when I found him passed out behind the

Flying Fish." He looked at Quinn, then Maddy. "Now you know."

"Yes, now we know," Maddy said. "Don't assume anything else, okay?"

"Okay."

Sheriff Danvers left after his shocking revelation, and Maddy let her shoulders slump. "Wow."

"No kidding." He paced from one end of the room to the other. "None of this is a coincidence. I feel like a puppet in a performance."

"I agree. Someone's setting everything up quite nicely." She walked to his refrigerator and snagged a bottle of water. After sipping on it in silence for a moment, she capped it. "Okay, I know what the sheriff thinks about Robert, but I doubt he's exactly objective. You think he had something to do with kidnapping us and killing eight, possibly nine, people?"

Quinn frowned. "If you'd asked me that thirty minutes ago, I would have said that I have no idea and I'm not speculating."

"Yeah, I seem to remember you don't like speculation."

"Who'd you hear that from?"

"Katie, I think. Or maybe it was Daniel."

He shot her a smirk, then sobered. "But *now* . . ."

"Yeah, knowing he's Ashley's father puts a whole new light on things, doesn't it?"

His phone rang and he glanced at it. His brows rose. "My mom. My mother never calls me and then all of a sudden she's started calling like once a week." It rang again and he looked at her. "Why would she be calling?"

"Um . . . maybe if you answer, you'll find out."

"What if it's bad news?"

She sighed and stabbed the screen with her index finger. "Ask her."

Quinn shot her a panicked look, then swallowed and held the device to his ear. "Hi, Mom."

·····································

Maddy was almost ashamed of herself, but Quinn really needed to work on things with his family. *Just like you do?*

She winced. Yes, just like she did. She and Quinn both had family issues they needed to resolve, and she had no business judging him—or forcing him to act to resolve his issues when she wasn't willing to do the same.

She grimaced. She owed him an apology.

Until then, she had some investigating to do. She headed for the connecting door that led to her room.

"Uh, where do you think you're going?"

She turned to find him still seated at the small table. He was off the phone and looking at her with eyes she couldn't read. "That was a quick conversation," she said. "How is she?"

"She's fine."

"Was it bad news?"

"No. She just wanted an update on the school situation. Since I have no new information, there wasn't a whole lot I could tell her."

"Was she calling for that or because she wanted to . . . put out feelers?"

He frowned. "What do you mean?"

She sighed. "Quinn, you're so aloof with your family—with everyone, really. But when one of your family reaches out to you, you should welcome it with open arms."

He sighed and pressed his fingers to his eyes. "I know."

"So why do you shut them down as fast as you can?"

"Because there are . . . circumstances, things that have happened that you don't know about."

"Oh. Things that have to do with your sister's death?"

His head snapped up. "You've been snooping?"

"What?" She crossed her arms and stared at him. "No! Really?" She planted her hands on her hips. "Have you forgotten what I used to do for a living? I'm pretty good at reading between the lines and figuring things out." She paused. "When it comes to other people and their problems, anyway. You already told me she committed suicide."

His shoulders slumped. "Sorry."

"Come on, Quinn. You know what happened with me and my family. I keep my distance from my parents and some of my cop brothers and sisters, but at least we talk. My mom believes in me. She knows I'd never do what I've been accused of doing, but with my dad . . . it's hard." She walked over to slump on the couch again. "This latest almost-dying thing has had my brain spinning in more ways than one."

"Like what?"

"Like I want peace. With my family, my father, the FBI, everyone I worked with. I'm tired of walking under the cloud that seems to follow me everywhere."

"You want to clear your name."

"If that's what it takes."

"Then let's do it. Who do you have working on the inside for you?"

"Quinn, I'm not talking about me right now. We were talking about you. Don't try to change the subject. Even when you were in the hospital for so long after your legs were hurt, your family came to see you. You pushed them out the door as fast as you could. What I'm getting at is, don't you want peace with your family?"

He continued that weird stare. Then he blinked. "Yes, of course. I just don't know that it's possible to achieve that."

She bit her lip, then closed her eyes for a moment. Finally, she opened them and walked over to him to place a hand on his shoulder. "I don't know either. I'm sorry for forcing you to talk to your mother. That was an impulse move on my part and it was wrong. But as for me, I sure want to try to get things resolved with my family—and if you do too, that means we're going to have to reach out. Both of us."

He looked down at his clasped hands and was silent. She'd give her right arm to know what he was thinking. He finally looked up. "I don't know if I can. I don't know if they can ever forgive me," he whispered.

She knelt in front of him. "Why? Forgive you for what?"

"For being the reason Stacy killed herself."

[19]

For a moment she didn't move, didn't blink. Quinn wondered if she'd even stopped breathing. It felt like at least a full minute passed before she wrapped her hands around his. "Tell me."

He let out a long sigh and wondered if he could even get through the recounting of it. He'd never told a soul what had really happened to his sister. "Stacy's husband, Reggie, was an accountant. A very successful one. He had a lot of big-name accounts and raked in an impressive salary. They were living the good life and then started their family after they bought their dream home. A six-thousand-square-foot mansion on a hill in one of the most prestigious neighborhoods in Columbia."

"Sounds lovely."

He cleared his throat. "Yes, it was. My parents were so proud. Appearances are important to them, you know."

"I didn't know that."

"Yeah. Mom grew up in a middle-class family, but Dad grew up on the streets of Columbia, scratching and fighting for every bite of food he put in his mouth."

"Oh, Quinn, how awful, I'm sorry," she breathed.

He shrugged. "It's okay, he's proud of what he's done, how he put himself through college and graduated from engineering school at the top of his class. I grew up hearing that story over and over and over." He pulled away from her and punched a fist into his palm. "Dad was always stressing how you work hard for whatever you get, you don't take handouts, however, you give to those less fortunate. And you don't ever steal something that isn't yours. Ever. Stealing, in his eyes, was about as low as a person could go. Second only to murder."

"Sounds like a man of integrity."

He grunted. "Yes. But also one of great pride. Pride in his family, pride in his accomplishments."

"Too much pride?" Maddy asked softly.

"Probably."

"How'd he feel about you going into law enforcement?"

"He was proud of that too. Especially when I made detective. Bragging rights, you know?"

"I'm sure."

"And then Reggie's boss came to me with a flash drive. He told me to take a look at it and get back to him." He pressed his thumb and forefinger to the bridge of his nose for a brief second, then dropped his hand. "I asked him what it was and all he would say was that I needed to look at the material on it and tell him what to do." He drew in a deep breath. "So I did."

"And?"

"Basically, Reggie had been keeping two sets of books." He snorted. "Just like something in a stupid movie. I compared them and it was obvious what he'd done. I called Reggie to come in and told him to explain himself." Quinn shook his head. "He didn't even try to deny it. He just broke down and started crying. Begged me to say nothing and to let him fix it. He promised to give the money back and no one would ever have to know. For Stacy's sake, he said. Think of the kids, he pleaded."

"What did you do?"

"I told him fine. Give the money back. He was to make sure every cent was returned to the rightful owners and he was to bring me the proof. Deposits, records, whatever. And I gave him a week to get it all done."

"You were going to give him a second chance?"

He looked away, then shook his head again. "I truly don't know what I planned to do. I was struggling. If I turned him in, my sister and her kids' lives would never be the same. Then again, could I look the other way when he'd committed a crime? No. I couldn't. So there you go."

"Yeah," she said softly. "That was a tough position to be in."

"However, if he'd followed through with it and returned the money and no one knew any better, his boss said the worst he would do would be to let him resign quietly and give him a two-months' salary severance package."

"Whoa, that's pretty generous when Reggie's actions could have destroyed the man's company."

Quinn gave her a smile he was sure didn't reach his eyes. "Well, appearances mean a lot to more people than just my parents. It wouldn't reflect well on the accounting firm for one of their own to be caught embezzling and arrested, now would it?"

"Of course not."

"So, he didn't want it public, but he couldn't keep Reggie on either. He couldn't trust him after that."

"How long had Reggie been embezzling?"

Quinn pressed the heels of his palms to his eyes. He needed sleep, but for some reason telling the story, *finally telling* this story, felt good. And he needed to finish it. "About a year," he finally said and looked at her. "He'd managed to siphon off about half a million dollars without anyone noticing."

"That's . . . insane."

He shrugged. "Anyway, while I was agonizing over what to do if Reggie didn't follow through with everything he was supposed to do to redeem himself, someone cut the brake line on my car."

Maddy sucked in a startled breath and her eyes went wide. "What?"

He nodded. "Three days after I confronted Reggie, I was driving home from work, lost control, and crashed into a tree. I was banged up pretty good, but walked away from the wreck."

"And you had the brake line inspected, of course."

"Yes. It had definitely been cut. But the clincher was when I had the line dusted for prints and a partial came back as a match to Reggie."

"He didn't even bother to wear gloves," she said.

"Nope. There was also footage from a neighbor's security camera of him under my car when I was visiting earlier in the day. He cut the line while I was inside the house celebrating my nephew's first birthday."

"Quinn . . ." She reached for his hand again and held on. Anchoring him.

He heard the agony in her voice, the hurt for him, but he was lost in the memories, his gaze on the floor. He couldn't let her distract him or he'd never be able to finish. "I waited for him to go in to work the next day and then went and arrested him in front of his co-workers for attempted murder."

She sucked in a breath. "Oh wow. I'm so sorry."

"I was furious. Hurt. I don't even remember how I was able to hold it together. I can't really describe what happened at that point. Emotionally, I mean. I just went . . . cold. Numb."

"I think that's understandable."

"But not excusable. My sister—" His voice cracked and he looked away. The memory of the betrayal in her eyes, her shock and disbelief, cut him. "My sister didn't handle it well. She'd suffered from depression as a teenager after her best friend was killed in a car accident. But after she met Reggie in college, she seemed to do better. He treated her like a queen and that made her happy."

"She didn't know what he was doing."

"No, no one did. So after I arrested Reggie, she stood by him. She refused to talk to me, to look at me, to even acknowledge my presence. If I walked into the room, she would leave. If I blocked the door, she'd turn her back on me."

Her fingers tightened on his and he felt tears crowd the back of his eyes. He swallowed. He hadn't cried at Stacy's funeral, he sure wasn't going to cry now. "And then at the trial, when everything came out, the evidence about the cut brake line, the embezzlement, Stacy turned into a zombie. She couldn't take care of her kids, she couldn't . . . function. I went to see her, to apologize for arresting Reggie like I had." He held up a hand. "Not for arresting him, but for doing it so publicly. I—" He cleared his throat. "I actually got on my knees and begged her to get some help and she just stared through me." Maddy's hands tightened around his, but she didn't make a sound. "As I started to leave, she finally spoke. She said, 'He really tried to kill you, didn't he?' I just nodded and then she nodded. She went to a bag that had been hanging on the back of one of the kitchen chairs and pulled out a Yankees baseball cap."

"The one you lost on the island?"

"Yes. And she placed it on my head and said, 'Reggie and I had a fun trip. I told Reggie I had to get you that hat. It looks good on you.'" He gave a short laugh. "I've pulled for the Yankees ever since my grandfather took me to see them play in New

York when I was eight years old. He bought me a cap at that game and I wore it for years until it finally fell apart. Stacy knew how much I missed that hat. She remembered and thought of me and—" He shrugged, unable to finish the thought.

"Quinn . . ."

He focused in on her and saw tears coursing down her cheeks. He raised a hand and thumbed them away. "Don't cry for me."

"I can't help it." She sniffed.

He sighed. "I was walking out the door when I heard the gunshot."

Maddy gasped. "Oh no," she whispered. "Please tell me she didn't . . . not with you right there . . ."

"She did. Right in the head. I ran back inside and . . . she was . . . just there . . . lying on her left . . . side . . ." His breath hitched. "Bleeding . . . the back of her head was gone, blood and . . . her brain . . . all over . . ." A sob escaped. And another. And then he was on the floor and her arms were around him, hugging him fiercely, while he cried into the side of her neck. "I killed her," he gasped. "I did. It's my fault."

Maddy wasn't sure how long she sat on the floor holding Quinn and she wasn't sure how long until his gasping sobs faded. She didn't care. She'd stay put with her aching shoulder and her now throbbing leg for as long as he needed her to. Her shattered heart beat in agony with his. She now understood so much more about this intensely private man. The amount of hurt he'd been carrying around was incomprehensible.

Still seated on the floor, Quinn pulled from her arms and leaned forward to press the heels of his palms against his eyes and sigh. "Sorry."

"For what?"

"That."

She shrugged. "You needed that."

"It's embarrassing."

"Okay, then it never happened."

He gave a choked laugh and turned to wrap his arms around her waist and bury his face in her neck. Then he pushed away from her to stand. He held out a hand and she grasped it. He pulled her to her feet and gave her a gentle push toward her room. "I can't do this."

"What?"

"I . . . I need to be alone right now. I'm going to take a shower and just chill. I'll see you in the morning."

She frowned. "I thought you wanted to go swimming."

"No. I . . . not now."

"Quinn—"

His face went blank. "I'll see you in the morning, okay?"

So that was that. "All right." She raised a hand, then dropped it. There was no reasoning with him when he was like this. "Fine. A shower sounds good. See you in the morning."

Once back in her own room, Maddy shut the connecting door and stood for a minute staring at nothing while her brain tried to process what had just happened. He'd cried in her arms like his heart had been shattered, then had turned around and effectively shut her out.

She got it.

He'd admitted being embarrassed about his little breakdown, but she didn't think any less of him. If anything, it had drawn her heart toward him, connected her even more fully to him.

And therein lay a huge problem.

She was so emotionally entwined with him at this point that she was going to have to go with her original plan to disconnect herself, distance herself from him, before she was an emotional wreck.

Only how could she do that when they were spending every single minute together because there was a killer after them?

Forget the shower, she needed a glass of ice water. She grabbed the ice bucket, stuffed her key card into the back pocket of her khaki shorts, and stepped into the hall. Maddy followed the sign to the snack area and found the ice machine. She sighed. Looked like she was going to be spending the evening working or watching television. She turned to leave.

And the lights went out.

Maddy went still and waited for the generator to kick in. When that didn't happen, she took a deep breath. Could it possibly be a coincidence that there was a power failure at the hotel where she and Quinn had rooms?

She was going to go with a *no* on that one.

Maddy set the ice bucket on the floor and drew her weapon. She moved to the opening and glanced down the hallway. Lights from the parking lot filtered in through the windows at the end of the hallway, but it wasn't much help. And while she saw nothing alarming, that didn't mean the coast was clear.

She hesitated to step out into the open, but she needed to get to Quinn. And while she'd brought her weapon, she'd left her phone in the room.

Then the doors started opening. People, dressed in robes and sweats, jeans and T-shirts, stood in their open doors and threw questions to one another. They also had their flashlight apps working and the hallway immediately brightened. Maddy holstered her weapon but kept her hand on it as she slipped from the snack room and walked toward Quinn's door.

As she approached his room, something pressed against the small of her back. She stiffened and started to turn.

"Just keep walking," a gravelly voice said in her left ear.

Maddy stumbled. His left hand came across his body to grip her left elbow. She winced as pain shot through her shoulder. Then focused on the pressure in her back. "Let go of the gun unless you want one of these innocents loitering in the hall to die."

Maddy let her hand slide from the weapon. "How did you know we were here? I thought we'd left you behind in South Carolina."

"Word gets around. Although truthfully, I thought it would be a bit more difficult to get to you than this. My intention with the blackout was to simply figure out which room you were in. What luck to find you in the hall of the first floor I tried."

"Glad I could make it so easy," she said through gritted teeth.

"Or maybe it's not luck. Maybe it's just divine help in fulfilling my destiny." He shoved her and she continued her trek down the hall, passing a number of hotel guests. All she could think of was that he had help. Someone had seen them and called him and told him where they were. But who? The only person who came to mind was the ferryboat guy. Robert. Or someone in the sheriff's office? Or Ashley's husband?

"Where are we going?" she asked.

"Just keep walking toward the exit sign at the end of the hallway."

He was taking her to the stairs. She passed Quinn's room and kept going, her mind racing, trying to figure out how to handle this new threat without getting anyone hurt or killed. Including herself. She continued to look at him from the corner of her eye. Red hair? Ball cap shadowing his features, five o'clock shadow. A long scar that ran from his temple to the bottom of his chin. "Is that a gun I feel in my back?" she asked. "I thought you were more of a crossbow kind of guy." She was proud of the steady calmness in her voice.

He actually chuckled under his breath as they arrived at the door with the exit sign just above. "Open the door and go down."

She pushed the door open and walked to the first step that would lead down to the third floor. She took a step, then pretended to trip. "Ow!" She grabbed the rail with her right hand, as though catching her balance.

He cursed. "You stupid—"

The pressure of the gun was gone and Maddy had the advantage she was hoping for. She leaned forward and, still gripping the rail, stepped down with her left foot, then twisted her lower body right while lifting her right foot. She kicked out, catching him in the stomach. He gasped and went to one knee. The gun tumbled from his fingers and fell through the railing. She had no idea where it would land and didn't have the time to worry about it.

In the stairwell, he was just a shadow, but Maddy aimed another kick at his face. He ducked, caught her foot, and shoved. With her just below him, gravity worked in his favor. This time, there was no pretending. She toppled backward, trying to catch her balance as she stumbled on the steps, her hand slipping from the rail. Maddy grabbed for it, caught it with her left hand, then went to her knee. She wrenched her sore shoulder and pain shot through her. "Ah!"

The door opened.

" . . . get a snack and wait this out, okay?" a deep voice said. A flashlight whipped across her face. "Hey, are you okay? What's going on?"

In the now illuminated stairwell, her attacker, caught between the man and Maddy, hesitated, glared at her, then shoved past the newcomer, causing him to drop his phone. "Hey!"

And up he went, headed for the fifth floor of the eight-story hotel. Maddy blinked against the pain and pushed herself to her feet.

She started up after him but turned to look over her shoulder. "Go to room 419 and tell the police detective in there that Maddy needs help and where I am. Hurry!"

He grabbed his phone and took off.

She went up, not sure if the stranger would follow her directions or not, but one thing was certain—she wasn't losing the guy who'd just tried to kidnap her for the second time.

[20]

Quinn knocked on the adjoining door for the third time since the lights went out. Again, Maddy didn't answer. The first time, he'd assumed she was taking the shower she'd said she wanted. He'd waited a few more minutes and knocked again. Then again. Now he was getting worried. "Come on, Maddy. Answer the door. I'm sorry! Let's go swimming!"

He frowned. That wasn't like her. To ignore him. He grabbed the spare key she'd given him for safety reasons and walked out in the hallway to open her door. "Maddy?" He peered in and didn't see her. Listened. The shower wasn't running. He checked just to be sure, calling her name so as not to scare her. She wasn't in the room. But her phone was. He picked it up off the bed, opened the adjoining door, and stepped back into his room. Then had a thought. He looked back at the small kitchen area. The ice bucket was missing. Relief flooded him. She was probably getting ice.

A knock on his room door spun him around. He walked over to it and looked out the peephole, but could see only a shadow of a man standing there. "Who is it?"

"Um . . . yeah. Someone named Maddy told me to come to this room and tell you that she needs your help."

Knowing it could be a trap, Quinn pulled his weapon from his shoulder holster and yanked the door open a crack, using it to shield himself. He peered around it. Thanks to the light coming in the end window, he could see a little more of his visitor. "Where is she?"

"I think something happened in the stairwell." He pointed. "There was a guy. It looked like he pushed her, but she caught herself about the time I opened the door."

Still aware it could be a trap of some kind, Quinn stepped into the hallway, holding his gun slightly behind him. "Which one?"

The man pointed. "The guy ran up and she followed him while she was yelling at me to come get you."

He couldn't take any chances. "Call 911 and tell the dispatcher Quinn Holcombe is requesting backup from Sheriff Danvers, got it?"

"Quinn Holcombe. Sheriff Danvers. Got it." The man was already tapping his screen. Quinn raced down the hall toward the exit, pushed open the door carefully, and scanned the interior as best he could in the limited light. When he didn't detect any immediate danger, he bolted up the stairs. He thought he heard footsteps, but didn't know if it was a guest or Maddy and the man after them.

"Maddy?" he called.

"Up here!"

He followed the sound of the pounding feet. Heard a door open, then close. Then open. "Going to the roof!" The door shut again. Quinn gritted his teeth and took the stairs two at a time.

He burst through the roof door and ducked low just in case

someone decided to start shooting. Bolts or bullets, he didn't care to be hit by either. "Where are you?" he called.

"Fire escape!"

He followed after her, heart pounding the blood through his veins. He rounded the air-conditioning unit just in time to see the figure Maddy was chasing jump off the roof.

And then saw Maddy follow. "Maddy!"

Quinn put on an extra burst of speed and came to the edge. His heart rate slowed slightly when he spotted the two going down the fire escape of the attached building. He jumped the three feet to the next building and grasped the wrought iron railing. By the time he was halfway down, the man in the baseball cap was on the sidewalk and racing for the street.

Maddy was right behind, but limping as she ran. She held her left arm tucked against her side. Quinn was amazed she'd made it this far. The sirens' wail registered, drawing closer. His friend from the hallway must have done his job.

Quinn pounded after Maddy and caught up with her. "I've got him."

"But I want him."

"Call in our location." Quinn snapped the phone into her hand and sped past her, confident she'd keep coming as long as she could. On the street, he saw the man dart around the corner of a store. Quinn bolted after him, rounded the corner. And skidded to a stop. The empty alleyway glared at him. He spun in a circle. No sign of the guy.

"Where did he go?" Maddy leaned over and tucked her sore arm under her once again. Her breaths came in short pants.

"I don't know. In the back of one of these buildings." He hurried to the door of the first building while Maddy went to the one on the opposite side.

She turned. "Locked."

"Open." Quinn stepped inside and found himself in the kitchen of a restaurant. He went to the nearest person. "Hey, did a guy just come through here?"

The fellow shrugged. "I don't know. I just walked in here."

Quinn groaned and turned to the next person. "You?"

"Yeah. He went out the front." The man turned to the others in the kitchen. "Whoever didn't lock that back door, you're fired!"

Quinn and Maddy didn't waste any more time. They bolted for the front entrance. Once outside, Quinn stopped again when he found himself in the middle of a bustling crowd of movie-goers who'd just exited the theater.

Quinn wanted to slam his other hand into the building. He resisted. "He's gone. We'll never find him in this."

"I hear the sirens," she said.

"Yes."

"Let's get back to the hotel and let Sheriff Danvers know what's going on." She sucked in another breath. "If he wants to kill you first, why does he keep coming after me?"

Quinn raised a brow. "Good question." His phone rang and he glanced at the screen. "It's Bree."

"Go ahead. I'm going to report in where we lost him." She got on her phone and Quinn turned his attention to his partner.

"Hey, Bree, what's up?"

"Hey, you sound a little winded. You okay?"

"Just fine. What do you need?" He'd tell her about this adventure later.

"I've been a busy bee doing background checks on all of the agents Maddy used to work with. The ones in the picture, anyway."

"Good. And?"

"No one's ringing a bell."

"No one?"

"Don't get me wrong. There are strong feelings where she's concerned. There are those who believe she set up their loved ones to get ambushed, but truthfully, there's no one who could pull off this stunt. That took some serious planning, not to mention traveling to Florida and back. No one fits that MO. And none of them have traveled to Florida—at least via commercial air travel—in the past year. And none of them have a pilot's license." She paused. "Not that they couldn't hire a private plane, but I don't think anyone did."

"Okay, thanks for looking."

"I also talked to a Nel Tarrington. Through some intense investigating, I learned she and Maddy were pretty close. She didn't come right out and say it, but I think she's running her own investigation into what happened with the ambush and who was behind it. She had only good things to say about Maddy— and she wasn't the only one, but I really think we need to focus our energies on the victims found in the mass grave and who they knew."

"Okay. Keep searching. I'll fill Maddy in."

"I told Special Agent Tarrington that we'd help look into the accusations made against Maddy and she said we were welcome to do whatever we could. But I keep coming back to the fact that we offered once before and Maddy said not to waste our time. I don't want to butt in where we're not wanted."

"I think if you find the person who set her up, then she's not going to be mad."

Maddy glanced up at him and narrowed her eyes, but didn't protest.

There was a slight pause. "Okay, we'll go with that instead of the victims," Bree said. "Stay safe."

"Working on it."

He hung up and found Maddy with a frown on her face staring at her phone. Two police cars, sirens blasting, zipped past them, lights glowing in the night. "What is it?" he asked after the ear-piercing noise faded.

"I told them where we lost him. Then my phone beeped with a text from Katie. We've got the link for victim number two."

"Great. What is it?"

"He was a character witness at a trial."

"Number two is the biblical number for witness or support, right?"

"Yes."

"Which trial?"

"David Rhymes."

Quinn felt his world tilt.

Maddy watched the color drain from Quinn's face. "David Rhymes," he said. "The serial-killer-I-put-away-six-years-ago David Rhymes. The one who killed Ashley Gorman? That David?"

"That very one."

He ran a hand through his hair, paced two steps up the side-walk, then back to stand in front of her. "Come on, we need to get out of sniper range. Let's get back to the hotel where we can think."

She agreed. Together, they walked and watched over their shoulders, but made it back to the hotel with no further incidents. "The lights are back on," she said.

"Apparently someone thought they were being funny and messed with the circuit breaker outside," a woman standing near the door said. "They got everything back on about five minutes ago."

"Good. Thanks," Maddy said.

They took the stairs to Quinn's room, not wanting to chance another power outage and getting stuck on the elevator. Quinn slipped to one side of the door and Maddy went to the other. She knew exactly what he was thinking. He wanted to clear the room in case the guy had doubled back, claimed he was the room's occupant, and managed to talk his way into a key. Stranger things had happened. Quinn swiped his key and pushed the door open. Maddy rounded the doorframe, weapon aimed into the room. She stepped inside. Quinn did the same. He motioned he was going to check the bathroom. She stayed silent and covered him while he opened the door. "Clear," he said. Next they did the same with her room.

"Clear all around," Maddy said and holstered her weapon. She followed him back into his room.

Quinn rolled his shoulders, then dropped his key on the dresser and took a seat at the table. He pulled his laptop over and opened it. "Gerald Haynes. One of the character witnesses," he said. "I remember him now. I don't know why I didn't recognize him or his name right off, but I don't think I was in court the day he testified."

"Quinn, how many character witnesses have you listened to? How many trials have you sat through?"

"I know, but this one . . ." He shook his head. "David Rhymes was special."

"Why?"

"Because I let him go," he said softly.

"You personally? Or the DA?"

"Well—"

"That's what I thought. But you caught him again."

"Yes, but it was awful for the families of those women, girls really. When I let him go, I had to look them in the eyes and tell them I knew he was the killer, but I'd been instructed to get more evidence." He sighed. "And in the meantime, I had to let him go."

Maddy sat up straight from her position on the couch. "So he killed Ashley before he was arrested for the final time."

Quinn rubbed his eyes. "Yes."

She bit her lip and moved to sit across from him at the table. "Anyone who vowed revenge?"

"Of course." Quinn met her gaze. "Her father, Leonard Nance." He leaned back. "I can't believe I didn't recognize him. I mean, I had twinges of 'that guy looks a little familiar,' but—" He tapped a few keys on the keyboard, then spun the laptop toward her. "This is what he looked like when I last saw him in the courtroom."

A well-manicured, well-dressed man stared back at her. But when she saw the eyes, she knew the two men were one and the same. "That's how I remember him too. I remember seeing him on the news, spouting his hatred for inefficient law enforcement." She leaned forward. "So what's he doing hanging out with the sheriff, being all helpful and stuff? How is it he's here where all these people are found murdered? There's no way you'll convince me that it's a coincidence. He's our killer, isn't he? He's the one who brought us here."

Quinn stood. "I don't know, but it's sure looking like it."

She frowned. "But it wasn't the same guy in the hallway. The guy who tried to snatch me had short red hair and a scar on his face. Then again, it was definitely his voice. I'll never forget that voice."

"He could have worn a wig."

She nodded. "True."

"But the guy I saw on the island didn't have a scar."

"He could have used some makeup or something to give himself one."

Quinn shook his head. "I'm going to call Danvers and see

if he's managed to pick up Tabor/Nance yet." His phone rang as he started to dial and he looked up at her. "Well, how about that? It's Danvers."

He pressed the speakerphone button. "Hello?"

"I'm at your door. Let me in."

Maddy crossed the room, checked the peephole, then opened the door. Sheriff Danvers stepped inside and shut it behind him. "We lost him."

Maddy rubbed her hands together. "Did you pick up Tabor?"

The sheriff shook his head. "No. Unfortunately, no one seems to have seen him since you two ran into him at the restaurant. We checked his home and the transport shop. Neither his son nor his wife have seen him since early this morning and he's not answering his cell phone."

Maddy tapped the table, thinking. "You think he found out you were looking for him and ran?"

"Maybe, I don't know. I can't imagine how he would have even known that I wanted to question him."

"Word seems to get around this little place quite effectively, Sheriff."

"You mean the fact that someone figured out you were staying here and attacked you in the hotel?"

"Yes. Keeping a low profile didn't exactly work for us," Maddy said.

He shook his head. "The only people we can connect that to are Brad and Tabor."

"And if one of them told the killer about our presence, he would have had plenty of time to hop in his plane in South Carolina and arrive in time to attack us."

"Or if Tabor is the killer," Maddy said, "he still would have had enough time to fly home and be here in time for us to run into him at the restaurant."

"Could have been someone in your department," Quinn said.

"You mean one of my guys is behind letting a killer know you're here?" He laughed. "Not likely."

"I'm not saying on purpose, but a slip of the tongue in the wrong place to the wrong person, or maybe not even aware someone is listening to your conversation about the two out-of-towners who have returned to help with the case?"

The sheriff shook his head and hitched his pants. "I'm not saying it couldn't have happened, just saying I doubt it." He sighed. "Most likely someone saw you down at the marina and word spread. Or Brad told someone. Whatever happened, the word is out. But there's another thing too. Tabor has a history. Every so often he goes on a binge."

"Drinking?" Maddy asked.

"Yes. He still hasn't come to terms with Ashley's death. Most of the time he does all right, but every so often . . ." He clicked his tongue and gave a slight shrug.

Quinn pinched the bridge of his nose. "Yeah. He was drinking when we ran into him at the restaurant, but said it was his only one because he had a ferry."

"If he had a ferry, then he would have been fine. He's never put a client in danger due to his drinking."

"But after he was finished with the ride?"

"Then I imagine he might have put away a few more and he'll go home and sleep it off."

"And it's also possible he found out you wanted to question him and took off. The more we look at this, the more it looks like Robert—Leonard—is our killer."

The sheriff shook his head. "He's a grieving father, but a killer?" He heaved a sigh. "All right, let's meet in the morning. I'll have two deputies stay the night. One outside the hotel in his cruiser and we'll plant the other one in between your doors. I'll give 'em an extra day vacation or overtime, their choice."

"You're sure you can spare the resources?" Maddy asked.

"Well, I sure can't have you two getting killed on my watch."

"Appreciate the concern."

"I am. Very concerned." He slapped Quinn on the shoulder and headed for the door once more. "I'll let you know when we've got an ID on the bodies."

"Wait, what? Did you just say *bodies*? As in, plural?" Quinn asked.

"I didn't mention that yet? Sorry. Yeah, there wasn't just one in that grave. There were three."

[21]

Quinn rolled over and looked at the clock on the nightstand. Twenty minutes later than the last time he'd looked. After Danvers's bombshell last night, they'd discussed their next move in this crazy game of serial killer chess. The connection wasn't a coincidence, of that he was sure. Now they had to figure out what to do with what they knew.

They had to find Leonard Nance, aka Robert Tabor. He swung his feet over the side of the bed and sat up. He'd shower, then knock on Maddy's door.

His phone buzzed and he picked it up from the nightstand to check the screen. His mother. He let it ring two more times before he answered. "Hi, Mom."

"Good morning, Quinn."

"What can I do for you?" He walked into the bathroom and pulled his toothbrush from his bag.

"It was really good to see you the other day—in spite of the circumstances."

He paused. "Yes, it was good to see you too." He hesitated and waited for the accusations to start.

"I . . . uh . . . called to see if we could reschedule our lunch since you . . . uh . . . had to cancel the last one."

He hadn't canceled, he'd stood her up. At least in her eyes. She didn't know he'd been running from a madman and fighting for his and Maddy's lives. And he wasn't going to tell her. He cleared his throat. "I'm sorry about that, Mom. I really am. Something came up at work and I had no choice."

"And you couldn't call?"

He sighed. "No. I couldn't call. I should have called after, though, and apologized. And explained. And I'm sorry I didn't."

Silence echoed back at him. Shock had probably rendered her speechless.

"Mom, I want to get together with you, I do. I want to . . . um . . . talk. And well . . . you know." A short gasp filled the line. More shock. "So, I'm in the middle of a case right now and I'm actually not even in town. But when I get back, I'll call you, all right?"

"Oh, that would be wonderful, Quinn. It really would. Your dad will be so happy to hear this too."

He paused. What was going on? Just the other night, she'd been tight-lipped and silent while his father reminded him how important loyalty and family were. And now she wanted to meet for lunch. And she hadn't thrown one verbal dart in his direction. "All right, Mom. I'll call you as soon as I get everything wrapped up."

"Does your case have anything to do with the officers I've seen watching our house and following us when we leave?"

Quinn pinched the bridge of his nose. "Yes."

"I see. Anything else you can tell me?"

"No, but when you don't see the cops anymore, you'll know the case is over. They'll make sure everything is fine and your lives can go on uninterrupted for now."

More silence on her end. "Are the children in danger?"

"I . . . can't answer that. Not because I'm sworn to secrecy, but because I really don't know. I don't think so. At least not right now." The killer was in Florida, not South Carolina. That much he knew. He just didn't know if the guy had help that might still be in South Carolina. "I'm sorry, Mom. I didn't mean to put anyone in danger. This is a special kind of case that's going to require my undivided attention. It's . . . personal this time."

"I see. Well, not really. Personal as in putting your father and me and the kids in danger?"

He sighed but couldn't lie. "Yes."

"All right, then. We'll make sure we're alert." She went silent for a moment. "Quinn, just be safe whatever you're doing."

"I'm doing my best." He swallowed. "How's Dad?"

"He's actually doing all right. He and Alyssa are down by the pond fishing. JJ is here helping me make cookies."

"Good. Good."

"JJ wants to speak to you."

"Sure, put him on."

"Hi, Uncle Quinn." JJ's sweet voice came through the line, and Quinn wanted to hug the little guy.

"Hey, buddy, how are you doing?"

"I'm good. We're making cookies. I'll save you some."

"Thanks, man, I look forward to eating a few."

"Bye! Gotta go."

"Bye, kid."

His mother came back on the line. She cleared her throat. "Just so you know, I told your father to keep all that family loyalty stuff to himself, that he needed to shut his mouth and leave things alone."

Stunned, Quinn couldn't speak for a second. "You did?"

He heard her sigh. "He just wants you back with us as much as I do, and he thinks beating you over the head about being loyal to your family is going to make you . . . well, never mind. I'll let you go. We'll talk about it when your case is over. Call me when you can."

"I . . . uh . . . I will. Thanks, Mom."

He hung up and stared at his phone for the next few seconds. What had just happened? His father wanted him back with them? What did that mean? He'd thought his father had been harping about family loyalty because he wanted to beat it into Quinn's head that he should have covered up what his brother-in-law had been doing.

Had he completely misread what his father meant?

Maybe Maddy was right. Maybe it was time to stop pushing people away. His mother appeared to be trying to bridge the gap. Quinn just didn't know if he could let himself do it. He'd cost his sister her husband. Then he'd taken his sister away from his parents. He didn't deserve to—

A knock on the door brought his head up. Maddy. He tugged on his sweatpants and crossed the room to open the door. She stood there looking beautiful in her casual blue jean shorts and green T-shirt, her hair pulled up in a ponytail. "Morning," he said.

"Morning."

"You look cute."

She blinked. "Thanks. So do you. Bed head really works well for you."

He gave a choked laugh and ran a hand over his unintentionally spiked hair. "Right. Give me ten and I'll be ready." He heard her phone ringing in the background as he shut the door and sighed. What was he going to do about her?

Marry her.

He froze. "What?" Speaking the word aloud pulled him from his . . . whatever. Craziness? Maybe. But the thing was, if he ever decided to get married, Maddy was definitely the woman he'd want to settle down with.

The fact that he didn't break out in hives at the thought nearly had him running out the door. Instead, he turned the shower on and waited for the water to get hot.

⸻

Maddy picked up her ringing phone. "Hello?"

"Greg Danvers here."

"Hi, Sheriff, what's up?"

"We've ID'd the first body in the grave."

"I see." She sat on the nearest chair. "Who is it?"

"Gabriel Clemmons. He went missing about nine months ago. He was a local architect. I suspect that the other two people in the grave with him are two more missing person cases I have on my desk."

"Who would they be?"

"Lamar Henry and Jason Roach. They were partners who owned a construction company. They disappeared about a month after Clemmons."

Maddy sat up. "An architect and two guys who knew construction."

"Yes."

"Our killer killed them too."

"Yeah. That's what I'm thinking. He grabbed the architect and had him design the building where he kept you, then the two construction guys who built it."

"And when he didn't need them anymore, he simply . . . disposed of them," she whispered.

"If it's them," Danvers said.

"It's them." She raked a hand through her ponytail. "This guy is more than just twisted. He's—"

"A psychopath."

"In some instances he comes across that way, yes," she said. "In others, he displays more sociopathic tendencies."

"What do you mean?"

The knock on the connecting door brought her head up.

"Hold on a second. Quinn's at the door." She walked over and opened it and motioned him in. "I'm talking to Sheriff Danvers. They've ID'd one of the bodies. He was an architect who disappeared nine months ago." She brought him up-to-date on the conversation, then put the phone on speaker. "So, Sheriff, as I was saying, the well-thought-out planning of the kidnappings, the patience that was required for the surveillance, et cetera, are characteristics of a psychopath. But the fact that I think he's being motivated out of anger . . . rage because someone he loved was taken from him—" She shook her head. "That's more than a psychopath. Psychopaths can disassociate from their emotions, which is why they can kill a person without remorse. And even find the killing amusing. Which I know is an emotion, but . . ." She sighed. "And then you have to factor in that he may have some OCD tendencies. It can be kind of confusing. Sometimes you can't just put a person in a category and stick a label on him. Humans are complex beings."

Quinn ran a hand over his head. "All of this doesn't sound like the same person."

Maddy nodded. "That occurred to me. On the one hand, you have the guy who thinks he's doing something that's been ordered from a higher calling."

"Psychosis," Quinn said.

"And then you have the cunning, the planning, the almost sadistic pleasure he takes in causing pain and fear in his victims."

"What if there are two of them?" Maddy asked. "What if we're not looking for one person, but for two who might be working together for whatever reason?"

"That's certainly possible," Danvers said.

They fell silent, contemplating that fact. Then Quinn leaned forward. "Have you found Tabor yet?"

"Yes, at least we think so. We got a report someone saw him arrive home about thirty minutes ago. We're getting ready to go out there and pick him up. And the hair from the island house is his."

"How do you know?"

"We talked to his son. He had a baseball cap that Robert had left at his house and it had some hair in it. We compared it and it was definitely a match."

"So what was his hair doing in the house that he hadn't set foot in since the owner died?"

"Yeah." The sheriff sounded subdued. "That's one of the questions on my list."

"Do you mind if we ride along?" Quinn asked.

"I expected you to. I've just pulled up to the entrance."

They ended the call and left the hotel room. Maddy noted the officer still outside the door. "Thank you for staying," she said.

He nodded. "No problem."

He and Quinn shook hands and they all took the stairs to the first floor and walked out of the hotel. Sheriff Danvers's SUV sat right outside the door and Quinn and Maddy climbed in. Maddy took the back, scooted over to the middle, and opened her laptop. She connected to the hotspot on her phone and pulled up all of her notes thus far. She started typing everything she'd learned since her last entry. "So how did he keep these men in line while they built the room?" She looked at the sheriff in the rearview mirror. "When did they disappear again?"

"The architect? About nine months ago. Then about a month later, the two construction guys."

"Right," she said. "Seems like the two of them could have teamed up together and escaped or fought back or . . . *something*."

Quinn shrugged. "Unless our killer had some kind of leverage to hold over them."

"Their families? A loved one?" the sheriff asked. He cranked the engine and sat there a moment.

"That's the first thing that comes to my mind."

Maddy narrowed her eyes as she thought. "And so Ashley Gorman was killed almost seven years ago. Someone who loved her is out for revenge by making a huge statement and giving the killings religious overtones."

"Like he's trying to justify killing innocent people," the sheriff said.

"Numbers are important to him, he quotes Scripture about how things need to be done in an orderly fashion," Quinn said. "He's got a twisted sense of religion."

"So where did he get that?" Maddy asked. "Who were the big influences in his life?"

The sheriff backed out of the parking spot and drove to the exit. He glanced left, then right, and pulled out of the parking lot. "Well, I can't attest to all of them, of course, but I do know that Robert's father was one of those fire-and-brimstone preachers back in the sixties," Danvers said. "I'm fifty-five years old, but I remember, as a kid, him coming to Key West and setting up his tent in an old field behind the courthouse before it was turned into a parking lot. I even went to one of his meetings. Scared the livin' daylights out of me. Wasn't until I was in my

twenties that I realized God wasn't out to get me or just waiting for me to make a wrong move so he could hand down the
punishment."

"It's possible that kind of upbringing could influence him
negatively," Quinn said. "I'm not saying that everyone who
grew up that way develops a twisted view of religion, but it's
definitely possible."

Maddy rubbed her eyes. "It's possible. Or it's possible that
his daughter's murder just sent him over the edge, and feeling
like he's the one who has to do something about it gives him
a special 'license' to kill to achieve the end goal." She leaned
over to look at Quinn. "Which is to make you suffer, make you
feel like it's your fault he's killing these people. Make you wish
you'd done your job 'right' the first time and not let the killer
out to murder Ashley."

He pursed his lips. "Yeah, well, he's doing a good job. I *do*
wish that."

She touched his shoulder. "It's not your fault, Quinn."

He nodded. "My head knows that."

The sheriff shrugged. "Bottom line is, someone saw Tabor
recently drive the boat into the boathouse, and he said he hadn't
been out to the island in a few years. So he lied and I want to
know why."

"What about the rest of Ashley's family? Mother? Siblings?"
Quinn asked.

Sheriff Danvers scratched his chin and made a left into what
had once probably been a nice middle-class neighborhood, but
had been neglected in recent years. "I did some investigating
yesterday when Burt became a suspect. Learned something I
hadn't known."

"What's that?"

"Robert . . . Leonard . . . was some sort of video game

producer. He made a fortune designing award-winning games. Then he sort of dropped out of the picture after his daughter was killed, and his son, Jacob—also known as Bobby Tabor— took over the business with Brad Gorman, Ashley's husband. Although, apparently, the last game Bobby and his company released was a huge flop, so he's been under some pressure to release a winner."

Danvers pulled to a stop at the front of the house, and three Monroe County cruisers did the same.

"This is the home of a guy who made a fortune?" Maddy asked.

"Yeah. This was where he lived before he hit it big. His son owns some huge mansion on a hill about five miles from here, overlooking the water. I think Mrs. Tabor stays with him when Burt has ferries to run."

"Why does he do the ferry thing?" Quinn asked. "He doesn't need the money, does he?"

"No, at least I don't think so. I think it was just something to do after he lost Ashley. Being out on the ocean, doing something productive." He put the SUV into park. "It kept him from sitting at home, dwelling on it, and seemed to make him feel better. I met him shortly after Ashley's funeral and he was a mess. He's come a long way."

"If he's not our killer," Quinn said.

"So when he goes on these binges," Maddy said, "how does he keep his business afloat?" She blinked. "No pun intended."

The sheriff barked a laugh and Quinn grinned. "His son, Bobby, takes over and does some of the runs himself. And, as you know, sometimes Brad helps him out. Bobby's a good guy. Seems to keep an eye on his father and makes sure his mother is taken care of when his father is off on his runs." The sheriff got out of the vehicle and Maddy saw him wave the others to stay back. "Let me handle this and see if he'll come in nicely. He sees a bunch of uniforms out here, he's going to get twitchy."

Quinn crawled out of the vehicle and Maddy followed. "You'll need backup," Quinn said. "If this guy is our killer, he's not going to come nicely."

Danvers frowned. "I've got backup," he said wryly. "You just want to be close by in case there's some action."

"I'm not denying it. And I'm not wearing a uniform. We should be good."

"I'm not in uniform either," Maddy said.

Danvers rolled his eyes, then nodded. "Let me knock."

Maddy skirted around the side of the house and unhooked the strap on her holster. She really hoped Robert wouldn't give them any trouble, but hopes didn't mirror reality most of the time. She walked up the back porch steps and slid up next to the glass-paned door. The position gave her a good view of the kitchen, and she saw nothing that alarmed her other than some dirty dishes still on the table.

"Burt, open up, will you?" the sheriff called from the front.

Maddy heard no response, but could see into the den where a foot hung off the edge of a couch. She banged on the door. "Mr. Tabor?"

The foot didn't move. She twisted the knob and the door opened. Maddy pulled the weapon from her holster and stepped inside. "Mr. Tabor, are you all right?"

Still no movement from the foot. She walked on quiet feet until she could see the front door. The sheriff spotted her and she motioned for him to come around the back. He disappeared from her view, and within seconds, she heard him enter behind her. She glanced over her shoulder and saw Quinn and two other deputies right behind him.

"I'll clear the back of the house," one murmured. He went down the hall.

Maddy moved into the den to get her first look at the man who belonged to the foot and gasped. A gun lay on the floor beside him. Blood pooled on his chest. She crossed the room and felt for a pulse. "Call an ambulance, he's still alive."

[22]

Quinn watched the ambulance drive off with Robert Tabor still clinging to life. First appearances said the gunshot wound was self-inflicted. If Mr. Tabor lived, he'd be able to tell them why he did it. If he died, the autopsy would reveal the truth about how he really died.

"Quinn?"

He turned at Maddy's call. "Yeah?"

"You've got to come see this."

Quinn noticed the gloves on her hands and frowned as he followed her back into the house through the front door this time. She handed him a pair of matching gloves. He pulled them on. "What is it?"

"Check out the dining room table."

Quinn walked into the dining room and stopped. The table was covered with papers and pictures. A small television sat at the end, with DVDs spread around it. He approached the table, his breath catching in his throat. "You're kidding me."

"Pictures like the ones we found in the room on the island."

Quinn picked up the remote and turned the television on.

When the screen flickered to life, he pressed play. And found himself staring at the madman with a bolt pressed into Maddy's back. He heard her gasp and glanced at her. "The cameras," she said. She came closer to the screen. "He wasn't just watching, he was recording. What else is on there?"

Quinn popped the DVD from the device and pulled another from the stack labeled "JM - #1." He inserted it in the slot and she pressed play. A woman he'd seen only in pictures appeared before him. "That's the first victim," he said, "Jessica Maynard."

On the screen, Jessica ran, gasping, terror seeping from every pore. She made it to the beach and then another camera caught her just as she disappeared from sight. Quinn flinched.

"She fell in the spear pit," Maddy whispered. He turned to see her pale and shaking. "That could have been me. If you hadn't . . ."

He grabbed her and pulled her to him. "But it wasn't."

"I know." She raised a hand to brush the hair back from her forehead, and he could see the fine tremor running through it.

He continued to hold her. Sheriff Danvers stood to the side and stayed silent until Maddy straightened and took a deep breath. She cleared her throat. "What else is there?"

"All kinds of evidence." Danvers shook his head. "I never would have pinned this on him."

"What about the fact that I saw him at the hotel and he had short red hair?"

"A wig, of course," Danvers said.

"And a scar."

"Makeup."

An officer stepped into the room. "I heard what you said about the wig. This guy has an entire room full of wigs and outfits and disguises."

The sheriff followed his deputy to the back of the house while Maddy ejected the current DVD and inserted the next. "Number two," she whispered.

A knock on the door distracted Quinn and he looked up to see four crime scene unit members enter. He thought he recognized them from the island. They nodded and got to work. Another figure stepped inside. The crime scene photographer. "Hi," she said and walked over to shake his hand. "Janice Young."

"Quinn Holcombe."

She frowned at him. "Wait a minute. I recognize you." Her gaze drifted to Maddy, who still had her attention on the television screen. "And you."

Maddy looked up. "Yes, we're still involved in this."

"What happened to Robert?"

"Looks like he shot himself," Quinn said. "You can start in the den."

"Is he still alive?"

Maddy grimaced. "Barely."

She nodded and made her way into the den where she began photographing the area.

Maddy turned away from the television. "Did we ever find out how old Robert is?"

"He's fifty-seven," the sheriff said, walking back into the dining room.

Maddy nodded again. "All right. Fifty-seven. He's in good physical shape." She walked into the den and stared at the couch where Robert had tried to kill himself.

"What are you getting at, Maddy?" Quinn asked, ignoring the flashes going off with each picture.

"I'm just thinking. He planned this entire thing out, meticulously. The kidnappings of the architect and the construction

253

guys, the buildings on the island, the booby traps, the cameras, everything . . ."

"Yes."

"He was obviously determined to kill us."

"I'll agree with that as well."

"So, he just all of a sudden grew a conscience and shot himself?"

Quinn gave a slow nod. "Maybe. He's done some pretty heinous things. What if he couldn't live with it anymore?"

She shook her head. "I don't know. Something's bothering me."

"What?"

She shook her head. "It's just a feeling, nothing I can put my finger on. Give me some time to think about it."

"He's had a rough time of it," Danvers said, "but I'm surprised he chose suicide."

"Why's that?"

Danvers clicked his tongue. "Mostly because of his wife."

"What about her?"

"After Ashley's death, she lost it mentally. She can't really be left alone, so when Burt was working, she'd stay with Bobby."

"What will she do now?"

Danver shrugged. "I guess Bobby will have to make those decisions."

"Sad," she murmured. "So sad."

Sheriff Danvers frowned at her. "Yeah, it's definitely sad."

"So, let's go over this again." Quinn ran a hand over his head. "You said one of your officers spotted him coming home about thirty minutes before we left to come over here."

"Right."

"And they didn't hear the shot."

"No. Their job was to just watch his house and let me know when he got home. They took off after that."

"They didn't stay to make sure he didn't leave again?"

"No. They know Burt as well as I do. Once he's home, he drinks himself into a stupor. He wasn't going anywhere."

Quinn looked at the sheriff. "Does Florida require gun registrations?"

"Nope. But the weapon looks like Burt's. He'd come over to the shooting range at the station and we'd shoot together a couple of times a month, and that's the make and model he had. He also carried it with him on his ferries, just in case he caught a bad client."

"Understandable," Quinn murmured.

"We'll run a trace on it and see who purchased it, but my guess, it'll come back to Burt."

"So . . . Robert is close to death, will probably die, and this is all over." She couldn't say she felt bad for the man. Not after what he'd put her and Quinn through.

The sheriff drew in a deep breath. "Looks that way."

Quinn sighed. "I have to say this is a relief. I'm ready to head home and reclaim my life."

Maddy nodded. "You and me, both."

Quinn took her hand. "Then let's do it."

"I'll call Daniel and he'll come get us." Maddy pulled her phone from her pocket and dialed the number she had programmed in. While Quinn wrapped things up with the sheriff, she and Daniel made the arrangements to get her and Quinn back to South Carolina. "Thanks, Daniel, I appreciate you rearranging your schedule."

"My secretary may require your firstborn, but I'm happy to do it. See you in a couple of hours."

Maddy hung up and walked back over to Quinn. "We're good. We just need to get back to the hotel and get our stuff."

"Sheriff," Quinn said, "is it all right if I leave the car at the station?"

"Sure. I'm going to be tied up here for a bit, so why don't you take my car to the hotel and pick up the other vehicle to drop at the station. I'll catch a ride with one of my deputies."

Quinn took the keys from him. "Thanks for everything, Sheriff."

"It's Greg." The three shook hands. "It was good getting to know you two," he said. "If you ever need anything else, let me know."

Maddy nodded. "Thanks so much."

"And I'll be in touch about what happens with Robert. I don't expect much to change, but if anything does, I'll let you know."

With one last goodbye, Maddy led the way out of the house and climbed into the passenger seat of the sheriff's SUV.

Once they were headed down the road toward the hotel, she let out a small sigh of relief. "It's over."

Quinn glanced over at her, then reached out to take her left hand. He squeezed her fingers and comfort immediately swept her. "Yes. It's over."

Maddy looked out the window and absently watched the passing scenery. "He killed so many people. Why do I almost feel sorry for him?"

Quinn huffed. "He was certifiable. He got what he deserved."

"Did he?"

He glanced at her again. "What do you mean?"

"He lost someone he loved. Ashley's death pushed him over the edge. His wife lost her grip on reality and he felt like he lost everything. How can that not damage a person mentally?"

"People lose people they love every day, but it doesn't turn them into serial killers."

"True."

Silence fell between them as he drove, and Maddy wondered

if she should bring up the subject of "them." Maybe. Maybe not. But if she didn't take a chance . . .

"Quinn—" "Maddy—"

She bit her lip. "You first."

He focused on the road and shrugged. "Nothing, I guess. Go ahead."

"It's nothing. Not really. We can talk later. I need to just . . . be."

"Sounds like a good plan."

Dread pierced her. She could feel him pulling away from her emotionally, bit by bit, as the minutes passed. Like a Band-Aid removed too slow, the hurt rasped against her heart. She clamped her lips shut and they rode in silence. Maddy watched the scenery go by while her mind spun. Should she say something? Confront him? Hope that he dealt with whatever it was he needed to deal with and found his way back to her? *God, tell me what to do, please.*

Once they got to the hotel, it didn't take long to gather their things and check out. They managed to do that and get back into the car with hardly a word passing between them.

Confusion rocked her. Why would he pull away now? They'd been through so much together and now he wanted to be all cool and distant?

Anger started to rise within her. She opened her mouth, then shut it. She needed to think, to choose her words wisely and not say things she might regret. Praying about it might help too. And so they continued in silence, the chasm between them widening with each mile.

He finally pulled into the sheriff's office parking lot and turned off the vehicle. Daniel's plane would land in about an hour. He looked at her. "You hungry?"

"No. Are you?"

"A little. And we have an hour to kill."

"So let's go inside and find a cafeteria or a vending machine and you can get something to eat."

Surface chatting. Shallow words. Her heart hurt. They walked into the building and identified themselves to the woman at the front desk. She waved them in and told them where the snack room was.

Once there, Maddy took a seat next to the window that overlooked the landing strip. She'd know the minute Daniel arrived. And he couldn't get there fast enough, as far as she was concerned.

Quinn held out a bag of trail mix and she took it. He had two more in his other hand.

She looked into his eyes. "What is it, Quinn? Just be honest, will you? Say what you're thinking."

He glanced at her from the corner of his eye and raked a hand through his hair as he dropped into the seat opposite her. "I'm sorry, Maddy. I don't mean to give you the silent treatment. It's just . . . I'm thinking."

"About?"

"Baggage. I have baggage, Maddy. A lot of it. Baggage I had before we even met."

"And that's supposed to surprise or shock me? Really?" She let out a low humorless laugh. "Well, all I can say is, join the club."

He blinked, seemingly surprised by her lack of emotion, but she was tired of reacting based on her *feelings*. Quinn was the only person who made her do that and it was time to stop. It was time to start *thinking*. "Anyway, these past few days have shown me some things," he said.

"Like what?"

"Like God works behind the scenes even when I don't think he is and I need to think about that."

She stilled at that statement. Quinn, who never had anything good to say about God, had just acknowledged his sovereignty. Hope flared. "I'll agree with that. What else?"

"You're right. I need to deal with my sister's death." This time, his flat monotone worried her. He was slipping back into his old patterns.

"How do you think that's going to happen?" she asked. "What do you need to do to *make* that happen?"

"I need to talk to my mother first."

"I think that's a good idea. Talk to your mother," she said, "your father, whoever you have to talk to, but do it and deal with it, then let me know if you still want me in your life."

He sucked in a deep breath and jumped to his feet. He stepped toward her and pulled her to him to grasp her in a bear hug. "No matter what happens, I want you in my life, but I'm fractured. I'm not—" he hesitated as though searching for the right word and finally said—"whole. And I can't be a good . . . whatever . . . until I'm whole again."

"I know you feel that way," she whispered. She looked into his eyes. "I love you, Quinn. Just the way you are. In my eyes, you're not incomplete or fractured beyond repair. To me, you are beautiful and whole in every way, but I understand that you can't see that yet." She smiled. "They say love is blind, but I say love sees all and still loves."

He gasped as though she'd punched him in the gut. Then he kissed her. Long, hard, sweet, and—desperate. She clung to him, hating the pain he was in and hating even more that she couldn't do anything to help him. Except let him go. Until he came to terms with his past, with God, she could do nothing more than she'd already done. She pulled away and he gave a low grunt of protest, but this time she insisted. And he let her.

She inhaled, loving his masculine, familiar scent. A musky mixture of soap, shampoo, and . . . him. She stepped back. "But how long do you think it's going to take?"

"Not long, I hope." As though he couldn't help himself, he pulled her back against him and buried his face in her neck. "You give me strength to do this."

"Don't rely on me for that, Quinn. You know where strength comes from." She turned her head and pressed another kiss to his lips, then forced herself to step from the circle of his arms. "Take as much time as you need." She blew out a slow breath and her phone buzzed. "Talk about rotten timing."

"Go ahead and check it."

She glanced at the text. It was from Nel Tarrington, her friend with the bureau.

Call me, I've got some news. Accessed the safe deposit box and you won't believe what was in there.

Maddy desperately wanted to know what her friend had to say, but she heard the drone of an engine that indicated Daniel was getting close. She shot back a response.

Will call as soon as I can. Might be a couple of hours. Getting ready to get on a plane. Stay close to your phone.

She looked at Quinn. "I'm going to be doing some of my own housecleaning."

"What do you mean?"

"Now that we've taken a serial killer off the streets, it's time to get serious about clearing my name and reconciling with my family once and for all."

[23]

Quinn's arms felt empty without Maddy in them, but the truth was, he probably needed the space. He knew she was right about everything she'd said. He needed to settle things. With his family—and with God.

She sat back down in her seat and he again took the chair opposite her. They munched on the bag of trail mix in silence, waiting for Daniel's plane to taxi in.

It wasn't a long wait and Maddy straightened when she saw Daniel taxi to a stop on the runway. "That's Daniel."

They threw their trash away and Quinn handed her the unopened pack of trail mix. "You have pockets."

"So do you."

"But I don't like putting things in them."

"Just *smooshed* loaves of bread and water bottles?"

"Yes, just that," he said without missing a beat.

She rolled her eyes and shoved the mix into her right front pocket. "Let's go."

They hurried out to the plane where Daniel had the doors open. He greeted them with a grin. "I hear you two are the heroes of the day."

Quinn snorted. "Just doing our job."

Maddy simply smiled and passed her bag to him to stash behind the seat. "Thanks."

"Welcome. Climb in and let's get you two home."

With perfect weather, the flight went about as smoothly as it could, and soon Quinn and Maddy found themselves on the runway in front of Daniel's hangar. Quinn grinned when he saw his SUV parked outside, and Maddy's as well. "We have great friends."

"You're just now realizing that?" she asked.

"No," he said softly. "I've known it for a while now."

"Good."

Katie walked out of the front door and made her way over to them. She hugged each of them. "So glad you two are home and that this ordeal is over."

Maddy clung to her friend. "Thanks for everything, Katie. We appreciate it so much."

"You bet."

Maddy pulled from her friend's embrace and turned to Quinn. The distance in her eyes cut, but he had no right to complain. He'd done that to her. To them. "Bye, Quinn."

He swallowed. "Bye, Maddy."

Quinn ignored Katie's speculative gaze and raised brow. And he didn't offer any explanations as he watched Maddy walk to her vehicle, climb in, start it—and drive off.

It was all Maddy could do not to bang her fists against the steering wheel. She'd managed to avoid Katie's questioning looks. She didn't mind talking to her friend, but the truth was, she simply didn't know what to say.

She knew Quinn loved her. He knew he loved her. But she

also knew he was right. As much as she hated to be apart, he needed the space. The time to get his baggage unpacked, so to speak. And she would use the time wisely herself, praying and settling her own family issues. She grimaced at the thought, but knew it was what she had to do.

At the next red light, she picked up her phone and dialed Nel's number. Nel answered on the first ring.

"Hey," Maddy said. "What did you find out?"

"Great timing, Mads, I was going to give you a try in about five minutes. I got into the safe-deposit box. She'd kept a journal, phone recordings, a laptop, and all kinds of stuff that prove you had nothing to do with that ambush."

Maddy almost had to pull over. "What?" she whispered.

"I'm taking it in now."

"Who was it?" she rasped through the lump in her throat and blinked against the tears in her eyes. "Who?"

"It all goes back to your ex-boss."

"Andrew was behind it?"

"No, Andrew's ex-wife, Chloe."

Maddy gasped. This time she did have to pull over. Through her shock and tears and renewed grief at the death of her friends, she managed to get the car off the side of the road and turn on her hazards. "What?"

"It's a long story."

"Tell me."

"Are you driving?"

"No."

"Kristy had started her journal years before she and Joe were dating and married." Joe, her partner. Hearing his name pierced her. She focused in on what Nel was saying. "Kristy had pictures and all kinds of stuff. It's really more like a scrapbook of their lives together. Anyway, after he died, she had a tribute to him on one page and then on the next page there was a picture with two people circled. Andrew and Chloe. They had a fight at Joe's funeral and Kristy saw it. She wrote a whole entry about it, including the fact that she didn't understand what the fight was about, but was mad that they would do that at her husband's funeral."

"I don't blame her." She pressed her fingers against her burning eyes. "I seem to remember seeing them arguing. They were trying to be quiet about it, but you could tell something was wrong."

"Yes, I noticed it too, but didn't think much about it. Anyway, Kristy had copies of Chloe's phone records and had a telephone number highlighted."

"How'd she get the phone records?"

"No idea, but I traced the number and it went to a burner phone that later turned up in the evidence room at the station."

"Oh!"

"Long story on how I tracked that down, but come to find out, it belonged to Nico Reyes, who was picked up for a murder last month—and is finally in prison where he belongs."

Maddy let out another gasp. "Nico Reyes! He's the one we were after in the raid, the one we're sure someone tipped off to enable him to set up the ambush."

"I know."

"What was Chloe doing calling Nico?"

"That's what I wanted to find out. I went to talk with her, told her I had evidence that she knew something, and if she came clean, it would go better for her. She broke down. Confessed she was trying to get back at Andrew about the divorce and custody fight. Andrew was suing her for full custody and she was desperate to discredit him in some way. She went up to his office and saw the information on his desk about the raid. She did a little more snooping and came up with Nico's cell number."

Maddy gripped the steering wheel as though it was the woman's neck. "I had given it to Andrew the day before, along with all of the other stuff I had on Nico."

"She called him and gave the details, and the rest, as they say, is history."

Maddy leaned her head back and closed her eyes. "I don't believe this. Did Andrew know anything about all this?"

"No. He's devastated."

"Guess he'll get his full custody now, won't he?" she whispered.

"Guess so."

"And Kristy Newman? Did Chloe kill her too?"

"Not intentionally. At least that's what she claims, and truthfully, I believe her. She said Kristy had figured out what she'd done and confronted her. Told her to come clean. Chloe refused and Kristy left, only to die in a car wreck the next day."

"Wow."

"Yeah."

Maddy cleared her throat. "Okay, so how do I ever repay you?"

"Well, you can rest assured your sister didn't have anything to do with it."

Maddy gave a low laugh. "I never believed she did."

"Not even a little?"

"No. Not even a little."

"How about resent her a little?"

Maddy found a smile at that. "Yeah. Maybe a little. Actually, it's not so much resentment as it is hurt." She paused. "I think she's the one who put those pictures in the break room." And had written: *Undercover or . . . traitor?* on each one after the ambush had gone down. She knew those pictures had just fanned the suspicion flames.

"I'm sorry, Maddy."

"I am too, but your news more than makes up for the lousy last few days I've had."

"The word will spread fast. Prepare for some apologies."

"Thanks, Nel."

"Anytime, Mads."

Maddy hung up the phone and sat on the side of the road. Tears coursed down her cheeks and all she could think was that she wished Quinn was here so she could share the news with him.

But he wasn't.

She tapped the steering wheel and let her brain process the shocking news. Chloe Williams had let her take the fall. Chloe. A woman she'd considered a friend. The knowledge of her betrayal hurt, but she would get past it. Somehow. In spite of the hurt, Maddy's baggage had just gotten a lot lighter. Maybe there was something she could do to shed a few pounds from Quinn's.

[24]

The Chosen One opened his eyes and looked around the hospital room. It took him a moment to remember where he was. Memory returned and he sat up in his chair. He looked at the man on the bed with the gunshot wound. The final word had come just a few hours before. Robert Tabor would live. The bullet had touched no vital organs and they'd managed to pump enough blood in him to keep him alive.

The Chosen One stared at Robert's chest as it moved up and down with each breath. He'd been too nosy for his own good, and when his snooping had led him to the evidence, he'd confronted the Chosen One in anger. Robert had been horrified and refused to listen to reason. He'd been almost *righteous* in his ire, quoting Scriptures about murder and whatnot and how God would avenge Ashley's killer. Robert hadn't understood that the Chosen One was to be God's tool in that. But in the end, it all worked out. The authorities believed they had their serial killer.

But most importantly, Quinn Holcombe and Maddy McKay believed it too.

The Chosen One gently removed the pillow from behind Robert's head, placed it over his face, and pushed.

Robert didn't even flinch as he slipped from this life into his eternity.

*   *   *

Quinn pulled out the chair for his mother and motioned for her to have a seat. She did as he bid and his hands started sweating. He rubbed them on his thighs, then settled into the chair opposite her. He grabbed the glass of water the waiter had been so thoughtful to have ready. He gulped half of it and set the glass back on the table with a thunk.

He winced. Why was he so nervous?

Because he was getting ready to bare his soul. To his mother. It had been hard enough with Maddy. This might just be nigh on impossible. His phone rang and he grabbed it as desperately as a drowning man would a lifeline. "Hello?"

"Robert's dead," Bree told him.

"What?" He forgot about his nervousness and focused on his partner. "What happened?"

"Looks like he just simply couldn't recover from the gunshot wound. They'll do an autopsy to be sure, of course, but thought I'd let you know."

"All right. Thanks. Will you tell Maddy?"

"Don't you want to do that?"

"No."

"Um. Okay. I'll do it."

"Thanks, Bree." He ended the call. He couldn't talk to Maddy yet. Hopefully, soon. He met his mother's very patient eyes. Time to do this. "I'm sorry about Stacy," he blurted. "I should have handled things differently. I should have given her a heads-up or delayed Reggie's arrest or arrested him at home and not in front of his co-workers. I should have seen how that would affect Stacy, but I didn't." He winced. Nothing like getting right to the point.

His mother stared at him for a brief moment. "Are you God?" she finally asked.

He blinked. Then barked a short, humorless laugh. "No. I am definitely not God."

"Then how could you possibly predict how Stacy would react?"

He sighed and dropped his head to stare at the table and think. While he was thinking, the waiter arrived to take their order. "A hamburger with the works and some fries," he said. He didn't hear his mother's order. When the waiter left, he looked up. "It's not that I think I should have been God, but with her history, I should have thought, should have put aside my self-righteous anger and . . ."

"And what? Let Reggie get away with what he did? He could have *killed* you!" Her voice rose and Quinn stared. Fire shot from her eyes and he realized she was furious. On his behalf.

"No, but I—"

"Stacy was depressed, Quinn, you know that. She came to me about two weeks before Reggie was arrested. She'd gone off her medication and said she was just tired of the side effects. I understood, but I didn't agree that it was the best thing to do." She spread her hands in a what-was-I-to-do gesture. "She was an adult, she made her decision. Yes, I tried to talk her out of it, but she wouldn't hear me. Then this thing with Reggie hit. She adored you and her husband tried to kill you." Tears welled in her eyes and threatened to spill over. "When she realized that, truly came to understand and believe that he intentionally tried to murder you, that was it for her. She just . . . snapped."

Quinn shook his head and fought his own tears. He should have picked a more private place, but he'd hoped in public, the two of them would keep their emotions under control. It was working, but just barely. "She just gave up, Mom, a family who loved her—and would have stood by her no matter what. Not only that, but she had two little kids that needed her and she just . . . quit."

His mother sighed. "Stacy fought a very courageous fight. She battled that demon of depression for so long, and some days I thought she'd beat it. But life just dealt her one blow too many, and to her, the only escape from the pain, that she could see, was death."

Quinn leaned back and crossed his arms. "I know. Still seems like quitting to me."

"I know it does. But you're only looking at the situation from the outside. You don't know how hard she fought, how much she hated what the disease was doing to her and her family."

"I have a good idea. I remember the psychiatrist appointments and the medicine and the therapy. But in the end, it didn't matter, did it?" he asked softly. "She still lost."

"In some ways, yes. In others"—she shrugged—"well, I don't know."

Quinn stared at her. "What do you mean?"

She waved a hand. "Don't misunderstand me. I'm not condoning what she did. I wish with everything in me that she would have chosen a different route. And for the longest time after she died, I was angry. With her, with God . . ."

"With me," Quinn said.

"No, never with you."

"Sure felt like it."

"I was jealous," she whispered.

He frowned. "What?"

She looked up, her eyes brimming. She nodded. "You were there with her when she died."

Quinn dropped his head into his hands. The food arrived,

270

allowing him to gather his composure, and for the next twenty minutes neither he nor his mother said anything as they ate. He had no appetite, but talking wasn't an option at the moment.

She finally placed her fork on the plate. "It's not your fault, Quinn."

"It feels like it is."

"I know it does. It's why you cut yourself off from us, isn't it?"

He nodded. "I couldn't face you. I'd taken Stacy away and felt like I caused you pain just being in your presence."

This time the tears ran down her cheeks. She mopped them with her napkin and kept her head averted from the other diners. "Oh baby," she said. "My baby boy. Honey, your pain is my pain. Staying away doesn't help, it just emphasizes the loss. Not only did we lose Stacy that day, we lost you." She sniffed and dabbed her eyes. "We can't get Stacy back, but you're here and we want you back."

Quinn wasn't sure he could get any more words past the lump in his throat, but he managed. "And Dad?"

She nodded. "Of course. I know he lost it a little after Stacy died. Said some things he shouldn't. Then he didn't know how to apologize. So he tried to talk around it whenever you two actually talked. Only I realize now that he was just making things worse. If I'd known sooner, I would have intervened. I thought you were just being stubborn and not listening. Then it hit me. Your perception of what he was saying was skewed. When he was talking about family loyalty and all that, he meant you'd left us and you needed to come back."

Quinn stared, then rolled his eyes to look at the ceiling while he fought to get his emotions under control. "I thought he meant I shouldn't have turned Reggie in and that I should have swept everything under the rug." He heard the roughness in his voice and cleared his throat.

She groaned. "It just occurred to me after our last conversation that you might think that. And you're so wrong." She slammed a fist on the table and Quinn jumped. Diners stared and his mother grabbed her napkin to dab her lips. "That darn pride of his. If he'd just said he was sorry . . ." A tear slipped down her cheek and she swiped it away.

Quinn sighed and wanted to join her. He'd cried more over the last couple of days than he had in his entire lifetime. "I get it now, Mom. If you're absolutely sure he feels that way, then . . . I get it."

He reached for his mother's hand and squeezed. She smiled through her tears. "Welcome home, Quinn."

A WEEK LATER

Maddy looked up from her coffee to see Haley come out of her guest room. She'd just fielded calls from her family who'd heard about Chloe's involvement and Maddy's newly cleared name. She appreciated their support, of course, but truly, she could have used it when everyone thought she was guilty. But for now, her family—and her emotions—were on the back burner. Something about Robert's death just didn't sit right with her. She was missing something. They all were. But what?

"You get some sleep?" she asked Haley.

"A bit. You?"

"A bit."

Haley made her way to the carafe and poured herself a cup. "I like your coffee."

"That's because you make yours so strong it sticks in your throat and makes you gag."

"Hmm. Probably. I can't seem to make it any different though."

"What are your plans for the day?" Maddy asked.

"Thought I might take the day off. I start a new case tomorrow."

"Ah yes, what's the client's name? Grant Harris?"

"Right. What are you going to do today?"

"Well, it's been a week since I've been free of the threat of death hanging over me and I seem to be done recuperating. I'm antsy and restless and ready to get back to work."

"Good, there's no shortage of that. What about Quinn?"

Maddy stiffened. "What about him?"

"What's going on with you two?"

"Why do you ask?"

"Because you've been as mopey as Eeyore and it's obvious he's not calling or texting. Quinn, I mean, not Eeyore." She paused and raised a brow. "Although, I must say, you might be more compatible with the donkey than Quinn these days, as down in the mouth as you've been."

Maddy stuck her tongue out at her friend, then sighed. "Obvious, huh?"

"Mm-hmm."

"You're very observant."

"And you're avoiding answering me."

Maddy groaned. "I don't know what's going on with Quinn. He's dealing with some stuff. We both are, actually. Although, I will say, I hope he's doing a better job of dealing with his baggage than I am mine."

Haley frowned. "I'm sorry, luv."

"Me too." She straightened and shook her head. "I think he feels like he can't tell me how he really feels until he 'cleans himself up,' so to speak."

"And how do you feel?"

Maddy smiled. It felt like a sad one, but that was okay, she *was* sad. "I love Quinn, Haley," she said softly. "I have for a long time. And I know he's got a past that haunts him." She shrugged. "I do too. Between the two of us, we have enough baggage to open a store. But I know him. I know his heart. And I know he loves me. He wants to be with me, he just won't let himself yet."

"I can see that."

"And while he's not perfect by any stretch of the imagination, he's perfect for me. I can't force him to see that, though, I have to let him figure it out. And he needs to figure out his relationship with God. And when—if—he does, I'll be waiting with open arms. If he decides that he's too damaged to love me . . ." Oh how that thought hurt. The tears wanted to flow but she refused to let them. ". . . then I'll figure out how to deal with it at that time.

Haley stared and Maddy thought she saw tears in the woman's eyes. Then her friend blinked and Maddy figured she was mistaken. "He doesn't deserve you," Haley muttered.

"It has nothing to do with him being deserving or not. It has to do with my love for him. I love him and that's that. Now," she said, "I think I'll go to the office and see what cases I have on my desk."

"There's not that many. Charlie and Lizzie are working one. Olivia has one that Katie's helping her with and I'm—"

"Still babysitting me. I'm not in danger anymore, remember?"

"I'm not babysitting exactly. Just want to make sure there are no lingering aftereffects of your terrifying ordeal."

"It's babysitting." She sighed. "And the aftereffects show up only at night. Mostly." Yes, she had nightmares, but she prayed those would fade with time.

"Well," Haley shrugged. "It's not like I mind a bit, ye know."

"I know you would and I appreciate you. But no need to hover, Mother. I'm going to the office. I'll catch up with you later."

"Fine, I'll probably see you there. And he still doesn't deserve you," Haley declared again as Maddy walked out the door.

Maddy smiled and climbed into her car.

WEDNESDAY MORNING

"You're an idiot." Quinn finished shaving while he gave himself a good tongue-lashing. "Maddy loves you, she's done nothing but show you that over the last three years. And what do you do? Push her away. Whine about your baggage and hurt her feelings." He set the razor on the side of the sink and patted his chin dry. Then he simply stared at his reflection. "You've had a week to obsess over this and think over this." And he'd prayed over it too. But now it was time. "Time to man up, Quinn. Be a big boy and tell Maddy you love her before you lose her." He drew in a deep breath and let it out slowly. "Right."

The scent of fresh-brewed coffee filled his home, thanks to the timer he set each night. He decided he would be glad to get back to his routine. Get up, run three miles, come home, shave, brush his teeth, shower, chuck three cups of coffee, and head to the office.

Sherlock and Watson bounded into the bathroom to remind him his routine was a bit different these days. And for now, it was time to eat. "All right, guys. Into the kitchen."

They took off. Funny how they seemed to understand him. And it was amusing to him how much he actually enjoyed having them around. They'd joined him on his morning run earlier and every day for the past week. Quinn had to admit he'd found himself smiling more.

He also had to admit he was surprised at how light his heart felt. The conversation with his mother had been a long time coming, and now he was kicking himself for putting it off. And for misinterpreting his father's words. Not that his father couldn't have made a better effort to communicate exactly what he meant, but . . .

Quinn sighed. No sense in rehashing it. He couldn't change it. There was only looking forward now, not back. He walked into the kitchen and found the coffee finished brewing. He inhaled the lovely aroma, even as his eyes fell on the picture he'd taped to his refrigerator. He and Stacy, Alyssa, and JJ stood in front of his parents' Christmas tree. JJ sat on his shoulders and Stacy held Alyssa on her hip. The picture was from their last Christmas together. It was one of his favorites because Stacy looked happy as she laughed at something he'd said. His mother had caught the moment forever with a lucky snap of the shutter. "I love you, Stacy," he whispered. He poured himself a cup of coffee, then came back to the picture. "I miss you and wish you'd chosen differently, but I hope you're at peace now because I think I finally am." He looked at his ceiling. "I'm working on trusting you, okay?" He got no answer, but smiled. God was there. Quinn was talking and God was listening. And Quinn was healing as a result. Maddy was right. One day at a time.

Watson sat in front of his dish and let out a low "Woof."

Quinn turned and breathed a laugh. "Not moving fast enough for you, huh, boy?" He scooped the dog food into the bowls and the two dogs chowed down.

Quinn checked to make sure the doggie door was accessible to the backyard, then grabbed his gun and slid it into the holster at his side. He clipped his badge to his belt, grabbed his phone, his keys, and his to-go mug of fresh coffee, and headed for his car.

While he drove to the office, his mind played over the fact that he wanted to ask Maddy to marry him. He ran a nervous hand over his lips and wondered if she would even give him the time of day. It had been a week and he hadn't so much as texted her. But he missed her in a way that surprised him to his core. He'd never felt that way about another person, except maybe Stacy. But with Maddy, it was even a different kind of missing. He almost felt like a part of him was incomplete, and the only way he would truly be whole was if she was beside him. Mentally, he knew that wasn't the case. She'd quickly set him straight on that if he even said it. He knew who made him whole. Having Maddy in his life, beside him forever, was just a bonus. No, a gift.

The thought terrified him and excited him all at the same time. He turned into his parking space at the station and felt his phone buzz on his belt. He turned the car off and grabbed the device. "Hello?"

"Quinn, this is Sheriff Danvers."

"Hey, what can I do for you?"

"I wanted to update you on a couple of things."

"Sure." Quinn got out of his car and started toward the entrance.

"First of all, Robert Tabor's—or Leonard Nance's—autopsy showed that his wound was not self-inflicted."

"What?"

"Absolutely. We've also learned that he didn't die from the gunshot wound. He was suffocated."

Quinn stepped through the glass doors and paused. "What?" He couldn't seem to find another word.

"You heard me. He was killed in his hospital bed."

"By whom?"

"Good question. We're going through security footage as we speak."

"I see." Quinn frowned, his mind spinning. "What else do you have?"

"That's it for now."

"Let me know if you come up with a face and a name from the security tape."

"Of course."

Quinn hung up and stood there thinking. So, someone else had known what Robert was doing and had killed him. This was no random thing. First the attempted murder at Tabor's house and then someone had finished the job at the hospital. The killer had taken a huge chance that he would be identified. Then again, if he was in contact with someone who knew Tabor, he'd have known Tabor was unconscious.

"Hey, Holcombe, you coming to the debrief or what?"

He looked up to find Bree standing in the door, waving him toward the conference room.

"Yeah. Yes, I'm coming." But his mind wasn't on what was going on behind the doors of the conference room. He was back on the island, dodging a killer. He also had a bad feeling that something else was going on. Something he was missing, something he needed to know, and when he figured it out, it might be too late to do anything about it.

Maddy hung up the phone with a frown and leaned back in her office chair. She'd made up her mind to do something for Quinn, and it looked like it wasn't meant to happen this week. Daniel's secretary had made it clear that her boss's schedule was packed and he didn't need to be running off doing favors for friends. He was busy with some big dinner thing for one of his restaurants and then he and Katie had several charity commitments.

Maddy grimaced. Fine. She wouldn't bother Daniel. He'd been more than obliging and she really didn't want to ask him to help her again. She'd just charter her own plane and be done with it. She googled private charters, then picked up the phone to dial the number.

Within minutes, she had her flight arranged. It would take a chunk out of her savings, but it was worth it. The pilot wouldn't take her straight to the island but would drop her at the local airport where she could catch a cab to the ferry stop and then get on the boat and ferry out to the island.

The thought of going back to the island gave her the shivers, but she had to do it. Not just for Quinn, but for herself.

She had to find a way to stop the nightmares. Maybe this would be the thing. The island wasn't dangerous anymore. It had been de–booby trapped and the killer caught, but she couldn't seem to convince her brain of that. Maybe seeing it, walking around the place, would help bury the nightmares and she could get on with her life. She prayed that would be the way it worked.

"Hey—"

Maddy jerked and spun her chair to face Haley, whose eyes went wide. "Oh, sorry. Didn't mean to startle you."

Maddy placed a hand over her racing heart. "It's okay. I'm still jumpy these days."

"And no one blames you."

"What's up?"

"I'm just going to run out and grab a sub at the shop. You want one?"

"No," she said, "but thanks. I've got something I need to do. I'll be back in tomorrow."

"Where are you going?"

"To run an errand."

"What kind? You want company?"

Irritation shot through Maddy and she squelched it. The feeling surprised her, because she knew Haley was only asking out of concern. But Maddy was fine. She was. Really. "No, I don't need company. Thanks, though. I just need to pick something up for someone and return it to its rightful owner. I'll have my phone with me if anyone needs me."

Haley shrugged. "All right then. See you tomorrow."

An hour later, Maddy pulled into the parking lot of the small private airport where she'd been told she would be met by a pilot by the name of Cody Granger. She grimaced. Small plane travel had never been her favorite mode of transportation, but she had to admit, it had sure come in handy lately. At her approach, a dark-eyed, dark-haired young man in his midtwenties looked up from his inspection under the cowl. "Are you Maddy?"

"I am." She held out her hand and he shook it. She liked his firm grip and friendly demeanor. "And you are?"

"Cody Granger. Nice to meet you."

"Likewise."

"If you want to throw your bag inside, I'll just finish up here and we'll get in the air."

"Thanks." Maddy checked her phone. Should she text Quinn? Just let him know she was going to be out of town for a day or so? She sighed and tucked the device back in her pocket. No. He'd call or text or whatever when he was ready. She'd left the ball in his court. When he was ready—if he ever was ready—he'd be in touch.

Cody climbed into the plane and soon they were rolling down the runway. Once in the air, Maddy yawned. "You mind if I take a nap?"

He grinned at her. "Go right ahead. I've got music to keep me company."

"Thanks." She closed her eyes and prayed, doing her best to keep the memories at bay.

Because while the danger was over, the terror still lingered.

[25]

Bobby Tabor stepped inside the Tabor Transport Office and let the door shut behind him. "Hey, Nathan, welcome back."

Nathan looked up from the newspaper he'd been reading. "Thanks."

"I appreciate you cutting your vacation short. Dad's death has kind of thrown us for a loop."

"Anything for you and your family, man, you know it."

Bobby nodded. "You got the list of passengers going out today?" he asked.

"Yeah, why?"

"Thought I'd do some runs if you need some help."

"Are you kidding? With your father dying so suddenly and Carl out with the flu, I'm having a hard time keeping up with the demand." He shook his head. "Who gets the flu in April? Whatever you can do would be appreciated."

Bobby held out a hand. "Let me see the list and what islands people are heading out to and I'll see what I can do."

Nathan fidgeted for a moment, then handed him the clipboard. "So, why aren't you with your family during this time? Your dad just died last week."

"You're as much a part of the family as I am and you're working."

"Yeah, but—"

Bobby grunted. "I didn't really expect him to make it. I sat at his side for a long time and said my goodbyes."

"What about your family though?"

Bobby snorted. "My father turned out to be a killer, my mother doesn't know what day it is and keeps acting like Ashley's just going to walk in the door at any moment, and once again my family is in the media spotlight. It won't be long until they connect the dots to Ashley. Frankly, I'm rather shocked they haven't figured it out yet." He blew out a breath. "Whatever. It's driving me nuts." He jutted his chin toward the water. "I'd much rather be out there where no one knows who I am." He frowned. "Much better than being at home with a mother who thinks I'm still twelve."

"Your mother's mind is messed up. She's hurting and she misses Ashley."

"Yeah. Well, who doesn't?" He looked around. "Have you heard from Brad?"

"Yes. He checked in first thing this morning."

"Is he making any runs today?"

"Said he didn't have time. He looked really agitated."

"I talked to him after those cops came by. They actually questioned him about being behind everything. He was ticked. First that detective lets a serial killer out so he can kill Ashley, then the man has the gall to come down here and accuse him of being behind whatever happened to them." He shook his head. "He's been a basket case ever since. The only time he's not muttering and moping is when he's working on the new game."

"How's that going?"

"It's pretty amazing."

"You guys make a good team." Nathan cleared his throat and ran a rag over the counter. "So, are you going to sell the business or keep running it?"

Bobby blinked. "I don't know yet."

"I mean, it's not like you need the money, right? What with your video game business, I mean."

Bobby narrowed his eyes and really looked at the man his father had entrusted the everyday operation of his ferry business to. "Why do you care?"

"Because I might be interested in buying if you're selling."

Bobby shrugged. "My father just died. I haven't gotten around to that stuff yet."

"Yeah, man, I'm sorry." He waved a hand as though he could wipe away the subject. "I shouldn't have brought it up."

"No, it's all right. You have every right to ask. You've been a part of our family for a long time." Leonard Nance had practically adopted Nathan after his father died in a boating accident when Nathan was twelve.

"I don't see how anyone can believe he's a serial killer," Nathan said. "I don't believe it, Bobby, do you?"

Bobby sighed. "I don't know what I believe. He had evidence all over his house. They found his hair in the house on the island and . . ." He sighed. "I don't want to believe it, but he changed after Ashley died."

Nathan glanced over Bobby's shoulder and Bobby turned, but didn't see anything.

"We all did," Nathan said.

Bobby hesitated. "You mind if I ask you a question?"

"What?"

"You and Ashley were pretty close. As close as brother and sister."

Nathan's fingers tightened on the rag he held. "Yes."

"She ever say anything to you about another guy that she might have been seeing?"

Nathan blanched. "Another guy? You mean like cheating on Brad?"

"Yes."

Nathan hesitated just a fraction too long. "No. Why?"

"You're lying to me."

Nathan shook his head. "Ashley's dead. Why drag her name through the mud now? What does it matter at this point?"

"So she was."

Nathan tossed the rag in the bucket on the counter. "I don't know, man, I don't want to have this discussion." He walked to the back wall and started straightening the pictures of Ashley.

Bobby narrowed his eyes, then lowered them to the clipboard. He didn't want to have the discussion either. But now he didn't have to. Nathan knew something. He'd get it out of him before it was all said and done. Bobby ran a finger down the list of names and stopped midway. "Wait a minute. Maddy McKay. I know her name."

"Yeah, she was the woman trapped on the island. The one that was in here with that detective that killed Ashley." Nathan glanced behind Bobby.

"Why do you keep doing that?"

"Looking for your television crew. They came by here earlier looking for you."

"I ditched them." But he couldn't help turning to look as well. As always, he expected to see the cameras aimed at him, but apparently he'd done a good enough job of sneaking out of the house and down to the marina. He wouldn't hold his breath, though. They'd find him again soon enough. Someone would spot him and try to be a big shot and call them. But for now . . . "I thought she and that detective would be gone for good once they got what they wanted. What's she doing coming back this way?"

"She wants to go back out to the island. She said she left something important there and needed to get it."

"Have the police released the place? Last I heard it was still a crime scene."

"Yeah. They released it."

"You're down to take her."

Nathan shrugged. "It's an easy run. It's quick and fast. I'll be back in no time."

"I'll take her," Bobby said.

Nathan frowned. "You sure? She's the only one going out there. You don't want a different run? One with more people?"

"Naw. Give Quan the one with the most people." He looked up and smiled. "More people, more tips. With a new baby on the way he needs them. And I wouldn't mind a few minutes alone with her."

"She might not go with you."

"Then she won't go."

Nathan studied him a moment longer, then made a notation on the paper. "Consider it done for Quan."

"When's McKay set to arrive?"

"She should be here in a couple of hours."

"Cool." Bobby hung the clipboard on the nail on the wall and rolled his eyes. His father had insisted on doing things the old-fashioned way. If he kept the business, he'd bring everything up to speed and incorporate technology. But he wasn't sure what he planned to do yet. He was still getting used to the fact that his father was dead.

Quinn tapped his pen against the yellow pad on his desk and leaned back in his chair. He mentally ran through the case. It was over, right? So why was he so restless? He checked his phone, but Maddy hadn't returned his text. He frowned.

She hadn't seen the message, according to his read receipt, but that didn't mean it hadn't come across her phone as a banner. Surely she wouldn't ignore him. No, that wasn't her style. That was just his own insecurities talking. And the fact that he wouldn't blame her if she *did* decide to give him the cold shoulder. He flexed the fingers on the hand he'd so foolishly tried to send through a wall and decided it was almost as good as new. A little sore, but nothing major. His leg ached, but that was a daily thing. Again, nothing that caused him too much distress.

He glanced at the screen. Still no text from Maddy. He stood and stretched, then walked to the window to look out. This was ridiculous. He wasn't accomplishing a thing. He returned to his seat and wiggled the mouse on his laptop.

Then let out a disgusted sigh and picked up his phone.

A tap on his door brought his head up. Julie Van Heerden stood there. She was a new detective, but one Quinn liked. She knew her stuff and did her job well. He set the phone back on his desk. "Julie, hey, what's up?"

She walked into his office. "Bree asked me to look into some things for you guys."

"Like what?"

She tapped her iPad. "Like the video game business run by Bobby Tabor and his brother-in-law, Brad Gorman."

Quinn nodded. In the briefing with his team, he'd discussed the fact that he just wasn't sure they had their guy in Leonard Nance, aka Robert Tabor. "So you found something?"

"Yeah. Maybe. Did you guys know that Tabor Games was founded by Leonard Nance and passed on to Bobby Tabor—

who was also Jacob Nance in another lifetime. The boys took the company straight to the top."

"Right, I know him." Ashley's brother had been barely eighteen when his sister was murdered and he'd sat in the courtroom day after day, glaring daggers at the defense of the man who'd killed her. And the detective who'd let her killer loose. But his appearance was quite different these days. Bobby Tabor had lost close to a hundred pounds and dyed his blond hair jet black. A very effective disguise.

"Anyway, take a look at this." She tossed a blown-up picture of an old newspaper dated about five years ago. Just after Ashley's death and as the media hype was dying down about the case.

LOCAL BOYS BECOME MILLIONAIRES OVERNIGHT WITH VIDEO GAME SENSATION

"Fortunately, Leonard Nance had some smarts and got the kids a lawyer right away to protect their interests," Julie said. "A year later they released another game. It was a total flop. Tabor Games is in trouble."

"So they're a one-game wonder?"

"Looks like it." She consulted her iPad. "And it looks like they're scheduled to release another game in about eight weeks. Just in time for summer vacation."

"What's it called?" Quinn asked.

She looked up and met his eyes. "Island Escape."

Quinn felt the blood drain from his face. He straightened slowly. Then he hit the desk with a fist. "The cameras. That's why there were so many cameras."

Julie frowned. "What?"

He shook his head. "Surely not." He ran a hand through

his hair. "Thanks, Julie. You just brought some new concerns to light."

She shrugged. "Let me know if you need anything else." She left.

Quinn grabbed his phone and dialed Sheriff Danvers and let it ring.

"Danvers."

"Hi, Sheriff, this is Quinn Holcombe."

"Quinn, didn't expect to hear from you so soon."

"Unfortunately, my mind won't quit this thing with Tabor/ Nance."

"Well, you've been through quite a traumatic event, I would think it would be normal to think about it, maybe even have nightmares about it."

"Yes, I know that. That's not what's bothering me. You said Nance was murdered. Suffocated."

"Yes, according to the autopsy."

Quinn leaned back and looked at the ceiling while he thought. "And in his home, he had the evidence just spread out everywhere, yet the rest of his home was immaculate."

"He had someone come in and clean. His wife just couldn't do it anymore. I remember him asking me if I had any recommendations as to who could help him out."

"And then it was awfully convenient that the shooting occurred when his wife was over at their son's house. And the fact that Tabor—as he's going by now—has a new video game releasing in less than two months called Island Escape."

Danvers fell silent on the other end of the line. Then Quinn heard the man sigh. "What is it you're getting at, Detective?"

"I'm sorry, I'm just thinking out loud and you're the only one as familiar with this case."

"All right, then, keep going."

"There was a young man with Nance at the bar when Maddy and I were having dinner at the Flying Fish. The guy was probably a little younger than I am. When he and Nance left, he shot me a look full of hate."

"That was probably Bobby, Nance's son."

"Yeah, that's what I thought." Quinn leaned forward and rested his elbows on his desk. "I'm going to fly back down there, Sheriff. I want to talk to Bobby."

"About what?"

"About who he thinks might have killed his father. And this new game he's got coming out."

"I've already had the conversation with him about his father. He says he doesn't have any idea who might have wanted to kill him. No one that would have suspected he was a serial killer. So why go back there? Not to mention the fact that you're not exactly his favorite person."

"I know. I'm hoping I'll get a reaction from him. I did the same with Brad. From what you tell me, no one had any inkling that Nance would do what he did—and I'm not saying that's reason to doubt—but I'm just kind of going with my instincts here."

"You don't think Nance was the killer."

"Let's just say the possibility that he wasn't won't leave me alone. Remember we discussed that there might be two people involved?"

"Yes, but we never found evidence of that."

"I know, but I can't help wanting to revisit that thought."

"So who killed Nance and who do you favor as the killer then?"

"His son."

"Bobby?" Quinn couldn't miss the sheriff's skepticism. Then the man sighed. "All right, come on down. What time will you land?"

Quinn's lips tugged upward. "In about two hours."

"I'll meet you at the office runway."

"Thanks." Quinn hung up and dialed the number to put in a request to use the department's helicopter. Now he just had to call Maddy and fill her in, then find Bree and see if she could chopper him to meet the sheriff.

[26]

Maddy didn't plan to stay on the island long. She just wanted to get out there, grab the hat, put her nightmares to rest, and get home to reunite with Quinn. Especially that last part. If he'd come to terms with his past and would let himself. Simple, right?

Right. She opened her eyes and was surprised to see she'd slept most of the flight. Seemed she did her best sleeping in the air. Probably, she subconsciously knew no one was going to try to kill her while she was strapped in a plane seat. She pulled her phone from the clip and checked it.

A text from Haley and a text from Quinn. The second one caused her heart to beat a bit faster. She responded to Haley, letting her know she was fine. Then she looked at Quinn's text.

Hey, I've got a lot to talk to you about. Would you be available to meet?

Maddy gnawed her lower lip. He sounded awfully formal. She texted back.

When and where?

She glanced at the time on her phone. She'd land in about an hour. If all went like she expected, she'd return home by midmorning tomorrow. Maybe they could do lunch. She added another text to her last one.

Lunch tomorrow?

Great. Looking forward to seeing you.
1:00 okay?

Sure.

Her stomach flipped. Yes, flipped. She almost laughed out loud at her response to the thought of seeing him. She'd missed him this past week. Missed him and prayed for him. Tomorrow morning couldn't come soon enough.

An hour later, Maddy grabbed her small carry-on and waited for the pilot to open the door. Was she doing the right thing? She could have simply called Sheriff Danvers and asked him to get the hat for her. She felt sure it was still in the cave. It wasn't in the evidence that had been retrieved from the island, so it had to be there.

So why hadn't she simply asked him to get it for her?

Because this trip was more than just getting the hat. It was facing her fears. It was her therapy. She stepped out of the cool plane into the south Florida heat and felt an immediate sweat break across her forehead. "Ugh."

"Yes, ma'am," the pilot said. "I share the sentiment."

She smiled. "Thanks for a smooth ride. I appreciate it."

"You're welcome. What time will you be ready to go in the morning?"

"Is six too early for you?"

He winced. "No, not at all."

She laughed. "Great, see you then." She'd be back home by

eight o'clock and would be eating lunch with Quinn. Sounded like a perfect plan to her.

She pulled up the number to the cab company she'd programmed in her phone and was told she would be picked up shortly to go to the marina.

Quinn stepped out of the helicopter and Sheriff Danvers was there to greet him with a smile and a handshake. "I've got eyes on the Tabor household. Both Bobby's and Brad's cars are in the drive."

"Great. We can talk to both of them at the same time."

They headed for the sheriff's SUV. "Why exactly is it that you think Bobby had something to do with your kidnapping and subsequent stay on the island? He's no hunter. He hates being outside except when he's on a boat."

Once Quinn had his seat belt fastened, the sheriff pulled out of the parking lot of the station. Quinn shifted so he could almost face the man. "I think we've been so focused on trying to figure out who had it in for me and Maddy that we missed a huge clue. How many cameras were found on the island?"

"Almost two hundred."

"So virtually every move we made was watched and recorded."

"Yes. I guess Leonard—or Robert—or whoever—didn't want to miss a minute of y'all's 'fun.'"

"Exactly."

They fell into a companionable silence. "What about Brad, then?"

"What about him?"

"I think we need to look a little deeper into him."

"You think?"

"I think."

Danvers turned into the drive and nodded to the two news trucks parked across the street. "They still smell a story."

"And I'm afraid we're about to give them one."

At the gate, Danvers lowered his window and flashed his badge to the guard. "Open up, Clay."

"What's going on?" The security guard stepped out of his little building and leaned down into the open window. "What brings you out here now?"

"Just paying one more visit to Bobby about his father's death." He jerked a thumb toward the vans. "Keep the vultures at bay, will you?"

"Of course." The gate began to swing inward.

"Nice neighborhood," Quinn said.

"One of the best. Right on the ocean. And only a few minutes to the marina when he's in the mood to make a run—or take his own boat out for a spin. The best of both worlds."

"He keeps a private boat at the marina?"

"Sure. I think he has one docked here too."

"Who needs two boats?"

"When you're rich, I guess it doesn't matter what you need. It's all about what you want."

"That's one way to look at it, I suppose."

Danvers shrugged. "I've never had that much money and don't figure I ever will."

Quinn laughed. "Join the club."

They walked up to the front door and Danvers rang the bell. "So is a butler going to greet us?" Quinn asked.

"No, probably Dottie, the housekeeper."

"Right."

They waited. Danvers pressed the bell again. Another half

LYNETTE EASON

a minute passed and the door finally opened. A woman in her
midfifties stood there in a silk bathrobe, her gray hair hung in
a long ponytail over her left shoulder. "Hello?"

Sheriff Danvers stepped forward. "Mrs. Tabor?"

"No, I'm Mrs. Nance."

"Ah, of course. I apologize. This is Quinn Holcombe and
I'm Sheriff Danvers. Do you remember me?"

Confusion flickered in her eyes, then they lit with joy. She
gasped. "Oh my, you've brought my Peanut home, haven't you?"
She looked behind him.

Danvers placed a gentle hand on her shoulder. "Um, no, not
today. She's still at school, remember?"

Mrs. Nance looked terribly disappointed. Then touched a
hand to her head like it hurt. "Oh yes, I know. That's right. It
just seems she's been gone such a very long time. She's going
to be a doctor, you know."

"I've heard."

"Is Leonard with you?"

The sheriff gave her a sad smile. "No, he's not. Where's Dottie
today?"

"She wasn't feeling well, so she didn't make it."

"I see. Say, do you mind if we come in and talk to Bobby?"

"Of course, of course." She moved back and Quinn shut
the door behind him. "Bobby's friends are always welcome
here. He's upstairs playing in his room. Follow me and I'll
show you."

She led them up the curved staircase, down a short hall to
a room at the end. As they got closer, Quinn could hear the
sounds of a video game behind it. "He's playing one of his
games, just go on in."

"Is Brad with him?"

She blinked, her eyes vacant. "Brad?"

"Ashley's husband?"

She laughed, a pretty sound that sounded young and carefree. "Silly, Ashley's not married."

Danvers sighed. "Right. So is Bobby's friend, Brad, here?"

"Oh! That Brad. He was, but I think he left a few minutes ago in the boat."

"Rats," Quinn muttered.

"That's fine," Danvers said. "We'll just talk to Bobby."

She motioned for them to go on in, then turned and floated down the hall to the top of the stairs.

"Sad," Quinn muttered.

"Very. You ready?"

Quinn nodded. Danvers turned the knob and opened the door. Quinn stepped inside the room and stared openmouthed at the sight before him. It was every gamer's dream. Multiple games, several computers, and a big screen on the far wall.

A screen where a cartoonized man and woman raced through the jungle dodging crossbow bolts.

Quinn's phone buzzed indicating a text. He tore his gaze from the screen and glanced at it.

It's time to take the game off pause. Ever heard of a red herring?

He frowned. Looked at the number and didn't recognize it. He texted back.

Who is this?

It's a literary term.

He knew what a red herring was. Why was—

It hit him and he froze. He looked at the man who was so

296

engrossed in his game that he was oblivious to their presence. He hadn't seen them and he hadn't sent the text.

Which meant his gut was right about Nance, but he'd just picked the wrong man. Bobby wasn't the killer, and he and Maddy were still in danger.

Do you know where Maddy is? Because I do.

Maddy tried to calm her nerves as the boat plowed through the water toward the place where her darkest nightmare had happened. The closer she got, the harder the panic wanted to hit.

"How much longer?"

"About fifteen minutes." Her guide, the young man she'd met just a few days before, looked back. Nathan Truett had helped her into the boat with a smile. "I'll get you out there and back in no time." Now he stood, left hand on the wheel, wind whipping through his blond hair. His tanned arms flexed with strength, and he simply exuded confidence in his ability to handle the craft.

"Not much longer," he called. He hit a wave and she held on tight. She liked the water. She liked boats. Especially on beautiful sunny days. But today, she just wanted to be in her home on the couch reading a good book, not going back to a place that held nothing but nightmares for her.

Her phone buzzed and she looked at the screen. A text from Quinn.

Nance wasn't our killer. Watch your back, you're still in danger.

Maddy's heart stopped for a full beat, she was sure. She stared, then texted back.

What do you mean? Who's the killer?

Not sure. Stay with someone, have someone
with you at all times.

"We're getting close to the island," Nathan told her.

She looked up from her phone, fear racing through her. Then she forced herself to take a deep breath. No one knew she was here. She was fine. This had been a spur-of-the-moment trip. So Nance wasn't the killer. The real killer had no idea she'd decided to return to the island. She was still safe. For now.

But her heart thundered and her damp palms had nothing to do with the humid weather. She drew in several more deep breaths and still felt light-headed, so she leaned forward to put her head between her knees.

"Hey, you okay? You feeling sick? We'll be there in about five minutes."

"I'm fine," she muttered loud enough for him to hear. And she was almost convinced she'd actually be all right until her gaze landed on some strands of gray hair sticking out behind the seat in front of her. She reached out, snagged the strands, and pulled. Then held up a long-haired gray wig.

"What are you doing?"

She looked up and into Nathan's eyes.

Terror ripped through her as she realized who the killer was.

[27]

Quinn dialed Maddy's number again and still got no answer. He left her another message while Danvers tried to get whatever kind of information out of Bobby he could. "This is the island, Bobby. Those are the people"—he pointed to images in Quinn's and Maddy's likeness on the paused screen—"who were kidnapped and held and almost killed on *that* island. Do you understand what I'm saying?"

"I understand, but I didn't have anything to do with that! I just write the code, dude."

"Who else is helping you? Who's giving you the information then?" Quinn asked while he sent another text to Maddy.

"Well, Brad's my partner, but Nathan is the real genius behind the games."

The sheriff blinked. "Nathan? Nathan Truett? The guy who works for your father."

Bobby crossed his arms and glowered. "The guy who works for me now. My father is dead, remember?"

"Yes, I remember. But, that Nathan?"

"Yeah." He shrugged. "He and Brad design the ideas and I write the code."

"Where's Nathan been lately?" Quinn asked. "He's taken quite a bit of time off from the marina, hasn't he?" He would have had to in order to pull off everything, from the surveillance of his victims to the kidnappings and construction of the building on the island.

Bobby shrugged. "Yeah. He gets vacation time just like any other employee. He came back a few days early after Dad died so he could help out. He's a good friend. More like family, actually."

Quinn dialed Haley's number. He knew she'd been staying with Maddy.

"'Lo?"

"Haley, it's Quinn. Do you know where Maddy is?"

"No, she said she had an errand to run and would see me tomorrow."

"You let her go alone?" His near shout turned heads and he grimaced.

"Quinn, she's a grown woman who's able to protect herself."

"She also has a killer after her."

"What's going on?"

"We got the wrong guy. Maddy might still be in danger. We need to find her."

Haley went silent. "I'm assuming you've tried her cell phone and couldn't get her, which is why you called me."

"Exactly."

"All right, then we'll track her phone. We all share our locations with one another." He heard clicking in the background. "It looks like she's just off the coast of . . . Key West? Could that even be right?"

"Key West? As in here?" Quinn paused. "Wait a minute, what kind of errand did she say she was running?"

"She didn't specifically say. Just that she had to pick up something that she needed to return to its rightful owner."

Quinn frowned. "I have no idea what that means."

"I don't either." More clicking.

"What are you doing now?"

"Looking up the last number she called." She fell silent. He listened, impatience clawing at him, the desire to act pushing him. "And here we are. She chartered a private plane."

"To Key West."

"That's what it looks like," Haley said.

"Send me her coordinates."

"Uh-oh."

Quinn tensed. "No, no, no. I don't do 'uh ohs.' What do you mean?"

"Her phone just went offline."

Quinn looked at Bobby, leaned forward, and stared at the sweating young man. "If she dies, you'll go down for murder." He wasn't actually sure he could make that stick, but Bobby didn't know that.

Bobby swallowed. "Nathan told me not to say anything."

"About?"

"He said she canceled, but they got on a boat together. He saw me watching and told me to keep my mouth shut."

· ·

Maddy watched her phone and sidearm sink in the aquamarine water, then turned back to the man who held the gun on her. Fury and terror raged inside her, but she'd not let this psycho see it. "What's the matter? You run out of bolts?"

"The bolts are back at the island," Nathan said.

Her fingers curled into fists. Self-defense moves flipped through her mind. She held still for now. "Why are you doing this?"

"He said it's time to resume the game."

"He? He who?" God? Or had their speculation been right and there were two people involved? Her fear mounted with each breath. "Haven't you heard? The island has been de–booby trapped and isn't available for your sick games anymore. And besides, I thought Quinn had to die first."

"Oh he does. He said he did. So I'm sure Quinn will be joining us shortly." He smiled. A feral stretching of his lips that didn't meet his eyes. "A good hunter always uses the perfect bait."

"And the bait would be me." Maddy felt a sinking in her stomach. "I really made this easy for you, didn't I? Chartering the plane, using your company."

"Yes. I was going to have to make a trip to come find you. But then your name came across the passenger list, so all I had to do was just sit back and wait for you to come. I appreciate it."

"Right." She saw the island growing closer. Fear threatened rational thought. She looked at the long gray-haired wig. "You killed Robert Tabor. You set him up as the killer, then murdered him. You killed eleven innocent people. Why? *Why* all the killing?"

He frowned at her. "I didn't kill Robert. He killed himself."

"The wound wasn't self-inflicted. Haven't you heard?"

His eyes flashed. "I'd never kill Robert. He treated me like his own son."

Doubt flickered. "If you didn't, then who did?"

His brow drew together over the bridge of his nose. "I don't know." His jaw tightened. "I thought he killed himself."

"Well, he didn't." Her gaze bounced around the boat and frustration clawed at her. Nothing to use for a weapon.

"Of course he did," Nathan insisted. "It was because of Ashley. He couldn't take it anymore. He missed her too much and he killed himself. Ashley needed justice and he couldn't give it to her."

"That's not—"

"She never should have died," Nathan continued as though Maddy hadn't spoken. "*He* told me I would be the one to help bring her peace in her afterlife. I would be the one to help her finally be able to rest. It's the only reason I agreed to help." His throat worked and his hand with the gun trembled slightly.

"And killing innocent people was the way to go about getting her justice?"

He frowned slightly. "It just had to be that way. Detective Holcombe was so wrong. He was slack in his job and an innocent woman died because of it. He deserves to pay."

"You loved her," she said softly. "You were in love with Ashley."

His eyes widened and his nostrils flared. "Don't talk about her. You're not worthy to say her name. And yes, I used the wig to make sure Robert was pinpointed as being on the island close to the time of your little adventure. He told me it was all part of the plan."

"Wait, Robert told you?"

"No, *he* told me. He said it was all part of the game. And now I have to deliver you to the island so the game can finally be finished."

Frantic, Maddy realized she was running out of time. She wracked her brain for an idea of escape. She could attack him, try to get him overboard, but wasn't sure she would actually be able to within the confines of the small craft.

"Killing is wrong, you know, killing innocents anyway," he said. "But even in the Bible, God allowed death to happen to those who deserved it. He killed them himself. Look at Ananias and Sapphira. It's all because the wages of sin is death."

"Yes, but God is God. He's a just God who acts accordingly. He's not an indiscriminate murderer."

"He told me the ones who needed to die."

"You numbered them."

"Numbers have much power and meaning in the Bible. He chose them. He gave me the list. I'm simply the tool he used to complete his work."

She wouldn't argue with him. And she wasn't going back on that island. She stood.

He blinked. "What are you doing? Sit down."

Maddy launched herself over the side and heard his furious shout just before she went under. She dove down, but realized in the clear water, she'd probably just delayed her arrival to the island. He would be able to see her. But maybe she could outswim him.

Maddy heard the boat turn. Her lungs started to protest and she headed for the surface. He might get her to the island eventually, but she was going to make him work for it. She struck out in the opposite direction of the island. One of the other islands in the area wasn't too far away. She could make it. The boat pulled up next to her. She didn't look at him. He wasn't going to shoot her in the back. He needed her alive. She continued to swim.

"Get back in the boat, Maddy."

Maddy ignored him and continued her strokes toward the land in front of her. Still not fully healed, her shoulder throbbed with the exertion. She did her best to put the increasing pain out of her mind. He pulled up beside her, the engine humming.

"Do you know who lives on that island, Maddy?" he yelled. "The Johnsons. Trey and Cecilia Johnson with their two girls, Harper and Nettie. The girls are six and eight. If you manage to get to that island, I'll kill them all. You'll try to stop me, but what if you fail? What if I manage to kill you? They'll still die."

Maddy wanted to weep. To wail. To rail against him. She couldn't take the chance. She had to get back in the boat and try to come up with another plan.

....

"She's going back to the island and he's got her," Quinn said.

Sheriff Danvers frowned. "I'll get a team out there."

"No. If he feels trapped, he'll kill her. We have to do this subtly. He wants me to come find him. Alone."

"I'm not leaving you to get yourself killed."

"I'm not too thrilled with the idea myself." Quinn's mind raced. He pulled up the text from the killer and replied.

I'm on my way.

Come alone or she dies first.

Quinn bolted from the Tabor house and threw himself into the passenger seat of Danvers's SUV. The sheriff was in the vehicle just as quickly and heading for the marina. "You sure you don't want to use the chopper?"

"No. I have to approach as quietly as possible. As inconspicuously as I can. He has to think I've come alone."

"You'll have backup. They'll be underwater and waiting for your word to close in. Before you get on the boat, we'll outfit with you with an earpiece."

"She's already on the way out to the island," Quinn said softly. "Her signal was lost while she was on the water, which means she's in trouble."

The sheriff was on his phone, but Quinn wasn't listening. He was praying.

....

Maddy shivered as the wind blew across her saturated body, but being chilled was the least of her worries. He still held the gun on her as he navigated the boat into the boathouse, then lowered the electric door to close them in. Maddy wouldn't have believed she could tense any more. Somehow, she had to get the gun away from him. Another boat sat in the second space.

"Who else is here?"

"He is."

"He who?" Nathan had referred to a *he* during the course of the conversation, but she'd just assumed Nathan had been talking about God. But maybe he was referring to an actual person. "You keep saying *he*. Who is *he*, Nathan? God?"

He blinked. "God?" He gave a small laugh. "No, not God. But he might as well be. He's the Chosen One," he breathed.

Chills raced up her arms. She and Quinn had been right. There were two of them. "Bobby wanted to bring you out here, but the Chosen One wanted me to, so I had to tell Bobby that you'd canceled."

Maddy barely listened to him talk as she scanned the interior of the boathouse. It was nice, nothing fancy, just functional. Surely there was some kind of weapon she could use. But Nathan waved the gun.

"Get out. It's time to go meet him."

"Who?"

"He didn't want me to tell you. Now let's go."

Maddy climbed from the boat, never taking her eyes from the man with the gun. "So where is he?"

"Waiting for you."

"I get that."

He motioned for her to go ahead of him. Maddy stepped in front of him and started toward the door. She took a deep breath. It was now or never. She spun and caught Nathan in the

306

stomach with a round kick. He gasped and went to one knee, the gun clattering to the wooden dock.

Maddy kept her momentum going and whirled once again to catch him in the chin. His eyes rolled back and he fell to the dock. Breathing hard, Maddy snagged the gun and checked the chamber.

"Very nice, Ms. McKay." Maddy froze as the voice from her nightmare returned full force. She glanced up at the speakers in the corners of the ceiling. That low chuckle grated across her nerves and fired her fear into full force. And her anger. "Quinn is on his way," the voice said. "Let the games begin."

Quinn cruised up as close as he could to the sand, then pulled the engine up. The boathouse was close by to his left, and he liked having that sense of protection on that side of him. He climbed over the front of the boat and jumped down to the soft sand. He grabbed the rope while his eyes scouted the area. No sign of Maddy, but the boat she'd been on could be in the boathouse. He and Danvers had stopped to check the records at the marina. There'd been no one at the desk, and disgruntled passengers had been in the process of leaving to find other transportation. When he'd taken the keys to the boat he arrived in, Bobby had been on his way to the marina to take care of the business. Brad and Nathan had been nowhere in sight.

He knew he was taking a chance on assuming the killer would either lure Maddy back to the island or bring her here if he had her. He had no concrete evidence, just her last known location. But deep inside, he knew he was right. He thought about what Sheriff Danvers had told him about the island. "The spear pits have been cleaned out and filled in. The room where you and Maddy were kept has been swept, the speakers and cameras removed, the lock disabled. Didn't want some adventure-seeking kids to wind up in the room, unable to get out. Eventually, we'll demolish the thing, but for now, it's safe enough. All the evidence has been removed, the cameras are gone, and the house is locked up tight, per the family's wishes."

Still, Quinn didn't put it past the killer to have something rigged and waiting. Feeling way too exposed in the open area, he stepped carefully, anxious to get to cover.

[28]

Maddy had stayed close to the shoreline, not too far from the boathouse, but under the cover of the trees. The weapon in her palm reassured her that this time could—would—be different. This time, she wasn't wounded or sick and she had a way to defend herself. Most importantly, she knew what to expect.

The main house loomed in the distance, but she kept her eyes bouncing between the ocean and the area around her. Nathan was still down for the count as far as she could tell. She wished she'd had time to tie him up, but once she heard the Chosen One's voice, she'd been anxious to get out of the boathouse.

She'd seen Quinn in the distance in the boat, and while she was relieved to see him, at the same time, she wanted to tell him to turn around and stay safe. Not bothering to go there, she watched and waited for him to pull up next to the boathouse and climb out. She held her weapon ready to shoot anything that moved. Even though he didn't know it, she had his back.

"Quinn!"

He spun. "Maddy!"

She moved to the left several paces just in case she'd given away her location and the killer had a bead on her. But she'd had to get his attention. He hurried in her direction. A loud pop sounded and sand puffed up around him. He put on a burst of speed and crashed into the safety of the trees.

Maddy raced toward him. "Are you all right?"

He nodded. "He missed."

"I'm having some serious déjà vu moments here."

Quinn pulled the weapon from his waistband. "Yeah, but this time the odds are better. We both have a gun."

"Nathan's knocked out in the boathouse," she said. "He's not the one after us."

"Who is it?"

"Someone Nathan likes and trusts and would do anything for."

"Bobby," Quinn whispered. "But that's impossible."

"Why Bobby?" Her eyes scanned the area, looking for movement, anything that would tell her where the killer was lurking.

"They were best friends as children. Robert practically adopted him into the family. Nathan has a loyalty to him and his family."

"Maybe."

A shot rang out and Maddy ducked, even though no bullet came near. "What's he shooting at?"

"I don't know. But I'm not waiting for him to come after us this time." He pressed against his earpiece. "Now would be a good time to make your presence known."

"Who are you talking to?"

"Backup. They're in the water making their way to shore."

"Good. Let's go get this guy while we can."

Quinn took the lead, his weapon held in front of him just as he'd been trained. She kept hers on the area behind them, even looking up to make sure no one was going to drop on top of her out of one of the trees. The path Quinn chose was an easy one. One that had been cleared by previous occupants.

Maddy broke away from Quinn and walked to the edge of the tree line. "Quinn," she hissed.

He stopped and spun back to her. "What?"

She motioned him over with a jerk of her head. "Look." A body lay sprawled just outside of the boathouse. "He shot Nathan."

"Why would he shoot him?"

"Because he had it coming."

Maddy spun at the voice. Quinn backed up to her, blocking her view. She stepped around him, her weapon trained on . . . nothing. "Where is he?"

"I heard your conversation," the voice said. "Every word of it. The cameras are gone, but some of the microphones and speakers are still here."

Quinn had his weapon out too but was walking in a half circle, keeping the trees between him and the unidentified voice.

"Nathan had an affair with my wife. He owed me."

"Brad?" Maddy said.

"Yes, it doesn't matter if you know who I am now, because this ends today. No more games, no more thrill of the hunt."

"That was you who found us in the hotel. You wore a disguise."

"Robert was involved in the local theatre. He had all kinds of good items that worked wonderfully to create disguises. Red hair and a scar."

"A gray wig," Maddy muttered. "Nathan was in love with Ashley, wasn't he?" she said in a louder voice.

"Very much so. When she died, a part of him went with her. He didn't realize that she would never be faithful to just one guy. I still don't know why she married me. Marriage vows meant nothing to her."

"And yet you've gone through all of this to avenge her murder."

"Detective Holcombe took her away from me. It was my

job, my right, as a husband, to deal with her unfaithfulness. Because of him, I never had the opportunity. And Ashley never had the chance to change, to realize that I was the only man she needed. I was the one who was going to show her how to be a proper wife. Everything should have been done in a fitting and orderly way. Only thanks to the good detective, that couldn't happen. Because a serial killer got to her first!" The agitation in his voice was increasing.

Quinn moved again, checked behind two trees, like he was clearing the area. Then froze. Maddy started to go toward him, then stopped when she saw the muzzle of the gun nestled just below his ear. Brad stepped from behind the cover of the tree and stared at her. "Put the gun down or he dies."

"Don't you have to kill him first anyway?"

His lips slid into a small smile. "Yes, of course."

"You put your gun down and I might let you live." Her eyes shifted from Brad's and locked onto Quinn's. Quinn stayed still, never even offering so much as a twitch. "I mean it, Brad. You have to the count of three to put your weapon down." Maddy made sure her weapon was aimed precisely. Quinn gave a slow blink of understanding.

Brad sneered. "Or what?"

"One—"

Quinn dropped.

Brad stumbled.

Maddy squeezed.

A small round hole appeared like magic at the center of Brad Gorman's forehead. He was dead before he hit the ground. Maddy stood still, her weapon still trained on the killer. Quinn rolled to his knees and pressed his fingers against the man's neck to check for a pulse. He looked up and met her eyes. "Now it's over."

[29]

"I can't believe we finally got around to going swimming," Quinn said as he settled onto the towel he'd spread out on the dock. He pulled the Yankees baseball cap down and let the warmth of the sun settle into his bones. Watson and Sherlock bounded over and flopped beside him.

Maddy nudged Watson away and dropped onto her towel next to Quinn. "Sorry, Watson, not today." The dog didn't seem to care and laid his head between his paws. Sherlock pounced at him and Watson was up and chasing after the puppy. They both splashed in the lake and Quinn smiled at their antics. They were good company.

Maddy's ponytail dripped and she wrung it out. "It's been a good day, Quinn. Thanks."

"You're welcome. Thanks for letting me invite myself and my canines over."

"Anytime. I mean, how could I refuse your obvious eagerness to show off your muscles?"

He scowled at her. "That's not why I wanted to come swimming."

313

"Really? What was your reason then?"

"I'll get to that in a minute." He sat up and ran a hand over his face. His nerves were getting the best of him. "How did the talk go with your dad?"

Maddy sighed. "Better than I expected. He actually apologized."

"Hmm. Really?"

"Yes. Seems he had some encouragement in that area."

"You don't say."

She sat up and faced him. "I was mad at you at first."

He frowned. "For what?"

"Interfering."

"Oh."

"But I know you just thought you were helping."

"Exactly."

"And you did help. So thank you. I think he's very regretful that he didn't have more faith in me. But I'm willing to forgive, so I think we're on the way to repairing our relationship."

Quinn saw the seriousness in her eyes and bit back the joking comment on the tip of his tongue. "You're welcome, Mads." He reached out and ran a finger down her cheek. "I only want the best for you."

"The feeling's mutual."

"Great. I'm glad you feel that way."

"I do. Which brings me to my question."

"What's that?"

"How are you and God?"

He smiled, a slow smile. "Well, thanks to your very helpful interference—" She punched his arm and he laughed, then turned serious. "God and I are okay, Mads. I'm praying and reading the Bible and taking it one day at a time. But I know he's the real deal and I can feel him working on my trust issues."

"Oh Quinn, I'm so glad." She leaned over and pressed a kiss to his cheek, then sat back.

"I'm glad you're glad. I am too. For more reasons than one."

"What do you mean?"

He gave her a faint smile. Then rolled to his feet.

She followed him with her gaze. "Where are you going?"

He grabbed the shorts he'd worn over his suit and dug into the pocket. "Stand up."

"What?"

He gave an exasperated sigh. "Must you always have a question on your lips?"

"What do you mean?"

He scowled and she laughed. Then got to her feet. He could see the anticipation in her eyes and he was relatively sure she knew what he was going to do. The fact that she wasn't running away bolstered his nerves. He cleared his throat. "Maddy, we've known each other for a while now. We've been through more in those few years than most couples experience in a lifetime."

"Boy, that's the truth."

"Sh."

"Sorry. Sorry."

He drew in another breath. "I know I can be a bear sometimes and I can be impossible to live with—or be around sometimes. But the truth is, you know me better than anyone and yet you're still here. By my side."

He saw the tears, but she stayed silent. Listening, encouraging him without a word. "You're my best friend, Maddy, my go-to girl, my . . . everything. I don't know what I'd do without you. And I don't want to find out." He opened the box and dropped to one knee.

Maddy's heart raced so fast, she thought she'd surely pass out. How long had she dreamed of this day? This moment? A lifetime. Her throat wanted to clog with tears, her eyes wanted to flood, but she refused to let either. She'd waited for this very second forever and she wasn't going to miss a moment of it. She looked down at the man she loved with all her heart. The man she wanted to grow old with. The man she wanted to have children with.

"Will you marry me, Maddy? Will you be my partner in life, for better or even better? Because I really hope and pray the worst is behind us."

A small laugh slipped past her lips. She looked into his expectant eyes and saw a hint of nervousness. Like he really expected her to say no? "Quinn, it would be an honor to be your wife."

He blinked up at her without moving.

"Quinn?"

"So that was a yes? I think I need to hear the word yes."

She laughed. A deep belly laugh full of joy. "Yes, you silly man. Yes! Yes, I'll marry you!"

"Dogs and all?"

"Absolutely."

He grinned and stood and pulled her in for a kiss like she'd dreamed of ever since the one they'd shared in the hotel room. A kiss that went on and on with no end in sight. She sighed and leaned in, wrapping her arms around his sun-warmed waist, feeling his heart beat next to hers. And then he pulled away. "When?"

She reined in her runaway pulse. "When what?"

"When will you marry me?"

"Tomorrow."

"That works."

His hand slid up her back to cup the back of her head. He

started to kiss her again, then stopped. She gave a small whimper of protest. "And Maddy?"

"Yes?"

"I picked out a perfect spot for our honeymoon."

Still slightly woozy from the effects of the kiss, she merely opened one eye. "Can we talk about this later? I'm rather enjoying myself."

He chuckled and reached for the shorts again. Maddy resigned herself to waiting on the kissing. He pulled a brochure from the other pocket. Curiosity made her force the other eye open. "Okay, I'm listening. Where?"

He handed her the brochure and she opened it. And stared, then read aloud. "'Rent your own private island. Just you and the one you love with plenty of sand and surf. Explore the jungle-like atmosphere. Hike to the waterfall and swim in the—'" She stopped and dropped the brochure to the deck. Then reached up and put both hands on his chest. His very nice chest, but she could focus on that later. "Quinn?"

"Yes?"

She shoved and he fell backward, arms pinwheeling to no avail. He landed in the lake with a surprised yelp and a big splash. He went under and she watched him from the edge of the dock with great satisfaction. When he came up sputtering, he grabbed his hat, then the nearest float they'd left in the water, and looked up at her. She lasered him with a look. "Really? A private island?"

He laughed and swiped the water from his eyes and face. "I'm sorry, I couldn't resist. I went looking for places to go and—"

She jumped in and grabbed him around the neck to dunk him. He went under once again. When he came back up, he snagged his hat and tossed it on the dock. Then turned back to her and kissed her. She forgot about trying to drown him and, instead, let herself be swept away by the man she loved. But she had to get one thing straight.

"Quinn," she muttered against his lips.

He leaned back slightly, letting the float hold their weight. "Yeah?"

"Just to make sure you understand one thing."

"Sure, hon, what's that?"

"I'm in charge of the honeymoon trip."

He threw his head back and laughter spilled from his lips. Laughter that she knew she'd never get tired of hearing.

She hugged him close. "I love you, Quinn Holcombe."

He buried his face in the side of her neck and kissed her ear. "And I love you, Maddy McKay. Forever."

"And ever."

READ AN EXCERPT FROM

CHASING
SECRETS

BOOK 4 IN THE

ELITE GUARDIANS

SERIES

Coming Summer 2017

[1]

The knock on the door jerked ninety-year-old Ian O'Malley out of his afternoon nap. He sat up and blinked at the shadow moving toward the foot of his bed. It took him a moment to realize it was Hugh McCort, his faithful employee. They didn't call themselves servants these days. "What is it?"

"How is your headache?"

Ian pressed a hand to his temple. "It's eased a bit. Is that why you woke me?"

"Of course not. There's a visitor here to see you."

Ian frowned. "I don't do visitors, Hugh, you know that."

"I do know that, but I'm making a judgment call on this. He's a member of the Gardai."

"The Gardai?" The Irish police. "What does he want with me?" Ian slid out of bed and pulled on the robe Hugh held out

321

to him. He might be ninety, but he still commanded respect with his straight shoulders and razor-sharp mind.

"I believe it has something to do with your granddaughter."

Ian froze. "Aileen?" he whispered.

"Indeed."

"What kind of news does he have?"

"I don't know, he wouldn't tell me. He said he would only speak to you. I allowed him to wait in your office. I hope that's all right."

"Of course." Curiosity and old grief ate at him. Ian threw off the robe that covered the lounge pants and T-shirt that he found himself wearing more often than not. "I need to dress."

Fifteen minutes later, Ian stepped out of his bedroom, dressed in his favorite pair of jeans and a crisp collared shirt, to walk down the stone-lined hallway to the other end of the house. He stopped at the entrance to his office to whisper a prayer. *Please let this be good news.* He breathed in, then out, and entered his office.

A young man dressed in full Gardai uniform stood from his perch on the love seat. He pulled his cap from his head and gave a slight bow. "Thank you for seeing me."

Ian motioned for the man to sit. "I hear you have news of me granddaughter?"

"I think so."

"She's been dead for twenty-five years. What kind of news could you possibly have?"

"My name is Duncan O'Brien. I work in the cold case department, and I've come across something that I thought you might find interesting."

"So my dear Aileen is a cold case." He sniffed. Of course she was. Her murderer had never been found.

O'Brien cleared his throat. "I asked for this case in particular because I've had an interest in it since I was very young."

322

"Why is that, lad?"

"I was supposed to be on the bus for that field trip."

Ian felt himself pale but stood statue still.

The young officer cleared his throat. "I'd fallen ill with the flu the night before the trip, and Mam kept me home. I remember Aileen clearly. She was me friend."

Ian fell silent for a moment as he felt the emotions of that long-ago day wash over him. It had been twenty-five years since the bus carrying his granddaughter and her nanny had exploded and killed all twenty-seven people on board. Twenty-one five-year-olds and six adults. Yet right now, it felt as though it had happened yesterday. Like he was reliving the news of that horrific moment all over again. He drew in a deep breath and tried to ignore the renewed pounding in his head. "I see."

"My sergeant honored my request to work the cold cases. This is the one I'm most desperate to solve."

Ian made his way over to the wingback chair next to his desk and seated himself. "What do you have on the people who killed Aileen?"

O'Brien reached into his pocket and pulled out a plastic bag that contained a picture. He passed it to Ian. Ian pulled his glasses from the desk and set them on his nose for a closer look.

He frowned. "What's this?"

"It was taken the day of the bombing."

"Who took it?" Ian asked.

"A mam whose wee one was on the bus. She brought her little girl and took the picture and then got in her car and drove off to head to work. She heard the explosion moments later, but didn't stop."

Aghast, Ian started. "Why not?"

"There was some construction going on across the street

from the school. According to the report, when the Gardai interviewed her, she said she thought the loud noise came from there. It was only when they showed up at her workplace that she learned the explosion was the bus her child was on."

Ian shuddered. "Poor woman." He knew exactly what she'd felt at that very moment. He shut his mind to the memory and focused on the innocent faces in the picture. He remembered quite a few of them. They'd been at the castle for Aileen's fifth birthday only a few weeks before they'd died.

"Do you notice anything interesting about the photo?"

Ian slowly realized what O'Brien was getting at. He removed the glasses with suddenly shaky fingers. "My Aileen's no' in there. She's no' in the photo."

"And neither is the nanny. If you'll turn the photo over, the mum had listed all of the names of the children. Then below, it says, 'Blessed to have escaped' and lists the four children who weren't there. Myself, Liam O'Reilly, Bailey Parker, and Aileen Burke."

Dizziness hit Ian and he leaned back to shut his eyes for a brief moment.

"Are you all right?" O'Brien asked.

"I'm fine. Fine," Ian said. He turned his focus back on the officer.

O'Brien nodded. "I know 'tis a bit of a shock for you, but I think yer probably wondering the same thing I am."

Ian looked down at the picture once again. "Where were Aileen and her nanny?"

"And were they there that day? And did they manage to escape the explosion somehow?"

Ian refused to allow himself to feel the hope that wanted to spring alive. He shook his head. "They must have just not been in the picture. Maybe they were late, maybe—"

"Sorry to interrupt, but they weren't late."

"All right. Can you possibly start at the beginning?"

O'Brien ran a hand through his hair. "I'm sorry. I'm no' doing a very good job with this."

"You're fine. Just keep going. How did you get the picture?"

"The woman who took the picture had another daughter named Megan, who was ten at the time of the bus explosion. Fifteen years ago, the woman committed suicide."

"Suicide?"

He nodded. "Her daughter said her mam had been battling depression since the explosion—"

"Understandable," Ian muttered. He'd battled it himself. Some days he wasn't sure he'd won.

"Anyway, she left a note that said, 'I'm so sorry. I can't fight anymore. Please forgive me.'"

"Awful. So much pain, so much grief."

"Indeed. Megan's father died last month, and when she started cleaning out his house, she came across some pictures. The date on the back said they were developed about three weeks' prior to her mother's death. Megan said something nagged at her. She knew Aileen had died in the bus explosion, so she wasn't sure why she wasn't in the picture, but thought it significant enough to bring it to me."

"As well she should."

"Megan feels like the pictures brought back all of the grief and her mother simply couldn't fight it anymore—as she stated in her note. As you can imagine, the daughter's followed the case closely, it being her sister who was killed."

Ian drew in another breath. It seemed terribly hard for him to get the air he needed at the moment. Finally, he pulled a tissue from the box next to his chair and swiped it across his eyes. He only just realized tears were leaking down his cheeks.

"Ian, let me—" Hugh, who had been standing silently to the side, stepped forward.

Ian waved him away, and the man stopped, then stepped back.

Ian kept his attention on the officer. "So they might not have been on the bus."

"I don't believe they were."

"You do realize that the day the bus exploded, most of my family members were killed in what I believe was a mafia-related hit? My son and daughter-in-law, Aileen's two-year-old brother, John . . . all of them," he whispered. "All gone. Slaughtered like they were worthless." His heart thudded. "A two-year-old!"

The young officer swallowed and blinked. "I know. And I believe the two incidents are related."

Ian snorted. "We all believe that. The problem has been finding the people responsible." He swallowed and paused, gathering his thoughts and his strength. "I should have been here, you know."

"Why weren't you?"

"My wife was having chest pains. We'd left around four in the morning to drive to the hospital. It's the only reason we were spared."

"You drove yourself?" O'Brien glanced at Hugh.

"I did. Hugh wasn't living here at the time and I didn't want to wake anyone." He ran a shaky hand across his eyes. How he wished he'd awakened someone. He drew in a deep breath. "All right, young man, if they weren't on the bus, then where were they?"

"That's what I was hoping to figure out."

Ian leaned back in his chair. "It's been so long. If she were still alive, don't you think she would have found a way to let me know?"

"I don't know, but she wasn't on that bus that day and neither was her nanny. Somehow she escaped the bus and I want to know if my friend is still alive."

"I want to know that too." He leaned forward and drew in a deep breath. "I've been hiding, you know."

"What do you mean?"

"I mean I've been a hermit for the past twenty-five years. I don't go out and I have more security than the president of Ireland. I work from my office."

"I'd heard you'd yet to retire."

He huffed. "Retire? And do what? Twiddle me thumbs all day? No, working keeps me on me toes and makes the days no' seem quite as long."

"I understand." O'Brien paused. "The people who tried to kill you and yer family were never caught. You think they're still out there?"

"I don't know about that, I just know there's not a doubt in my mind we were all supposed to die that day."

O'Brien nodded. "Every last one o' you."

"Every last one."

Acknowledgments

Huge thanks to my brainstorming buddies: Colleen Coble, Carrie Stuart Parks, Ronie Kendig, and Robin Miller. I couldn't have put this story together without your input! I'm ready for our next retreat!

As always, thanks to Dru Wells and Wayne Smith for your invaluable input on all things FBI.

Thanks to Tamela Hancock Murray with the Steve Laube Agency, my fabulous agent. Love you much!

So, I just have to say thanks to Michele Misiak and Karen Steele with Baker Publishing. You guys are amazing in getting the word out about the books. I love working with you!

And God bless you, Barb Barnes, for your brilliant work on whipping this story into shape. Your input is priceless.

I have to give a shout-out to my family, who supports me through it all.

And thank you, Jesus, for letting me do what I do.

Lynette Eason is the bestselling author of the Women of Justice series and the Deadly Reunions series, as well as *No One to Trust*, *Nowhere to Turn*, and *No Place to Hide* in the Hidden Identity series. She is a member of American Christian Fiction Writers and Romance Writers of America. She has a master's degree in education from Converse College and she lives in South Carolina. Learn more at www.lynetteeason.com.

Come meet
Lynette Eason at
www.LynetteEason.com

Follow her on

 Lynette Barker Eason

 LynetteEason

INTENSITY. SKILL. TENACITY.

The bodyguards of
Elite Guardians Agency have it all.

"This is one of the best romantic suspense novels I've read in a long time.
Highly recommended!"

—**COLLEEN COBLE,**
author of *The Inn at Ocean's Edge* and the Hope Beach series

 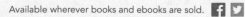

Also from Lynette Eason:
The WOMEN OF JUSTICE series